Conflicted Interest

AVA STARKE

Athenian Press

1172 South Dixie Hwy., #466,

Coral Gables, FL 33146

First Edition: February 2017

ISBN: 978-0-9986837-0-6
ISBN: 978-0-9986837-1-3 (ebook)

Ava Starke

ROMANCE THAT INSPIRES

THEO

I MET HER on a three-day weekend in May — a perfectly beautiful one — very much worthy of the extra day of holiday. In Greece it was particularly hot under the Athenian sun, which seemed to burn the city into a smoldering decay. The noble, sandy-white buildings alluded to a former grandeur; the authority of the country's history was undeniable. Ancient landmarks set the scene for today's bars and restaurants creating a centurial harmony between the capital and its inhabitants that appeared unbound by time.

My luggage, lost on my short flight from Turkey, was not expected until the following afternoon. By then, I would already be back in Istanbul.

Desperate to find a stand-in suit for David's wedding, I ducked into an anonymous shop on my way into town.

The men's atelier was buried among a long line of identical one-story storefronts that descended from the mountains down into the city. The shopkeeper, however, was one in a million.

"Welcome. I'm Angelo," he said while shaking my hand incessantly. The instant I walked into the small operation with its old, half-empty glass display cases and tired sixties tiling, he swept me off to the back room where he kept his prized collections. There, Angelo handed me a dark-blue linen suit and told me this was the one for me as if it had been divinely chosen. It was a perfect fit, and the fabric rivaled the fashion houses of Italy.

"Where did it come from?" I asked curiously. The suit seemed oddly placed in this local outpost of a store.

"It was ordered from Milano for the wedding of my friend's son."

"He didn't want it?"

Angelo turned around and began fidgeting with a stack of pocket squares on the opposite counter. "The boy was very wealthy. When my friend passed away, his son inherited a large shipping company; but he was too young — too stupid. He went bankrupt. Lost all his money. When he lost his fortune," the shopkeeper turned back around to face me, "he lost the girl."

I slipped off the jacket and leaned my back against the edge of a display case. "I'm not sure I want to wear that kind of karma," I said laying the suit coat on the scratched glass of the counter.

"Of the suit?" Angelo exclaimed. "Don't be stupid." He draped the silky linen back over my arm. "The suit is meant to bring the next man good luck. It wasn't meant for my friend's son, but it is meant for you."

I liked the guy. He was persistent and reminded me of my father as he rubbed the tips of his thumb and middle finger together.

"Look, you try it. If it doesn't bring you luck, you bring it back to me; and I'll give you a refund."

An involuntary smile curled at the sides of his mouth. We both knew when I left the shop, I wouldn't be returning. He had the mad passion of a good shyster, and my options at this point were limited. The wedding was set to begin in ninety minutes.

Angelo quickly settled my purchase and walked me to my waiting cab. His sweaty palm shook my hand no less than four times on the way out.

My taxi deposited me in front of my hotel leaving me just enough time to check-in and take a quick shower before the wedding. An hour later I was sweating under the heated rays of the sun. I looked great though, and I knew it.

This was my first time in Athens. I'd never before had a reason to come, and even this visit was limited to a strict twenty-four hour window. I had tickets for the Turkish team's football match against Spain the following afternoon in my home city of Istanbul. Wedding or no wedding, this was a match I would not be missing. There were few things I cared for in my life: family; work; football; and, of course, women — predictably, in that order.

The church was tucked just beneath the overbearing hilltop of the Acropolis, a minor player within a much larger scene. Feeling the steam rising from beneath my suit, I stepped into the entryway of the tiny Orthodox enclave and peeked my head in the door to add my face to the congregation.

My mind was wandering, and I imagined how the night would end. Given the last minute brevity of my visit, I hadn't precooked anything on Tinder, my preferred "dating" app. As a member, I could arrange meet-ups in the days leading up to my trips from anywhere in the world; and that suited my frequent-flier lifestyle perfectly. The application was not without its socially engineered "bugs" though. In London, I had to screen for prostitutes; and in Russia, I once matched with the ex-mistress of a local billionaire who insisted that her former boyfriend had bought her a five million dollar flat in the Khamovniki District of Moscow. Apparently, she was ready for an upgrade. Having far more interesting investments to make, I never heard from her again.

A man couldn't lose with the app. Either one had a fun hook up or collected excellent cocktail party fodder; and given the grueling travel and difficult hours of my job, I didn't have time for anything more.

Tonight's wedding reception party would inevitably go on late. This was more or less the Mediterranean after all; but I was in a state of detox from an intense week of business travel to the U.S., London, Munich, Istanbul, and now this crumbling relic of classical antiquity. I was tired, and it was entirely possible I'd end up in my room asleep before the dancing even started.

An elderly woman tugged at my sleeve, telling me she wanted to inch by me. Stepping aside, I saw the church was painted in white with gold and light-blue accents. Dark, ornately-carved wooden doors created a dramatic scene behind the altar; and large bronze chandeliers with red stained glass hung from the ceiling.

I surveyed the crowd. There were clear distinctions between the locals, probably family, and the wedding couple's more international friends. I assumed the global constituency was mostly David's American friends from home, with a smattering of the occasional coworker. There weren't many young women, maybe fifteen at most — a small pool to pick from.

I redirected my attention to the bride and groom at the front as they walked circles around the altar together. I always found this to be a strange yet amusing custom at Orthodox weddings. Delia, David's new wife, was beaming with honest joy; and he stood beside her in muted delight. Delia was elegant and statuesque in a long, figure-hugging silk gown. She was a well-known model in New York, and David had scored above his bracket when he landed her as his fiancé. I felt a pang at witnessing their mutual happiness.

My last significant relationship had ended abruptly following my move to Istanbul. I had invited my then girlfriend, Susanne, to move to Turkey with me; but she'd insisted her work in Berlin was too important to her. Nevertheless, I'd really wanted to start a family. At the time we'd been trying for a baby, so we continued on for a few months flying to see each other weekly until I came to the stunning realization that she was cheating on me back home with our neighbor.

It was just as well, since now I questioned whether having a family was even realistic given my lifestyle.

I hadn't procured anything of lasting importance since; but then again, I was always working. In my thirty-five years of wisdom, love seemed fraught with disappointment.

I'd yet to find a relationship that was worth its intensive investment; and while I knew my energy was better spent at the office, I still held out hope that one day I might find someone who would prove me wrong.

I continued my survey of the little room farther to my right and spotted a row in the back filled with more guests.

Rising from the back corner, she slowly stood up from her wooden seat and signaled to an older man to take her chair. He rejected her proposal and stood taller in his dignity. Smiling, she signaled again to the chair before turning in my direction. In her sky-blue dress and shoes in hand, she made her way toward where I was standing. I wanted her to slide by me as she was sliding past others: the skirt of her dress sweeping their knees as she moved out of the narrow row. She was American; I knew it. European women wore their shoes in church, and they remained for the entirety of the ceremony out of polite obligation.

The straps of her dress were thin and taut against her skin, bracing themselves to hold her breasts in place. I pictured the straps snapping upon the slightest touch. As she passed by me, her shoulder brushed the fabric of my suit jacket. She left out the back doorway as the growing crowd increasingly cornered me into a rear pulpit.

There must have been a hundred people captured inside the small gilded room of spiritual fortification that had a capacity for thirty. I could feel the waves of heat swelling and swirling between the congregation. The ceremony was wilting us all like flowers in a febrile summer; so with no end in sight, I sneaked back out the door to follow her.

SHE WAS SITTING under a tree that shaded the sidewalk just beyond the church at the limit of the Acropolis Park. Her long, dark hair was draped along the curves of her breasts in stark contrast to the light color of her dress. Still in bare feet, she'd pulled up her skirt showing off more of her legs — and I was caught. She smiled, staring right at me. Feeling curious and obedient, I went over to play.

"Hi." Her voice was low and soft.

"Hey," I replied with a cautious smile. As I crossed over the broad dirt path to where she was sitting, my shoes kicked up hot dust, covering them in a powdery film. "What are you doing out here?"

"It's so hot in the church. I'm getting some air and making new friends," she said, winking at me with presumptuous intimacy. She tapped on the curb of the sidewalk next to her and invited me to sit down. "Don't I know you?"

I took my place beside her under the tree. Her eyes shone in the persimmon sunlight; and looking into them, a faded familiarity tugged at me as if I'd known her for ages. I was sure we had never met before, but there was something comfortable and easy about her. "You do?" I came back, bemused.

"Yes, I'm sure of it."

I was certain I would have remembered her if we'd met before. "I don't think so."

While her head was turned, I let my eyes graze down her slight form. I wanted this woman. I wanted to taste her. We were sitting side by side, but I wanted to see her standing again. I always struggle to picture women naked while they are sitting down.

"How do you know David then?"

"We're working together on a project and became friends. You?" I didn't know David terribly well; I'd met him on a deal, and we'd gone out a few nights together. The reality was that I didn't have close friends, so I tried when possible to support those that I met through work.

"So you're a consultant?" She didn't seem impressed by the revelation and continued before I could answer. "David and I were together in New York for a couple years," she continued, "but when we broke up, I decided to go back to school and get my masters."

"Wait, are you Audrey?" I asked.

"Yeah, that's me," she sighed, as my naked expectations for the night instantly deflated. Audrey wasn't just any ex, she was THE ex: the one who got away. David had spoken of her bitterly one night over drinks; and even if he was now in love with another woman, there was no way I could touch Audrey now; David would never forgive me.

"What's your name?"

"I'm Theo," I said extending my hand to shake hers. I was despondent but curious. "Isn't it strange to be at the wedding of your ex-boyfriend?"

"To be honest it's really weird. I was surprised to be invited. I think on some level he's still angry with me; but I decided it would be good form to attend, support him, and put the past to rest."

"Do you suppose they will live happily ever after, as you Americans like to say?"

"David and Delia?" She turned from me and an

awkward pause hovered between us. "Maybe, although, I don't really believe in marriage anymore."

I could smell the heat coming off her skin — it was sweet and feminine. I closed my eyes and let the hot air fill my lungs. I tried to imagine being on a Grecian beach rather than in Athens' city center. The more Audrey-filled breath I took, the more addicted I became. But I needed to relax. She was off limits.

In the faint breeze, I could see her dark, wavy hair lifting off her shoulder as the air tried to carry it away. Other strands were caught in the light perspiration on her skin — prisoners of her body in the sultry weather. In my desperation to touch her, I imagined my hand brushing her hair away from her tanned, glowing shoulder, feeling its way down her back — my fingertips gliding along her skin.

I needed to move on but couldn't help myself indulging in a few more minutes with her.

"Where are you from?" she asked, diverting my attention.

"I'm German, born in Munich." If the wedding were to end at one in the morning, that meant I had eleven hours to find someone else to seduce. I looked around at the amassing crowd outside the church, trying to identify another target.

"Where do you live now?" she asked, also staring at the crowd.

"Istanbul."

"Really? Why?"

"My parents were Turkish, so I'm taking some time to reconnect with my roots." I surveyed the long, elegant line of her neck while she was turned from me. "Exploring my heritage, I suppose."

"What do you mean they *were* Turkish?"

"They were both killed in a car accident when I was fifteen — a drunk driver."

"Oh, no. I'm so sorry." Her face scrunched, trying to find something more appropriate to say.

"I was recently able to move teams so I could be based in Istanbul," I added. "It was doable since my partners are all over the world. This week alone I traveled to five international capitals." In my rush to leave the subject of my parents behind, I now sounded like a pre-pubescent boy, desperately trying to impress her.

She was a perfect example of impervious beauty: light, charismatic, relaxed, indifferent. Beautiful women were my vice.

"Do you feel at ease traveling abroad?"

"I do, but I miss my family . . . or a sense of belonging to a family."

"Of course. That's understandable." Audrey looked at me with softened eyes. "I feel perfectly at home on my own also," she asserted.

"Family is important to me. Don't you want one of your own someday?"

"No, it's not something I think about. My career doesn't support the weight of having a family. My parent's relationship was a mess, and I don't want to be held back by personal drama."

At the end of the day, having a family was the only thing I was really searching for. "Where are you from?" I asked in an effort to lighten the mood.

"Nashville."

"I've been there once. I ended up downtown in a country bar with some colleagues."

"Oh, well, you went right to the heart of it didn't

you?" she laughed as she spoke. "I confess I've only made it to one of those once in my life. It wasn't exactly my scene, but I have friends who practically live in the honky-tonk bars. They play for tips and phone numbers."

I couldn't imagine her coming from such a place. Admittedly, it was charming; but with the veil of religion that engulfed the city, one could feel the repression like a thick fog. She seemed anything but repressed; her calm steady way made me strangely anxious.

"I have to admit, it's hard to picture you there," I confessed. "You don't have an accent."

"I lost my accent in New York. After I finished school, I moved there for work. Banking." She said it casually, but she was proving something — to herself, I think, rather than me.

"Ah, so you're a brain."

"Well, it depends on your perception of the finance industry," she joked.

"Fair point. I fight with your people every day, and they are exhausting — valuations and market receptiveness."

"Mergers and acquisitions?"

"It seems to be what I've been specializing in lately." That wasn't a complete truth; although, it wasn't a lie either. I wasn't ready to play my entire hand. I wanted this woman tonight, anonymously — if only David hadn't dated her.

She exhaled, "How many minutes do you suppose stand between us and champagne bottles."

"I think that number just reduced dramatically," I said, nodding at the couple as they exited the church. "Wait, you'd better put your shoes back on!" Audrey was already on her feet, skipping toward the crowd.

"Hurry! You don't want to miss the rice. It's my favorite part," she called, stopping to hold out her hand and pull me along with her.

AUDREY

I OPENED THE DOOR to my hotel room as the relief of cold air conditioning billowed over me. The cleaning lady must have turned it on high; and at this very moment, I was incredibly grateful to her, whoever she was. I dropped my clutch on the hardwood floor, kicked off my heels, and placed my room key on the credenza in the entryway. Twenty-eight years of losing things, keys especially, had instilled the habit.

Heading toward the bathroom, I purred in relief as my feet sought out the expansive cool, white-marbled floor. What was I doing here? It had been a mistake to come. I was sure that David had invited me to prove how much he'd moved on. If I was honest, I'd probably accepted just to substantiate the same; but the whole thing was incredibly awkward. I couldn't ignore the harsh stares of both his friends and Delia's family anytime I walked by them. I'd survived the ceremony, but the reception loomed. *Maybe I could feign food poisoning and stay in my room tonight?*

David was a model of American upper-class accomplishment. His father had been successful in commercial real estate up and down the East Coast, but David had paved a new path for himself in the prestigious banks of New York. On paper he'd been perfect, but he had secrets — secrets that ultimately destroyed our relationship.

I turned the shower on and attempted to slide off my light-blue dress. Sweat was dripping from every corner of my body, and the satin lining clung to me all the way up until it was over my head. I deposited the wet heap on the marble. Turning toward the shower, I cautiously threw in a leg to test the temperature. It was perfect: cooling but not cold. I jumped in just as my phone rang.

"Damn." I stepped out of the shower and into the frigid air of the bathroom. Dripping water all over my now useless dress, I scrambled to reach my phone which was ringing from inside my small, formal clutch, an Art Deco keepsake from my paternal grandmother. She had passed away ten years before, but there were still some treasures of hers I clung to. I was sure that when I opened the clutch and smelled the white satin lining inside I could smell the calming comfort of her Southern countryside home.

"Hello."

"Hello, Audrey?"

"Yes. Hi, Nick."

Nick, my V.P. and direct line of reporting, was my boss at the bank. I was sure he got off somehow by calling the team on weekends. He had a tough exterior at the office, but I liked him. We'd seen a lot together in my few years at the bank in London, and I felt we didn't have anything left to prove to each other.

But his wife had recently left him; and with their mortgage and a second rental for himself, he was increasingly panicking over his team's performance. London was an expensive place to go through a divorce.

"Listen, Audrey, I just spoke with Angela at National Motors; and she has reservations about the French acquisition we proposed."

"Well, can you blame her? We aren't sure Riviere's French diesel technology can be adapted to gas hybrids for the U.S. market." Why Europe still ran on diesel technology was beyond me. It was smelly and dirty: encasing the old buildings of beautiful European capitals in black soot. I understood diesel had better fuel efficiency; but nevertheless, it was disgusting.

"It doesn't feel right to me either; and admittedly, I'm embarrassed we haven't come up with any better alternative," Nick said.

Shivering now as the cold air evaporated the water on my skin, I resigned myself to the thought that this might take a while. I shuffled back into the bathroom to grab a towel, my feet tripping slightly on the slippery and now soaking wet dress that was still a mess on the floor. I tucked the towel under my arms and around my body with the phone wedged between my wet ear and shoulder before walking back out.

The last thing I wanted my boss to hear was the echo of my voice in a bathroom. "Yeah, me too; but it's not as if this is a saturated space. We're talking about a niche market; there isn't a lot of research and development being allocated to hybrid technology in the United States. With the drop in oil prices, car companies don't expect consumers to demand it in the near to medium term."

I was at a loss. My team had been researching the players in the hybrid market for months. We hadn't come up with anything new to propose to the client, and I could feel Nick's disappointment all the way on the other side of Europe.

"I agree, but we still have to solve the problem for the National Motors' team. They must show investors they are putting cash into advancing their technology."

I sat on the edge of the bed, wet and still wrapped in my towel. I was reminded again of my grandmother in that moment. She never traveled much; but when she did, she always insisted on removing the top cover from the hotel bed. Grandma called it the "wet-butt blanket," insinuating that hotel guests sit on the top cover with their wet butts when they come out of the shower. I was sure, that at this very moment, she was chiding me from Heaven. I looked up and gave her a smile.

"Perhaps hybrid technology is putting a Band-Aid on the issue," I floated. "Many consumers will soon leapfrog hybrids and go straight into electrics."

"I'm not sure it will happen as soon as you think. It's is a controversial investment choice for an industry hooked on oil."

He was dismissing the idea without even thinking about it thoroughly. I would have to work it in another way.

Nick was conservative but consistent. Clients liked that about him. He wasn't a revolutionary, but he could predict the steady stream of deals that kept the markets aflutter. He would rather place a safe bet giving a client a small but predictable market boost than steer a client to a riskier deal with a potentially larger upside. He was the yin to my more aggressive yang; but at the end of the day, he was still my boss. And most importantly, he controlled the allocation of bonuses.

I couldn't move on without seeding the idea further. "I respectfully disagree. We're seeing some interesting development come out of Germany, California, and Japan."

"Yes, but so far they are unproven in the market. The way I see it . . . we have two options. We can either retool the pitch for the Riviere deal and try to convince National Motors that it's the best course of action to take, or we can identify other potential acquisitions that would make more sense strategically."

My heart sunk into my stomach. Nick was signaling that I had to go back to the drawing board; but it was Saturday, and I was in Athens.

"Are you in London? Could you work up a few ideas by Tuesday?" he asked, without asking.

Shit! I had done all of the manic prep on the Riviere deal in the weeks before I left to make sure I would have a work-free weekend. This was precisely my largest hang-up with banking. The industry had a knack for making a person regret stepping out of his or her apartment to get a haircut on Saturday, let alone booking a long weekend in Greece.

"No problem, Nick. I'll work up something and pass it by you in a couple days.

"I want ideas by Tuesday and a solid proposal by Thursday, Audrey. We have a meeting with National Motors on Thursday afternoon."

"Yup, no problem."

"Okay, great. Have a nice weekend," he said as he hung up.

I dropped the phone on the bed and pulled the towel closer around my body to shield myself from the stark air. *How am I going to fix this one?*

"IT IS HOT in this city," Gina wailed as she walked into the lobby bar. "I just held ice under my arms for five minutes."

I kissed her cheek; and we eyed the large, tufted leather couch just ahead of us. It cooled the back of my naked legs as we sat down.

"I can't believe my parents used to live here," she added.

Gina was one of my dearest friends from our graduate class. An international mix of Italian, Bulgarian, and Greek, she was beautiful and spoke more languages than I had fingers. She'd worked with David on a few transactions back in New York, so in a way I'd known of her even before she and I met at business school. After graduating with her MBA, she had set her sights on the art world. Now the director of a medium-sized gallery in Paris, the exact content of her job was lost on me. Cocktail parties and jet-setting seemed to be the core function of her role.

"Hey, have you seen Nir?" she asked. "He borrowed my phone during the wedding and hasn't given it back."

"That was brave of you!"

Nir, an Israeli friend from school, was the craziest of them all. He was absolutely unpredictable, but his kind heart always won me over. "I haven't seen him since the ceremony, but he should be popping up soon."

The waiter came by, and we ordered sparkling mineral waters with extra ice. As he turned to leave, Gina called after him.

"Also, an Old Fashioned on the rocks, please."

"Isn't it a little early?" I asked. I was fairly sure I would throw up if I had anything strong to drink now. I was all nerves from my phone call, and the scorching temperature was testing them.

I looked around and took in the smoky Grecian room. The ceilings were high and covered in bright cherry wood, but the floor was stained in a more subtle ash. The windows went from the floor to the ceiling and could open out onto the patio. They were shut, and an inadequate air conditioner labored endlessly to keep the room as comfortable as possible. The chairs and couches were covered in aged, brown leather which gave the bar an air of conservative fatigue. The shutters, drawn over the windows to keep the sun from breaking in, cast a hue of dark masculinity around the room.

"I'm feeling festive, and I want to drink." she explained. "So how is life in banking these days? You still doing a lot of mergers and acquisitions?"

I knew she was happy in her new life, but I sensed she still liked to hear about her former one.

"I'm working a deal my client is sweating over."

I shifted in my seat. The short pink dress I'd changed into was out of place in the old-styled bar, but Gina in her black gown looked every bit the part.

"The acquisition doesn't feel quite right. I need to find a new one to propose to the client immediately."

The waiter brought over the two waters and Gina's

cocktail. It was four o'clock in the afternoon, which I suppose qualified for aperitif hour, albeit an early one.

Gina smiled as she pressed her iced water glass to her neck. Her entire life had changed over the course of our twelve-month program. When we started, she was a dog mom, a banker, and was married. The only thing remaining of her previous life was the dog.

Truth be told, I was jealous. Who wouldn't be? I had managed to change countries, but I was still in finance and weaving in and out of unremarkable relationships. The rumor, which she had never confirmed nor denied, was that she'd had a wild affair with a musician, a guitar player to be precise, whom she had met at a Singapore bar while we were there for school. I was sure it was true — although, I wouldn't have put it past her to have made up the rumor herself.

Gina had taught me a lot in school as a model of liberation. Having grown up in the conservative Southeast, sensuality was synonymous with temptation in many minds back home; and no young girl wanted to be accused of such ethical decay. I struggled with that all throughout my teens and early twenties.

She was incredibly sexy but not in a traditional way. Everyone in school had a crush on her, but it wasn't her looks that made heads turn. It was her unequivocal disregard for caring what other people thought.

"I'm displaying a Simeti next month at Frieze in New York. I know you like him."

"Oh, I do," I sighed. "Simple, controlled, and provoking." I knew little about art really, but I knew very well that I was far from being able to afford one of his pieces. My father was a big fan of his work in the seventies. He'd even bought one back in the late eighties, but he'd given it to one of his girlfriends. An investment that never paid off — I made sure to remind him whenever the opportunity arose.

"I've started sleeping with my favorite client," she said somewhat acerbically. On some level, Gina was an inspiration; and on another, I was concerned about her. I shot her a look, and she read my mind. "Don't worry. I'm just having fun."

She reached down and picked up her glass of ice water. It dripped a stream of beaded perspiration as she lifted it off the table. Gina reveled in the drops that fell onto her bare legs which peeked out from the slit in her dress. She rubbed the water deliberately into her skin before taking a drink.

"I'm not sure I could ever do that. Don't you worry about damaging your reputation?" It was impossible for me to imagine a situation at the office where dating a client would be considered acceptable behavior.

"Darling, I see it completely differently. I am building my reputation."

"I think I'll stick with banking." *I couldn't sleep with clients; but I wouldn't want to anyway*, I grimaced. Gina may have been able to do whatever she wanted and be celebrated for it, but I'd already been involved with someone in my industry, and I ended up vilified. Besides, guys working in finance weren't known for their sex appeal anyway. They were known for their money and buying their way out of boredom. At this point in my life, I needed more in a man than just a full bank account.

Gina looked straight through me and set her drink back on the table. "Oh come on; it's a miracle you are even here this weekend! I was in London for my art fair in October, and I never saw you. You were so busy at the office. That is depressing, Audrey. You can't stay in banking forever. Who does that?"

"Our bank was the top adviser on M&A last year meaning nearly $1.7 trillion in deals. A lot of that came through London." I hated when people assigned me to a stereotype, even if it was true.

"Didn't you tell me once you had a dream to create your own advisory company?"

That was a dream born out of the optimism of being a student. It died as soon as I returned to banking. "Corporate feels more secure. At the end of the day, I just want to make a lot of money and be on my own — completely independent."

"That's the first time I've ever heard anyone refer to investment banking as secure!" Gina laughed. "You need to lighten up, lady. I think you've been in the corporate world too long. All the fun is being sucked out of your life. Are you still not dating anyone?"

"As if there is any time. What time I do have, I catch up on sleep."

I could see Gina's eyes roll just outside of my view. "Well, when someone worth it comes along, you'll make time."

"Maybe," I said unconvincingly. "I tried in New York, and that relationship promised me everything but almost destroyed me." We both relaxed a little deeper into the sofa. As the banana leaf inspired ceiling fans whirred overhead, neither of us wanted to talk badly about the groom at his own wedding.

"And what's the story with Mister Tall, Dark and Handsome? I saw the two of you talking outside the church."

"There isn't any story," I replied. "His name is Theo

by the way." My mind wandered to him, and I thought of his smile. "He's beautiful though, isn't he?"

"Gorgeous. And he seems like a lot of fun. Why aren't you making a play?"

"I don't make plays. I'm too proud; and besides, I think it's bad form to pick up men at your ex's wedding."

The truth was that I was sure Theo was something of a womanizer, and I had no interest in indulging the delusion he'd bestowed upon himself. Playboys bored me to tears, and I found it unjust that I never seemed to receive as much from them as I had to relinquish. I always ended up fantasizing about them a little after the affair had finished, and that wasn't productive. "Besides, he lives in Istanbul. It's far, and I don't see that city anywhere in my future."

"Don't be ridiculous, Audrey; you don't have to marry the guy," Gina said, launching into a whiskey-infused lecture. "You know, you don't have to control the situation to enjoy it."

"You know me. I don't know how to do one-night stands. I tried it once and ended up engaged." I tried to deflect her spotlight. "Why don't you go for him?"

"Oh, no, he's not my type," she explained. "He's too buttoned-up for me. I like my men messier, less tamed."

I laughed. Sometimes, she just sounded ridiculous. "He's in a suit; but Gina, we are at a wedding."

"Unless he has a few tattoos hidden under his suit somewhere, I'm not interested." She leaned back on her side of the couch; content she had effectively asserted her alternative palate.

"Doesn't he look familiar to you?" I was so sure we had met before, and I thought Gina might be able to help me remember.

"Right? I wondered the exact same thing. I actually thought he was with us at school."

I didn't remember him being in our class. "Maybe we've seen him in some of David's photos on Facebook or something?"

"That's probably it," she corroborated. "Less exotic, but more probable. Look, if you end up not going for him, you can take comfort in knowing the memory of a love affair is always more romantic if the affair never actually happened."

I wasn't sure I agreed, but I felt like indulging her. "How is it living the life of a gallerist?" I asked.

"I'm in a bit of a mess at work, honestly. The owner of the gallery has taken on a lot of debt to finance commissions. There's no way we can get out from under it. I think we're going to have to fold. The owner, Damien, has been bankrolling all of his friend's projects without any paper trail, meaning the gallery was far more indebted than anyone had thought."

"Yikes. How much of a liability are we talking about?"

"Nine hundred thousand euros."

"Gina! Are you kidding me? That's a lot of debt for a gallery, isn't it?"

"I know," she said. I reached across the couch and took her hand in mine. It felt remarkably cold even in the heat. "I certainly can't sell my way out of it quickly, and further financing will cripple us. We would have to make some serious sales to get the gallery above water or at least current on repayments."

"Gina, I'm so sorry."

"I know it's horrible, but we'll see. It's not over till it's over. There are two other partners that are considering buying out Damien; but the problem is, Damien has all of the connections. If he stays, it's bad. If he goes, it's worse — all of the artists will leave with him. They all love him, of course, because he's the magic money man. A gallery is only as strong as the community of artists it works with."

Gina looked up behind me and smiled.

"What is it?"

"That guy, Theo, you were talking to at the ceremony is on his way over here," she said, beaming with delight. She had the capacity to change on a dime. How she could be so happy in the middle of such pressure was beyond me, but that was just like her. She really did live in the moment.

"Hello," she said to him as he approached. "I was just leaving."

"Don't leave on my account. I was just coming by to say hi," he offered with a smile. "I'm Theo by the way," he said, extending his hand.

Gina stood, showing off her tall-elongated frame. "I'm Gina, and I know all about you," she said with a wink sliding her hand into his. I could feel my face flush with embarrassment. She picked up what was left of her melted cocktail and headed off to her room, squeezing by Theo as she passed him. "I think I'll have another cold shower before the reception," she said looking squarely at him.

"WHAT ARE YOU doing here in the lobby?" he asked, as I motioned for him to take a seat.

"Trying to stay cool. I just had an obnoxious call with

my office in London," I affirmed. "And I'm processing it, slowly committing myself to action."

"Really, on a Saturday?" His eyes searched me for an explanation.

"It's banking. We're always on the clock."

His hair was dark like India ink and wavy, cut short enough to be a consultant, but just long enough to prove to himself that he was a rebel. The chiseled features of his face were softened by the kindness of his eyes, and he had a slight dusting of a beard that cast a hue of savage beauty over his face. I was dying to put my hands on it. But it was the smile — the bright grin that shone across his face — that weakened me. It was quite possibly the most memorable smile I'd ever seen.

There had been only a few times in my life that I saw a man and was struck by our immediate chemistry. I saw cute men every day, but I see a beautiful man only once every few years. At twenty-eight years old, I could count on my left hand the number of times it had occurred.

He glanced toward my feet. I was wearing the latest fashionable stiletto sandal; the magazines had said it was the most comfortable sandal to ever be released; and just like everything else those magazines ever said, they were full of shit. The strap on the back of my left heel was already starting to cut into my skin. It was its own form of torture, but the shoes looked so great they were worth it.

"I like your shoes."

"Are you into women's shoes?" I joked.

"No, I'm just trying to make conversation to keep you next to me a little longer."

His flattery made my cheeks flush. "They were an experiment."

"How so?" he asked. His eyes lingered at the meeting point where my legs crossed.

"A friend of mine started a fashion-related tech company. Imagine pre-ordering fashion."

"Pre-ordering?" His eyes narrowed on mine and then shifted off behind me. I was losing him to something — a thought. *Maybe I was boring him?*

"Yes, it's like crowdfunded fashion. If the company gets enough pledged orders, they'll make the item and ship it out. Anyway, I tried out the platform by ordering these."

"Interesting. I like that idea. So you follow the tech industry?"

His voice was deep with a subtle German accent that seemed to stir desire. First, I imagined him naked; but quickly my thoughts escalated to dreaming about him in my bed while his accented voice whispered in my ear. "I do, but it doesn't pay as well as banking."

"Well, it might if your startup takes off."

"Ventures are risky. I don't mind placing such bets for my clients; but when it comes to my life, I prefer safer investments."

"Are we talking about your personal life or your professional one now?"

"Both," I said with a laugh while grabbing my glass of water off the table. "What about you?"

"I'm always attracted to risk," he said, giving me a small nudge. What game was he playing? Surely he wasn't trying to pursue me. David and I may have been pretending to be friends, but I knew very well that anything with Theo would be crossing the line.

Theo was scrolling through his phone, and he'd checked out of the conversation abruptly. I was contemplating a quick exit to my room to change my dress, but I wasn't ready to leave just yet. I enjoyed talking to him, but I knew better than to linger too long.

"Are you ready for champagne?" I asked, trying to keep the conversation afloat and get him to put down his device.

"No. I need to focus and keep my head clear." He gave me a careful look. "I have a big project at work, and you might have actually given me an idea," he continued.

"Are you a recovering alcoholic?"

"No. You are awfully suspicious."

"Not at all. It's just most of the people I know who don't drink, are, that's all.

"Really? He looked at me skeptically and then leaned in closer. "Who do you hang out with?"

He was inches from me now — his eyes piercing through me. I wasn't even sure what we were talking about anymore. I was done talking, and I wanted him to finish what he'd started. *Maybe just a quick kiss? No one would ever have to know.*

Silence fell over us, and I could feel the tension in the air that separated us. I could smell his masculine scent; he was so close. I breathed in deeply. I wanted to feel his lips touch mine.

"Bankers," I said, my mouth inches from his.

He smiled and pulled back to his corner of the couch. I internally celebrated my small victory. There was an entire night ahead of us; and anyway, he was forbidden. "Right, of course," he said.

"So if you're not drinking, then what is your vice tonight?" I asked.

"What makes you think I need one?"

"Weddings are so much more fun if you corner off your own pocket of pleasure."

"Is that right?" He looked around the room for a moment and rubbed his manicured beard with his hand. Then looking back at me, he said, "Well, I haven't committed to one yet."

We both knew he was lying.

THEO

THE EVENING WAS COMING TO AN END. Dinner had been extravagant and delicious as far as wedding fare goes, and the dance portion of the party on the rooftop of the hotel had erupted hours ago outside on the terrace that overlooked the golden-illuminated Acropolis in the distance. Audrey had been assigned to a table on the other side of the room, and I silently cursed David for such unfortunate table planning. I was jealous of those seated around her. The people at my table were boring and desperately single. From my seat, I had a perfect view of Audrey's naked back thanks to the plunging black jumpsuit she'd changed into.

I wasn't in the mood for dancing. Rather, I was focused on finding a way to make it back over to Audrey. She had spent the past hour in the adjacent rooftop garden talking with her friend Gina, and I hadn't found an opening to interrupt their conversation.

Emerging from the garden, Gina headed to the dance floor with her hands swaying above her head. Audrey looked across the terrace at me with a look of respite and headed to the bar with a smile. I took it as an invitation to join her.

"Clearly, *you* haven't been to rehab, yet," I said over her shoulder. She coughed up the sip of champagne she had just begun to swallow and elegantly turned her head away from me to recover from her clumsiness. A fog of awkwardness filled the space between us.

"What are you trying to say?" she rebuffed.

Her lips were still wet from the sip she'd just taken, and I wanted to taste the champagne from them in a kiss. "Only noting your fondness for champagne. I've never had it before."

"How is that possible?" she asked.

"When my parents were killed, I promised myself I would never drink."

She looked shocked but then softened her eyes.

"It's not that hard really. Don't get me wrong; I love to have fun, but drinking isn't my gateway to fun like it is for others." I could feel her withdraw slightly, searching me to know whether I was judging her. Perhaps she wasn't as confident as she let on. Probably not — who is?

"Does it bother you when others drink?"

"No, not at all. I've just always felt this promise was a special one to keep."

"Do you think you'll keep it your whole life?" she asked while coming again closer to me. "I mean, it seems extreme to make such a long commitment." She looked off to her right, pulled away, and raised her glass while smiling. David was across the way looking at us. She pulled the bottom of her dress down.

When she refocused her attention, I continued, "I'm not sure, but it's important for me to keep it. It keeps the memory of my parents alive in my heart; and no matter where I am in the world, it's a grounded connection I have with the family I still have in Germany. It's an association that is triggered constantly. Every time I go to a restaurant or bar or party or celebration or wedding, it's triggered."

The distance of her withdrawal was diminishing, and I could see her becoming more at ease. I could hear her breathe, and I felt her warming again. She was still searching for something more to say.

She picked up her glass from the bar and stood, brushing my hand as an encouragement to pursue her. I followed as she led me to a table closer to the dance floor. She sat first and smiled while she waited for me to sit down. We were sitting closer here than we had been able to at the bar.

I was surprised at how much I was sharing with her. Very few knew this story, but I couldn't stop the flow of endless expression. I yearned for something to break the conversation, something lighter to pull us out of the depths of my personal history.

"I have a rule about dating," she divulged.

"Is that right?"

"Yes, there are three parts," she teased, her eyes now shimmering in the evening light.

"Well, you must tell me." In the distance I caught the eye of Mitch, a mutual friend. He smiled and raised his glass to me; I winked back to say "hello."

"They are quite simple," she continued. "The first is I never date bankers."

"Well, that seems justified."

"Second, I never date consultants." She paused to give me time to react surprised.

"Really? Keep going . . ."

"And, third, I never date entrepreneurs."

I certainly wasn't winning this game but not for the reason she assumed. I wanted to keep playing though. The record could be set straight some other time.

"I know you don't like consultants, but why the entrepreneurs?" I asked, unable to conceal my curiosity.

"Because they live for their companies and nothing else. They stay awake at night working on improving products, hustling for financing, proving there is a market for their service."

"Do you really think entrepreneurs are more committed to their work than you as a banker?"

"Absolutely. I work in banking for the thrill and for the money. I can walk away any day and pick up something new. Entrepreneurs cannot."

I could smell the reaction of her perfume on her blushed skin. The light moisture that condensed on her from dancing earlier in the thick, thermal night air made her scent seem muskier than I'd noticed before in the lobby. I wondered what she would smell like up close. How would her neck smell? Her shoulder — her upper thigh?

If we disappeared tonight together, no one would ever have to know. "Well, you are going to break one of those three rules tonight," I said, as I slowly stood. "Come with me."

AUDREY

HE PAUSED, presented me his hand, and guided us to the dance floor. Turning me, he placed one hand just above my hip as I raised mine to his shoulder. He kept my other hand in his and dropped his head slightly to breathe in deeply at my neck. My lips parted as I let out a silent sigh. I knew I shouldn't be dancing with him, but I was having too much fun to decline his invitation. I'd find a way to take some distance when the song ended.

The music was slow, loud, and consuming; but the silence between us was awkwardly intimate. Each moment stretched and filled the room completely as if time was suspending itself between the hold of our bodies.

I had completely forgotten the rest of the room when I felt the cold wet of a glass press itself against my bare back. Startled, I turned in shock. It was one of David's friends from New York who I didn't know very well. The music muted his voice, but I could tell he was apologizing for his clumsiness. I hated it when drunks brought their sloshy drinks out on the dance floor.

I turned into the serenity of Theo's warm body; the side of my face pressed into his chest, but the chilled traces from the condensation of the glass still burned on my back.

When our intimacy became uncomfortable, he spun me around to air out the increasingly delicate connection. As he caught my hand, our eyes fixed and smiled. Again, he turned me; but it was too fast, and our hands missed each other; my heart stopped for a sliver of a second until he caught me again and drew me back into him. He was a good dancer: light and elegant. Someone must have taught him. His mother? An ex-girlfriend? No matter — I was grateful to whoever it had been. My body continued to pendulum between his arms — the tension between us expanding and contracting.

As I spun out once more, I saw David watching us; but when I turned back around to find him, he'd disappeared. He looked elegant in his black tuxedo — a model husband. At twelve years my senior, he'd grown into forty without gaining a wrinkle. His wavy, blondish hair hid any grey that might have crept up on him; and his sculpted face was just as beautiful as when he'd first approached me on the beach in the Hamptons. I hated him for looking so well.

Watching him declare his fidelity to another woman was more jarring than I'd anticipated, yet I couldn't stem the thought that maybe today was all a duplicitous sham. Could a deceitful man really change his nature in so little time? I'd come here to move on and make amends, but I now doubted whether I had succeeded. Maybe coming here really had been a mistake after all?

Theo was overheated in the Athenian spring air, and I could feel the subtle dampness beneath his shirt when my hand lingered across his back. The heat had forced him to remove his tie and then his jacket. I'd been watching him all evening strip off layers from the other side of the room. When the cufflinks were sacrificed, he'd rolled up the sleeves of his white dress shirt, revealing his strong forearms. I felt them now flex under my fingers each time we would catch each other between turns.

The song faded, and I realized there were maybe a dozen guests still remaining. I feigned fatigue to queue up my exit. Theo led, and I followed him back to the table. He gathered his clothing and slid his long arms back into his jacket. Collecting my things, I paused to catch a steely look from Delia, reminding me how uncomfortable my presence was for everyone. No doubt they were surprised I'd turned up at all. Perhaps the invitation had been meant more as a notice than an olive branch.

She and David looked tired; in fact, looking around, I saw the room was descending into its evening slumber. Athens was falling asleep; I was eager to join her.

Sensing a break in the traffic leaving to the elevators, I started toward them to dodge saying farewell to David. I could feel Theo some yards behind me: far enough to go unnoticed but determined enough, I was sure, to be transparent to anyone paying attention. I reached the elevator and pressed the button to call it.

Theo joined me, and we exchanged smiles. Was he nervous? Did he have a plan? The truth was that I loved it when a man had an agenda, but I didn't want to know it. Not yet — I was enjoying the suspense of not knowing how the next moment would unfold.

"You're tired," he said, fishing for a hint of my intentions. "I can see it."

"This is an excruciatingly slow elevator," I replied, refusing to confirm whether I was tired or interested. I wanted him to work a little more. I wanted to see him flex his power. Theo was tall and sexy, but he hadn't yet made a bold enough move. I made enough of those in my job that I didn't want to have to make them when it came to romance.

THE DOORS OPENED, and I stepped in. Theo quickly looked over his shoulder and followed me in as the doors lazily closed shut in the merciless pressing heat.

"What floor are you?" he asked.

"Six. You?"

"I'm on four," he said, pushing them both.

Could it be, I wondered? *Is this it? Are we going to our rooms separately? Is he that tired?*

I suddenly felt a surge of resentment. The truth was, playboy or not, I wanted him tonight regardless of any lingering emotional consequences. I'd deal with David's ghost another day. He smiled at me with his beautiful mouth. He was going to say goodbye, and my ego panicked as the elevator started its languid descent toward the ground floor.

Theo touched my shoulder with his fingers and turned me around to him. His hands then gripped my waist, pulling me into him as he backed me up against the wall.

In my heels, he still was at least twelve inches taller

than I was. He leaned into me — his right cheek brushing mine — his slow deep breathing in my ear. His lips crossed my forehead, and he pressed his nose slightly into my other cheek. The tension was thick and progress was painfully slow. Thankfully, the sluggish elevator was moving at the same pace.

He pulled away from me slightly and then lifted my entire body to match his height. The rush left my head spinning, and I felt weightless as he pulled me up to meet his face — my eyes widening while I tried to keep up. Wrapping my legs around him, I pulled myself back slightly as my thighs locked tightly around his hips. A wide smile peeled across his face, and I couldn't help but answer with my own.

I searched his brown eyes while his arms enveloped me and pulled my torso closer to his. I felt him inhale deeply while we stared through each other, searching one another for permission. He exhaled and then pushed me completely into the wall of the elevator, breaking off our stare. His focus shifted to my lips as he kissed me — lightly at first — but desire took over as he pressed into me harder. His kiss was deep and consuming. He was looking again for something, and I let him search for further consent.

The elevator doors opened on six, and he walked us through them and into the hallway.

"What room?" he asked as he turned right out of the elevator, my legs still wrapped around him with my wrists meeting behind his neck.

"What makes you think you are invited?" I demanded with a smile, still not ready to give up the play.

"Oh, I'm invited."

"637." I gave in easily.

I pulled back to look at him; and he smiled his gorgeous, wide smile back at me and gave me a wink. I kissed him again, sighing between my breath as he continued to walk us down the hall. The play was over.

"When was the last time you were tested?" I asked between kisses.

"Last week and clean," he replied. "I'm a little OCD about it." He pulled back abruptly, concerned he had revealed too much; but I was relieved. "You?" he inquired.

"Nine months ago." He stopped walking and paused to look at me inquisitively. "Clean . . . and no partners since."

I pursed my lips, embarrassed. *He must think I'm a loser.* But no matter, he had no idea about the power of the toy box I kept at home. A toy box is always there and never disappoints. The same could not be said about men.

We smiled at each other for completely different reasons and continued on down the hallway.

"But still, I prefer to use something." I never understood how people could sleep with strangers without using something. It was just too intimate for me.

"Not a problem," he said putting me at ease.

He let me down as we turned the corner into my hallway, and I fumbled for the card in my purse. I found it and slid it into the slot. The door beeped, and the light turned red. *Shit,* I thought. *It's not possible.* Worried my phone had deactivated it, I tried again while holding my breath.

The moment had been so perfect, and I was imagining myself embarrassed and awkwardly locked out of my room. The door beeped again; my heart stopped, and the light turned red. I'd been defeated by a door.

Theo, behind me, removed his hands from my waist and took the card. He warmed it between them and then slid it back into the slot as I contemplated whether it was better to retreat to his room or descend frustratingly to the front desk. The door beeped its third and final time as the light turned green. Theo was already pushing us through the door.

I recklessly kicked of my shoes and ran further into the room searching for a light switch. He let the door shut silently behind him. I found a switch; and soft, yellow light gleamed into the room from a corner floor lamp. I looked in his direction and locked into his predatory gaze. He walked slowly toward me, momentarily tripping on one of the stiletto pumps I had flung earlier. I smiled as he laughed off his flash of distress.

He walked across the living-room of the suite toward the bedroom and reached for my hand. He pulled me into to him. For the first time, I felt his hard length forcing itself against the fabric of his suit. As his hands wrapped around the back of my neck, he pulled me into his kiss. I was intrigued — my mind suddenly silent and suspended. I let my hands feel up under the front of his jacket; heat radiated from his body. My fingers plotted the lines of his torso over his white dress shirt. He was strong and built; I was dying to confirm with my eyes what I was feeling with my hands.

I slipped his deep-blue suit jacket off his shoulders. With a small tug at each wrist, it fell, crumbling to the floor. I brought my hands higher onto his chest and touched the bulging curves that lay under his tight, buttoned, white shirt. My heart was beating hard in my chest, and I could hear my pulse in my ears.

All of a sudden, a phone began vibrating urgently between us. "What is that?" I said jumping back.

"Oh, no. I'm sorry," he said searching his pocket for the device. He pulled it out and looked to see who it was. "I think I need to grab this. I'll be right back." He shot me a wink as he sneaked out the door. "Don't move."

Who would be calling him at three in the morning on a Sunday? I wondered. Feeling defeated, I collapsed on the bed and stared up at the ceiling.

And why couldn't he take the call in my room?

THEO

WITH MY PHONE RINGING, I slipped out of the hotel suite and shut the door quietly behind me. *Terrible luck,* I thought, adjusting myself slightly to get more comfortable.

"Hello?"

"Theo, It's Richard."

I looked down the hall searching for a place to talk so I wouldn't wake the entire floor.

"Hi Richard. You're in the office on Saturday night? I hope it isn't only on my account," I said, heading for the common area a few meters away at the end of the corridor.

"I don't believe that for a second," he replied. "You know, you might want to take a break sometime so that those who work with you can do the same. Hell, don't do it for you, do it for me."

Richard was one of the sharpest and shrewdest lawyers in New York. My firm consulted with him on nearly every deal we pursued, both in the United States and abroad. His loud mouth and brash style was effective in getting us what we needed but not to the detriment of the regard he commanded in the industry. In reality, he advised on much more than just the law. He was also an excellent strategy guy. Princeton and Harvard educated, he was a character that seemed to belong more in a Jersey-mafia film than in some of the more respected boardrooms in New York City; but he was what he was — and he was great at his job.

"Listen, we have ongoing tension among underwriters between their obvious enthusiasm to fully price the offering and the longer term strategic view requiring we anticipate sufficient upside for secondary investors."

Audrey has a nicer floor than I do, I realized as I reached the outdoor balcony and looked up at the golden Acropolis again in the distance. My floor didn't have this open terrace. I suppose it was my own fault for booking only the night before.

"I agree, Richard."

"With that in mind, we're going to struggle to raise the five hundred million you need. Let's take another look at the figures this week. I think, at this point, we're only halfway there; and the other issue that is concerning investors is whether or not there is demand in the market. Right now, it's theoretical; but it's not yet proven."

"I know; but I'm working on another idea that might help us close the gap," I said, wishing this call would wrap up quickly.

"I wouldn't have expected any less. What are you cooking up?"

"It can't be pitched just yet." In truth, Audrey had only just given me the idea.

"Okay, moving on, there is something else . . ."

I sighed silently in frustration. I really didn't want to be on this call, but I knew Richard was doing his best to help. His time was money, so I let him continue.

"Given the current burn rate and cash still available, this company will need to raise capital again before we see the end of five quarters."

I was growing tired of bad news, and it seemed to be swarming all around me like fire. However, at the moment I couldn't have cared less. All I really wanted was to get back into Audrey's room. "Look, I have to get back to something; but let's touch base after the weekend. I'll have some of the consultants outline other scenarios. The more minds on the problem, the better."

"I couldn't agree more. Have a good night. And sorry again for disturbing you."

"Good night, Richard. And get out of the office."

"Sleep is for the dead."

"You don't have to sleep. You just have to leave." I ended the call and looked down at my phone. It was 3:18 in the morning. I would be in the air on my way back home in less than ten hours. A faint wind of delirium swept through me as I remembered what was waiting for me behind the door down the hall.

I walked back to Audrey's room and knocked lightly. Suddenly, I wondered if she'd fallen a sleep. It was late, and it had been a treacherously long day in the sultry heat. And then rescuing me from my distress, the doorknob turned like a page.

AUDREY

A KNOCK FLIRTED AT THE DOOR. I bolted from the bed and slowly with frosty undertones opened the door, inviting him back in.

I'd taken advantage of Theo's fleeing the room to collect myself. Breathing deeply, I brought my arm to my face and searched for the remnants of his cologne that lingered on my skin. I rolled onto my stomach and crawled across the bed until I was sitting on the edge — my eyes still closed and my body focused on its breath. Arching my back, I let my hand fall along my face slowly, taking in its curves as my fingertips dripped down to my chin and then my nape. Stopping there, they lingered, seduced by the heat of my neck.

I grew more peaceful as the seconds ticked by until I

realized the gift that had been bestowed upon me. My eyes shot open; and I ran to the bathroom, kicking my shoes further out of the way. Reaching for my perfume, I spritzed the air and myself before returning to the entryway. I waited a full ten seconds, staring at the door, before giving up and collapsing back onto the bed in the other room. It was another five minutes of restlessness before he knocked on the door.

"I'm sorry. I apologize for my rude and badly timed exit," he said.

"Why on earth are you getting calls so late on a Saturday night?" The moment it escaped from my mouth, I regretted it. I had thought he was working, but maybe it was a woman. A girlfriend? A partner — I couldn't stop my mind from playing out its insecurities.

"I'm in the middle of a really tough deal. The stakes are extremely high. I'm really sorry."

"But still, your client calls you so late on weekends? Are you sure you're not a banker?" I joked, my defense softening now that he was standing before me.

He laughed and then smiled with a huge grin. "It's only eight o'clock in the evening in New York. And yes, it's true; some poor soul is at the office ruining my night."

"Consulting is the worst, really. I don't know how you do it." I took a look around the living room. *How to get him back to the bedroom elegantly,* I wondered.

His eyes smiled at me as he closed the gap between our bodies and slid his arms under mine.

"Anyway, I think I should start working on my apology for running out," he said before plunging his hands into my hair and kissing me.

His lips were warm and firm against mine as he

playfully licked my tongue with his: at times — controlling aggressive yet at others — relaxed and playful. His breath was sweet and warm; and with every inhale he took, it felt like he was stealing a little bit of my soul. *It was a pleasure kissing him*, I thought, as I felt myself warming inside his kind and generous embrace.

The strained tension returned under his suit. He was betraying himself, but he no longer had any shame. He wanted me to know.

As he explored my neck, my nipples tightened; and my breasts lifted slightly. He turned me around; and with his hands firmly gripping my hips, he started undoing the bow behind my neck with his teeth but not without distraction. His mouth deviated from the bow to explore my back with soft licks. My stomach contracted, and my thighs softened: my body willowy, seductive, and animal-like.

I broke away from his grasp and turned to face him. We stared at each other in silence as I unfastened the top button of his shirt and then the second. As I made my way down his torso, our eyes continued to search one another.

What was beyond those eyes, I wondered, *lust? Indifference? Was it arrogance?* It occurred to me that I knew very little about the man who stood before me. It felt dangerous — forbidden.

I released the fifth button on his shirt, revealing his brown chiseled stomach. As he breathed, his muscles expanded and constricted. Dark soft hair lightly wisped across his stomach, converging at the center and pointing to a trail that led downward to his groin.

As I unlatched the final two buttons of his shirt, his breath became more rapid. I peeled the unbuttoned shirt off his shoulders, and it too surrendered itself to its fate as it fell.

Then, out of blind desperation, he swallowed me in a kiss. With his hands at the back of my neck, he finished untying the bow he'd struggled with earlier. My slow game was over.

The silky one-piece slid down my body, catching at my hips. My breasts were exposed; the nipples taut and hard in the stiff air of the room. Theo backed away to take in the view.

I stood there in full confidence, letting him map me in his mind, until I raised my left hand to my hip and tugged at the fabric.

"Don't," he commanded. "Let me."

Defiantly, I continued to push the fabric down. His eyes raged at my disobedience. I knew that the moment I followed through my outfit would fall to the floor, and my naked fate would be sealed. So, I lingered two seconds too long: torturing him with time and letting him weigh his prize. He took a step closer to me; and I flicked my fingers, the fabric wilting. His eyes narrowed sharply.

"Really?" he said, surprised and amused.

"Really," was the extent of the explanation I felt like giving as I stepped out of the outfit — pantiless.

He smiled and took half a second to determine how to punish my display of rebellion.

"Come here," he ordered.

I took three steps forward, and he pulled me back up into his arms while I wrapped my legs around his waist once more as he walked us back to the bedroom of the suite. The damp between my legs was pressing on his stomach as we walked. There was nothing left for me to conceal from him.

He bent over, laying me onto the bed; and he straightened back up. I pulled on his belt; and it unwound itself from his body, bringing the heat of his erection closer to me.

Stepping out of his suit, he started to crawl over me, forcing me to my back. Surprised, I tried to find a counter move; but he was too fast; and his deep urgent kisses were paralyzing me with distraction. His attention moved quickly to my breasts; and my nipples sprang back to life under the magic of his bite, while the softness between my legs blossomed. I could feel the layers opening, exposing themselves. But, no . . . I wanted to taste him first. I craved it.

I extended my arms out and pressed on my forearms for leverage. As my chest rose, I pushed him back onto his knees and, with a little extra force, finally to his feet. Kneeling on the bed, I reached for his hips and pulled his stomach in for a light kiss. I dropped my face slightly to smell him. The perfume of his perspiration and tired cologne filled my lungs, and I selfishly breathed in a second time. He jolted in my hands.

I slid my fingers under the elastic band of his briefs and pushed them down. The head of his cock was swollen, with a distinct lip that dramatically separated itself from the broad shaft. With my arms wrapped around his hips, I led his cock into my mouth slowly, letting my tongue swirl beneath him in circles, massaging the underside of his shaft as I took him deeply into me. He gasped for deeper breath. He was big and just at the limit of what I could comfortably accommodate. Even so, I wanted him so much that I took him deeper into my throat.

Stifling my choking reflex, I slowly slid him out, my tongue continuing to circle and explore him.

He moaned through his breath as I retreated; my lips parted farther, lingering as they drew back over the tip. Again, I slid my mouth over him, consuming him. I was showing off.

His thighs shook; and I withdrew myself again, lifting my mouth off him. Obscenely, he remained in front of my face as I lowered his shorts down from his thighs, letting them pool around his ankles. He smiled at me with his big smile as he stepped out of them, one foot at a time. I watched him from under my eyelids, giving myself away with a grin.

He pursued me back onto the bed, and I surrendered willingly as he once more took my left breast into his hand, teasing the nipple between his fingers. He lowered himself to my stomach, which had tightened again in my aroused state, and kissed around my navel until my hip caught his eye. Tracing circles around my hipbone with his tongue, he made my stomach spasm from the pleasure.

He grabbed for the back of my thigh and lowered himself farther under the shadows of the room. With two fingers he entered me, and the swollen walls of my sex gripped around him. The tips of his fingers began a slow walk summoning me; Theo watched me intently. My back arched when he reached a feverish spot; and his mouth descended to my clitoris, flicking and teasing as if playing me like an instrument. It was sweet, burning torture. He began pressing deeply up with his walking fingers, and a rush of new currents shivered down the back of my legs.

"Stay right there," I whispered desperately.

My breath deepened and slowed for what seemed like

an eternity while he continued to play me. The brittle air of the room hardened my nipples further as breath caught in my throat. The back of my legs tightened moments before my body began its release, pumping hard against his hand and mouth. I came as he gently sucked my clit; his eyes alight with triumph — another conquest made. I obviously wasn't the first, but I didn't care.

I recovered my breathing as he crawled to lay next to me still fully erect. Selfishly, I disappeared out of my head for a moment, silent, feeling no obligation to speak whatsoever.

I turned to face him. He smiled generously and full of pride; his hand was lightly stroking himself. His touch was lazy and slight, just enough to tempt me. He was too proud to beg. I continued to watch to learn how he liked it; and once I was confident of the rhythm, I rolled onto his body and slid myself down until I fit between his thighs. I took him again into my mouth: one hand at the base of his cock and the other planted next to his hip to help me keep my balance. With my hand I continued the rhythm he had taught me only seconds before; and with my tongue and lips, I sought out his secret spots with care. His sex engorged even more, and his breathing deepened.

He grabbed me around my abdomen, lifting me off and placing me to his side on the bed. Crawling toward the edge of the bed, Theo was careful to regain control; but he was close. I could taste it.

Reaching into his pants, he ripped apart the foil wrapper, and rolled a condom down his long shaft — one foot on the floor and the other knee bent on the bed. Still sitting in front of him, I watched the swells of pleasure chasing up his torso as he did it.

"I can't take you anymore, Audrey. I'm going to come so hard," he spoke as he began to crawl over me again.

He laid me back down on the fluffy, white hotel comforter and wrapped his arms under mine, taking my upper shoulders into his hands. I felt him pressing against me as he hovered close. Slowly, he entered me; and we both inhaled before collapsing in a tense surrender. He quickened his thrusts, pushing deeper inside me with each one. As my breath began to catch again, I wrapped my arms around his body, burying myself into him as I surrendered to another eruption of waving pleasure. His breathing slowed and regulated until it seized in his lungs; and he came too, pulsing deep inside of me as the surges of my own orgasm began to subside. It ripped through his body, shaking him involuntarily. His warm breath exploded in short bursts at the side of my cheek. He clung to me as he finished — unmoving for a few moments, lost to the world and hidden in my arms.

When he stirred, he took his place next to me.

Maybe I had been wrong, I thought. *Apparently toys have their limitations after all.*

The room fell silent, and the yellow light of the room crept in and out of my view as my eyelids grew heavy.

"*Guten nacht,*" he whispered, rotating me onto my side and curling his body intimately around mine.

I had completely forgotten he was German.

"*Schlaf gut.*" I whispered back, kissing the arm that was holding me. That was nearly all of the German I remembered from my grandmother.

As sleep began to overtake me, I fleetingly wondered if I'd need to learn more. Unlikely as it was, it would depend entirely on if, when I woke up, he was still in my bed.

THEO

I WAS GRASPING onto the final, elusive moments of sleep when I heard her voice — soft and muffled; she was trying not to awaken me. It was kind of her, but the effort was useless.

I lingered there between the sheets that had just hours before been saturated with sweat and exhaustion. Now, in the golden light of the morning, they were dry and cool; and in the earliest moment of my wakening, I wasn't completely sure where I was. I clung to the ambiguity for a moment longer until it inevitably escaped, chased away by a startling surge of reality.

Clumsily, I searched for my phone to see the time. The tired illumination told me it was ten o'clock in the morning. My flight back to Istanbul was in three hours. I ran the math. Taking into consideration checkout and the taxi to the airport, I had one hour to spare. Forty minutes if I adjusted to allow for finding my clothes and stuffing what I had in my room into my small carry on.

I rolled back onto my stomach; my face turned as I observed her unseen. She was dressed in nothing but unquestionable confidence. I studied from a distance the lines of her curves: the delicate arch of her back that emptied to her tight, round ass. She hung up the hotel phone on the large wooden desk in the living room and turned around toward the bedroom.

"What are you working on?" I floated.

Facing me, her breasts hung abundantly on her small frame. I retraced in my mind the places I'd discovered only a few hours earlier while I twisted again onto my back.

"Coffee," she said as she walked back toward the bed. I wasn't sure how you took it, so I ordered it with options. I like a good option."

She was playing with me. "I take it black," I told her.

"Of course, you do." She slid back under the sheets, her hand traveling up to rest upon my chest. "Is it because you like it that way or because of some masculine obligation?"

"Definitely obligation," I said. "I don't want you to judge me for taking sugar."

"I totally would have if you did."

"How do you take yours?" I smiled.

"With sugar and warm, frothy milk."

"You are so soft."

Her hand traced down to my lower stomach. "I'm indulgent; there is a huge difference!"

I was sure of that, and I confirmed it silently to myself as the memories from the night before began flickering in my mind: the curve of the small of her back gliding across the bed, her arm muscles contracting as she crawled on top of me. I started to become turned on as she slinked around beneath the sheet. She was exposed but guarded — conflicted somehow.

I wondered if I would see her again. *Could I manage to fly up to London?* I wanted to, but it was unlikely. I didn't have time for women right now, especially women living in another country. Even here in Athens, I could feel the pressure from work mounting all around me. Yet, there was something about her. She would be hard to forget.

THE ROOM BELL RANG. "You stay there; I'll get it," she said, throwing a mint-green beach cover-up over her naked figure.

I crawled back under the sheets while she signed for breakfast.

She wheeled in a cart covered in crisp white linen and topped with silver. "Your coffee," she said pouring out an Americano. Reaching for her frothy cappuccino, she made her way back to the bed. Waking up with her seemed overindulgent, probably because it wasn't my habit to sleep over.

I could just make out the outline of her curves under the sheer cover-up. Her nipples were hard, the silky fabric catching on them as she moved about the room. I wondered if I had time to take her again: one last tryst before we left the city.

She handed me the coffee as she crawled onto the bed. "Are you specialized yet as a consultant?" she asked.

"Well, I used to work on a lot of manufacturing cases;

but now I seem to spend more time working on financial transactions." That was mostly true.

"Sounds riveting."

"Hey, I really like my work. You shouldn't knock it. Not everyone is cut out to be a banker like you."

"Maybe not even me," she said lowering her eyes over her mug of coffee.

"It seems to be going well for you."

"It is, but I'm not sure it's a sustainable lifestyle. I come here and see my friends; and I realize that back in London, there is a lot missing in my life. And all for what? A nice flat and a full bank account?"

"Maybe you should go into consulting?" I joked. "Why do you dislike consultants so much?"

"I find most of them to be content light — always selling; and I've dated enough of them to know it's not what I'm looking for in my life."

"Ouch. And me?"

"Still assessing," she said with a wink. "I think I'm frustrated. I can't even get away for a weekend without work following me here."

"What would you do if you weren't a banker?"

"That's the problem. I have no idea. I'm really good at this." Her eyes fell down to the coffee cup she was now holding in her lap. She swirled the frothy liquid around like a whirlpool, completely somewhere else. I was losing her.

"Look, I have a big deadline at work. I should probably get to it. What time is your flight?"

Uneasy and surprised, I was sure a woman showing me the door had never happened to me before. I looked at my phone. It was 10:30 a.m. There was no time left to play, but still I wanted her again.

"My flight is at one o'clock. I should probably head back to my room, pack, and head to the airport."

"Okay," she said, revealing the slightest air of disappointment. She stood placing her coffee back on the silver cart and tightly wrapped her cover-up around her body. She was withdrawing, and I felt an involuntary sense of urgency as I looked around the room to collect my clothes.

I dressed myself enough to make it through the halls and back to my room — not exactly a walk of shame, more a walk of disheveled pride. She was nervously scrolling through her phone waiting for me to leave. She was gone, somewhere else entirely — no longer with me in this room, in this city.

I made my way toward the entryway of her room and placed what was left of my coffee on the cart as I passed. Walking toward her, I took her phone out of her hand and brought her back into my arms.

"This was one of the most memorable nights I've had in a long time," I said, eager to leave an impression on her amidst her indifference.

Her chilled impassivity melted, and she smiled while looking straight into my eyes. "You were an absolute pleasure," her voice thick with sleep and seduction. "Thank you for a wonderful night."

I leaned down to kiss her. We both lingered — our lips hovering together for an instant too long. Breaking the moment, I slowly pulled away and made my way to the door.

I took a step out of the room and then turned to see her in the arch of the doorway. A blade of panic crashed through me, and I grabbed her arm. It was a slightly awkward move following such an intimate night.

"Come see me in Istanbul," I sputtered. It was an involuntary reaction. I knew it, and I could see in her eyes that she knew it too.

"Let's not kid ourselves," she replied hesitantly. "Neither of us needs a relationship right now."

"No, I mean it." I said, again unable to stop the stream of dribble flowing from my mouth. I was talking just to have an excuse to stay a moment more with her. "Just come. It doesn't have to be any more complicated than just a visit."

"I'll think about it," she said. It was the empty promise to match my desperate but empty request. It was my ego longing for what it couldn't have.

I pulled myself closer to her, my hands now gripping her upper arms, and leaned down to kiss her one last time. My lips trembled slightly as they touched hers, and I felt closer to her now in our separation than I had when we'd awoken together.

She was kind; but as I let go of her arm and turned down the hallway, I knew I wouldn't see her again.

AUDREY

"THIS IS A GREAT FIND. It's perfect," Nir said looking around the tiny outdoor terrace bar. His eyes, distracted by the energy of the strangers moving around him, darted around the breezy space.

Athens was a funny mix of grunge and splendor, and the former certainly was the prevailing element when the sun fell beneath the horizon. Young people on the streets were decked out in their most alternative attire, parading through the ancient and narrow pathways of the city. The bar I'd found had been highly rated online, and it was nestled into the street like a diamond wedged into kimberlite. The tiny road curved around the bar, and a small local park filled with olive trees was located just across the street. The terrace of the bar naturally overflowed into the public garden.

Nir, a mutual friend I shared with David, lived in New York and had dated a semi-famous actress a few years back. Ever since they'd split, he'd been floating around like an untethered rope in the wind. We were the only two guests left in Athens on Sunday night: wedding exiles lost in an unknown city.

Since Monday was a day off in the United Kingdom, I'd decided to stay until the next morning to get away from the pressure of London. I knew if I went back home I would end up in the office during the holiday, so I thought it best to stay far away. In the end it hadn't made a difference since I spent the entire day working in my hotel room from the moment Theo left until Nir texted me to hurry and get my ass in the cab he had waiting downstairs.

My initial plan was to be alone for the night in Athens to relax and sleep, but I realized that would never materialize once I discovered Nir had also stayed the extra night. On top of that, it was his birthday so I traded in my earned night of relaxation to take him out to celebrate. It was a lot of pressure — nights out with Nir were notoriously insane and mostly illegal, and I was out to show him a good time in a city I didn't know.

Neither of us had ever been to Athens, so we were making up the evening as we went along. Nir's suggestion had initially been to book a night at a discovery dungeon. *Whatever that is?* But I'd succeeded in shifting his birthday party to the quaint local find where we now sat drinking gin cocktails. This was as far as my planning went, but he was cheery and seemed perfectly content with his lazy birthday party of two.

"That is an amazing dress you're wearing tonight," Nir said, taking a cigar out of his jacket.

He was right. This dress was special. It was a light, cherry-red with a deep, wine-colored lace appliqué on the front. The best part though was the wispy ties that held the dress together at my shoulders. I'd stumbled upon it last summer at the Bon Marché, the oldest department store in Paris. Having loved it so much, I'd bought it in duplicate since it was on sale.

"Thanks, luv. It's one of my favorites."

"I really like how it shows of your shoulders. Sexy."

I looked across at Nir as he lit his cigar. I've always loved the way men look when they puff on cigars. The smoke floated from his mouth into the dead of the night. I'd never noticed before how attractive he was since my souvenirs of him were blurry flashes of wild parties and tripping laughter; but now in the calm glow of the sleepy city, I saw his shadowy sultriness so plainly. He was a little shorter than the men I was usually attracted to; but with his linen white shirt mostly unbuttoned in the still feverish city, I could see that his figure was slight and toned.

It was only now, on this weekend, that I was truly coming to understand the depths of my friend beyond the limits of his feral reputation. Nir was an amazing pal, and I especially loved the way he talked about women. He truly loved all things feminine and appreciated the finer divine details of my gender. I could listen endlessly as he explained his attractions with the romanticism and fluidity of a prized poet. Being Israeli, he personified living in the moment like so many of his compatriots. I suppose not knowing whether one will live to see the next day conditions a person to fully experience the present.

The night air filled my thoughts of Theo, and I wanted to hold on to the memory of him a little longer before it would eventually fade. We'd exchanged numbers during the reception at the wedding before the destiny of our affair had been clear. As my cocktail began to go to my head, I found myself tempted to message him. Amidst the warm calm of the night, my body longed to be close to his again, yearning to feel his soft skin silkened with light perspiration. I tried to picture him in Istanbul, but I'd never been there before and had trouble imagining a scene that wasn't here in Athens. *I should go visit him there,* I thought, before dismissing it as a terrible idea.

Nir's phone lit up with a message. "David's on his way. He's parking."

"You invited David?! Are you mad?"

"Yeah, why?"

"Yes, you're mad?" I asked, raising an eyebrow. "He just got married yesterday. Why would you invite him to hang out with me, his ex-girlfriend?"

"Well, first of all, it's my birthday, so I can do whatever I want. I invited him to hang out with me, actually. And second, he's coming, so . . . guess it isn't a big deal?"

I rolled my eyes into the back of my head and wished that I'd stayed in my hotel room. The wedding had been uncomfortable. Being an adult was harder in reality than how I'd imagined it to be sitting in my London apartment weighing whether to RSVP "yes" or "no."

In my foolish fantasy, Delia would have embraced me as a postmodern sister; and David would have thanked me for coming and told me that he was sorry for what had happened between us. *But it's all water under the bridge,* he'd say.

"Who was that guy you were dancing with last night?" Nir asked, swallowing a sip of his cocktail. Apparently,

Theo's and my chemistry hadn't been as discreet as I'd hoped. I set my cocktail on the table between us as I prepared to explain myself.

"Hey, sorry it took me so long," David shouted as he arrived in understated fanfare. I turned around to greet him but not before Nir shot me a knowing look. I prayed that he'd remain silent.

"This is a great spot, guys. I didn't even know it existed," David admitted. "It reminds me of that tiny place in Paris that Gina always took us to in the Sixth Arrondissement."

The Sixth was a trendy neighborhood on the Left Bank, and Gina always insisted we meet there since that was where she lived.

"Yeah, except that one doesn't have a terrace this cute." I said, setting my drink back down on the bar.

The corners of David's mouth curled into an intended smile, and I wondered if Delia knew that her husband was out partying with his ex — especially given the shadows of jealousy she'd cast in my direction during the wedding.

"I think my favorite bar is this little place in Japan I went to once by accident. I walked in and was asked to take my pants off. Then the hostess asked me to sit naked on a chair that had a box of kittens underneath."

"What the hell are you talking about?" David shouted.

"It's a really great place, and they make their own whiskey." Nir continued, "but the kicker is the kittens paw at your naked balls while you drink. It's remarkably delicate and soft, aside from the occasional claw."

David and I looked at each other with wide eyes while Nir made kitten clicking sounds with the back of his throat and mimicked ball-pawing movements in the air with his two hands.

I worried David could sense what had happened between Theo and I the night before. Each time he looked in my direction, I felt the cringe of shame for having slept with his friend.

Did he know? No, it's impossible for him to know.

He would have been too preoccupied with the finale of his wedding. I needed to shake it off. Gina would never worry about such a thing. I regretted on some level that I couldn't be more relaxed like her.

"Right, okay, guys let's go," David said saving the night. "I'm going to take you to The Deuce."

I closed out our tab, and we headed back to a main road that seemed to act as an artery through the city.

"Audrey, give me your dress," Nir shouted as we walked among the background noise of the traffic.

"What?" I asked, not paying much attention to him.

"I want to wear it," he insisted.

"I'm not giving you my dress. What would I wear?"

"I'll give you my clothes."

"No," I said, trying to end the conversation.

"But, it's my birthday," Nir pleaded. The personal capital that Nir was spending on his birthday was starting to run out.

David continued leading the way, and I looked around at the traffic that trickled down the four-lane thoroughfare. There was a small park off to the right; and with the guys a couple steps ahead, I took my phone from my bag and quickly sent off an intrepid first message to Theo: *Thinking of you in Athens.* It was as creative as I could manage while trying to keep up with the guys.

There were two ways this "Theo-thing" could go.

Either it would die on the vine once a few more days passed, and we forgot about each other; or we would continue to flirt by text message every so often and maybe hook up if he ever came to London on a project. I was fine with either option but slightly preferred the latter. In any case, if he never wrote me back, the alcohol in my blood told me that at least I wouldn't have any regrets.

I dropped my phone back into my bag and ran a few steps to catch up with the guys. "Okay, Nir, you can have my dress but only for two minutes."

"Great! Yes, fine," he said as he started a series of imperfect cartwheels through the park.

David looked at me with his eyebrows raised, and I rolled my eyes. "It's his birthday," I reminded him.

Nir took off his white linen shirt and handed it to me in the park. *What were the indecent exposure laws here?* I wondered.

I untied my red dress at the shoulder and buttoned Nir's shirt over it. Sliding my dress off, I felt the hot evening air against my bare ass. I regretted not having thrown on panties before running out the door.

I handed my dress to Nir and confessed, "Darling, I'm not wearing any underwear." David shot me a wide-eyed look that I pretended not to see.

"Like I care," Nir replied throwing my dress over his head and shimming it down his body. I couldn't believe it fit him.

He slid off his jeans and handed them to me. His white shirt just barely covered my butt; so with the grace of an egret, I slipped my legs into his jeans and pulled them up. They were big on me; but with the belt, I was able to keep them on.

I looked over at Nir. He was actually pulling off the dress. I was impressed.

"Okay, let's go. Everybody have some clothes on?" David said, eager to keep us moving.

Nir ran ahead and was dancing in the street while David and I hung back watching on like exhausted parents.

Arriving at The Deuce, David found a corner outside for Nir and I to change back. "I think this is a good spot," he said walking up close to me.

"It's perfect," I said looking everywhere but at him. The small space was dark and had three brick walls around it. "Where is Nir?"

"I think he went straight into the bar." David said.

"Shit, he's going to get beaten up," I exclaimed, as we headed in to find him.

David held the door open and smiled, first with his eyes and then with his mouth. "You haven't spent much time in Greece, have you?"

FROM WHAT I COULD SEE in the obscurely lit and narrow place, The Deuce was a genuine dive but wallpapered with character. The bar was to the left and ran all the way along to the end of the room, which was dimly lit in red hues. A long mirror hung just behind the bar allowing guests to survey the entire room from wherever they stood.

Nir had already established himself at the center of the bar with a stool saved on either side of him. David and I went to take our places in his court. The bartender was already pouring out Nir's drink order when he turned around on his stool to face the room. "I like this place, David. Good pick," he declared.

"Nir, I think we should change back." I requested.

"Just a little longer," he said, eying a woman across the room. "It's such a great dress."

"I know, dear. That's why I'd like it back."

The bartender placed three drinks in front of us. Nir, picking up his drink, ordered another round to follow and stood up to walk over to the woman who'd caught his eye. We were already a few drinks into the night, and I was starting to faintly worry about my inevitable hangover in the morning.

"To Nir," David toasted.

"To Nir," I seconded. We looked on as our friend tried to make new ones.

"He's working so hard," David observed.

I turned myself back in toward the bar. "I think he's disadvantaged trying to pick up a girl while dressed like one." I smiled and picked up my drink again. "To Greece," I said. "What a magical place."

David moved over to the middle seat that Nir had been sitting in and continued to make jokes at Nir's expense. When those ran out, he hesitated and then asked his question. "So what's going on with you and Theo?"

My face flushed, but I continued to look forward as if his inquiry was no big deal.

"I mean you two seemed to talk a lot last night."

"Did we?" I paused while contemplating which card to play: truth or harmless deception? "He's nice. Not really my type, of course."

"Is that right?" David floated while Nir returned with his head hanging low.

"So how did it go?" David asked.

"She wanted to keep hanging out with her friend. I took the hint."

I knew Nir didn't speak Greek so I was curious. "What language did you speak with her?"

"I'm not sure."

David and I exchanged a laugh together as Nir stood back up and went toward the front of the bar to try again with another target.

It was awkward sitting with my newly-married, ex-boyfriend exchanging lighthearted laughs as if he'd never broken my heart; but I was determined to put the past to rest. We had too many mutual friends to maintain any lingering bitterness.

"Maybe we should change back," I yelled after him.

"It's like watching a puppy try to make new friends with cats," David remarked.

Again, Nir returned with disappointment in his eyes. By now there were twice as many people in the room than when we'd entered. It was getting crowded, and Nir stumbled into a man on his way back to the bar. I held out my hand, and Nir pulled me off my stool to dance to the eighties remix that was waking up the room. I needed a little space from David. We danced together laughing as David documented the scene with the camera on his phone.

One of the locals left his crowd to come over to us. *Oh no*, I thought, *this is going to be a fight.* I was sure that we had offended at least half of the room, if not the majority.

The guy was on the short side with dark, wavy, wild hair. He looked like a musician, wearing apple-green pants and a pastel-paisley buttoned shirt. He spoke directly to Nir, out of my range.

The two guys exchanged smiles and a high-five. Nir

grabbed the motorcycle helmet from the guy's hand, put it on, and turned to me. Sweeping me up in his arms, he went to fake kiss me; but my face collided with the helmet. I burst into laughter and fell backwards out of his arms. His pal in the green pants was quick to catch my fall. The local musician gazed at me with intense hunger. Nir spoke into the ear of his new friend as the stranger began unbuttoning his wild shirt.

It had been an hour since I'd texted Theo, but he'd not yet messaged me back. As brief waves of semi-soberness ebbed and flowed, I began to feel uneasy over having messaged him in haste. Embarrassment crept at the corners of my mind.

Handing his shirt to Nir, the musician turned back to face me. Now that he was fully naked from the waist up, I could see that his torso was completely ripped. I wondered what they put in the water here as I looked around and realized I was surrounded by attractive men.

"Hi," the artist said, directly into my face. He was so close I could feel the heat from his half-naked body. Just behind the hot newcomer, I could see Nir pulling my dress down to his waist to put his friend's shirt on before continuing to dance with the strangers who walked past him.

"Hi," I returned reluctantly.

The handsome stranger continued in Greek which I couldn't understand. I smiled politely and shrugged to show my incomprehension.

I turned around to David who was watching my every move. "You know, there's a point in every night when it occurs to me to go home; and every time I ignore that cue, I regret it in the morning."

David smiled wistfully. "Maybe we should get going;

but for the record, I think we passed that point a while ago."

He moved to talk to Nir, and I could see he was engineering our exit.

I smiled again at the artist and turned back toward the bar to pay Nir's birthday tab. Two pairs of hands slipped under the shirt I was wearing and made their way easily to my hips. His grip was strong, and for a moment I felt myself seduced by the momentum of the night. His hands continued to explore further up my stomach, and I hurried to finish closing out the bill before he went too far.

It was a bold move, but it only reminded me of Theo's resilient hands around my waist the night before. I could feel myself surrendering to my anonymity in this city. I turned to him as he swept me out to the center of the room.

I looked toward the door. David had succeeded, and he and Nir were already on their way out. The stranger held my face in his hands, lustfully; we were paralyzed by the loss of language, neither one of us capable of communicating with the other.

Then in a thick Grecian accent, he said, "Maybe we should . . ." He struggled to search for the remaining words in the depths of his English vocabulary but came up empty. He wanted to take me home. I knew that someone like Gina would totally have been up for it, but I was incapable. The energy of the city was compelling, but my fantasies still lingered on Theo.

"I can't," I said as graciously as possible. All I really wanted was another night in Theo's arms. Anything else would have been riddled with disappointment.

I slipped out of his strong, persuasive embrace and made for the door — chasing after the guys.

My phone beeped, and I picked it up in an instant to look at the message. *Missing you in Istanbul,* was all it said; but on some level I knew it meant trouble.

THEO

My eyes were still heavy with sleep when I opened them to appease my ringing alarm clock. It wasn't until focusing up at the ceiling that I realized where I was — home in Ulus. It was six o'clock in the morning, and the rest of the neighborhood would be asleep for another hour or two. I was expected at work, and there was much to accomplish this week.

I rolled from my back onto my stomach, half-committed to getting out of bed. I wasn't ready for the day yet. Laika, my dog, stretched out lazily at the foot of the bed, pushing my leg out of her way with her own.

My thoughts wandered back to Athens — waking up to see Audrey's naked silhouette. Thinking of her began to turn me on, but I couldn't. I had to get to the office. My ears were still ringing from the roar of the stadium during last night's football match. We'd won. It had been a great weekend.

Standing up, my feet shuffled across the dark wood floor; and Laika sprung off the bed. She was always ready to face the day at a moment's notice. I envied her early morning enthusiasm.

I made my way down to the open kitchen to make coffee as Laika circled her chocolate, furry mass around my legs.

Looking out through the giant living room window, I was reminded of what a luxury it was to live here. Ulus was a posh neighborhood in Istanbul, set in the mountains with incredible views on the Bosporus Strait and the Anatolian side of the city. The sun had risen just minutes ago; and the city to the east, across the water, was awash in a rose glow. The view overlooking the Bosporus was worth every cent I'd paid for the place. Views like this could not be found in Berlin.

As the coffee brewed, I thought about how much it felt like home to live here — or a home. The machine whizzed and whirled. The smell of fresh coffee filled the room, and I started to fully awaken. I went to the dining table with my mug and flipped open the computer. There was still no news from New York, but it was just as well. I was due in Gebtz where our manufacturing plant was located, and I had my own mountain to climb this morning. Our team of consultants had been working on financing for months, but each improvement was marginal. Now, we needed a big idea — and Audrey had given me just that.

My mind wandered from the computer back out the window to Audrey. I pictured her still in Athens asleep in the cool white sheets I'd woken up in yesterday. I wanted to see her again, but I chased the idea away with pragmatism. It was impossible right now with work.

Looking at my phone, I pulled up a photo she'd sent me of herself, David, and another friend out in Athens the night before. It was a messy scene; but her beautiful, green eyes drew me into the picture. I looked at David with his arm wrapped around her waist. I felt a jolt of envy each time I looked at it but managed to dismiss the feeling. David had just married after all. *But why was I jealous?* She wasn't mine — *or was she?*

Best not to tell him about our fast affair. *Would she have told him?* I wondered how close they remained. I wanted to text her, but my sense of self-preservation told me to cool off.

I swallowed the final sip of coffee from my mug. There was no denying it; I was now committed to the day. I walked back over to the large window and looked out over the water. Laika came and sat next to my feet while I imagined the immensity of the Asian continent that spread out beyond my window. *The world is so vast,* I thought, *so many people: only a minuscule probability of a chance encounter with a stranger.*

Laika's attention shifted to a ball that was stuck under the couch, and she went over to it scratching carelessly at the dark-blue Belgian linen that covered the sofa. I walked over to rescue my furniture and reached under for the ball. She looked up at me with shameless optimism. "Okay, okay, I'll play, but only for a minute." Her face erupted in pure joy as I drew back my arm to toss the ball. Work could wait a few extra minutes.

GATHERING UP my things, I got out of the car and started to walk toward the platform. The air was humid and thick, but the temperature was mild. It was cooler for May than I had remembered from last year, and it was certainly fresher than Athens had been.

"Good morning, Azra," I said, walking up to my assistant. Her long, dark hair was blowing in the wind of the rotor blades.

"Morning," she replied trying to hold her hair back with her empty hand. There was a coffee cup in the other, and I hoped it was for me. "Did you have a nice weekend in Athens?"

"It was nice but very hot. The airline lost my bag; could you sort it out for me?" I asked, tucking my boarding passes into her leather bound portfolio.

"You got it. Anything else?"

"Is that coffee for me?"

"As if you even have to ask," she said, handing me the paper cup and turning toward the helipad.

I HAD just settled into the office in Gebtz when Malik peeked his head through the door. A little younger than I was, he was one of my best: fresh, hardworking, and creative. An engineer by training, he now was a link between business operations and manufacturing. I'd brought him with me from our team in Berlin.

"It's time we prove the demand for the product," I declared.

"But we already have orders from all over the world on Model I that we still need to fulfill."

"That isn't enough. We're having trouble coming up

with the full amount of cash we need to raise in the initial public offering, so I'd like to pivot."

Athens had proven useful to my problems at work. This company was running out of cash, and we needed to convince its investors to provide capital. I'd been grappling with the mounting tension from them for months, but Audrey's shoes had given me an idea — a risky one.

Malik leaned forward. "What did you have in mind?"

Audrey's sexy legs flashed in my mind. "I want to make the new Model II available for pre-order. We can use the deposits that customers make to hold their place in the queue to finance production."

"Aren't you worried about the mechanical glitches we are still testing."

"No, those will be solved in a matter of time."

"That's true, but we don't have a feasible manufacturing plan yet in place." He was right, but the truth was it didn't exist because it hadn't been made a priority given all the other urgent cases these last months.

"Exactly, so our task today is twofold. We need to develop and launch a pre-order event. I want it to build anticipation in the market, and it needs to be huge. Our challenge is to have the event within the month."

"What?!" he exclaimed. This was a big ask.

"At the same time, we need to develop a solid manufacturing plan that accounts for the range of possibilities we might see in terms of orders."

"Okay, but I'm going to need more resources on this."

"Take the consultants you currently have working on manufacturing to sort out that piece. I'm going to ask for another team to work on the ordering process and event while collaborating with the in-house publicity team in

London; both will report to you. You need to know what they are projecting in terms of final orders so you can work on the manufacturing problem."

"Okay, yeah, that's clear." Malik leaned back in his chair as if to relax, but I could see his brain overheating.

"This needs to be a huge publicity win. If it flops, it will kill the company's IPO later in the year. There is a lot on the line."

"I got it. I'll have a plan in motion by next week, and I'll keep you informed."

AUDREY

ARRIVING AT MY APARTMENT DOOR, I slid my key into the keyhole with the precision of a surgeon. Two years of this daily routine had made me an expert on the exact sweet spot of the locking mechanism. I hoisted the weight of myself and my weekend bag through the door. I was happy to be home — I was always happy to come home.

It had rained in London while I was away, and the grey of the still-threatening clouds outside cast the apartment in a heavy shadow. Mother Nature would inevitably troll through May with a few showers. She was an evil sort of seductress this time of year, washing away ideas for family picnics and rooftop meet-ups. Yet when the storms cleared, there was nothing more magical than the sunny days that arrived later in the month — when days grew longer and the smell of springtime grass bewitched an entire country.

I dropped my bag in the hallway and walked to the large bay window in the living room. Lifting my hands to feel the thrill of the cool glass on my fingertips, I stared out the window and let my mind wander to Theo. Some hours ago, he'd been in my arms; now reality had placed him some fifteen hundred miles, ten countries, and eight languages away.

I wondered why he was still on my mind but then remembered that I wasn't hardwired for one-night stands. Our goodbye had been incredibly awkward. What had he been trying to achieve by asking me to come to Istanbul? Had he been trying to make me feel our night together had been more than what it was? Was there more to it than I was admitting?

I cursed him for leaving the notion unfastened in my mind. The man would now occupy my thoughts for a few days. Had it been worth it? The sex had been great; but in a very dark corner of my mind, I knew I was only one of his many conquests. He hadn't yet texted anything more which confirmed my mounting doubts.

With the cool shock from the window came the acceptance that my short-lived affair was coming to an end. I struggled to hold the exact details of him in my memory. There would be a few more futile texts; and then he would fade into the shadows with all my previous inconvenient romances, broken off not for a lack of attraction but to appease an unwavering devotion to my career. Except the one — the one poor investment I'd made that I buried deepest of all — the man who'd just gotten married.

Hunger raged though my stomach and drew me from

the window. Opening the door to the empty fridge, I saw a bottle of white wine and a box of baking soda. Relieved to have no other option, I went back to my weekend bag to dig out my laptop. I was always delighted to have a reason to order from my favorite Indian restaurant, and I always did so via Lickity, an online delivery bicycle service.

Ordering was always something of a gamble, but I liked to fervently support startups even if it might be to the detriment of my sanity. The knot in my stomach grew as I made my way through the service's online checkout cart. There was no shortage of problems I might encounter — the restaurant could be closed, the website might be overloaded with traffic, the restaurant might not have my order. However, the uncertainty was worth not having to step out of my door to search for dinner, especially with the pending rain.

At last the confirmation window sprung to life with my Primrose Hill address highlighted in green.

When I'd arrived in London, I fantasized of living in Notting Hill and owning a beautiful two-story white townhouse with a bay window. However, with my office in the east side of the city, living on the west side would have made for a miserable commute. When I lived in New York, I was a mere twenty minutes walk from my office in the Financial District; and that was a luxury I was hesitant to give up. Even in Primrose Hill, I had to take a car in the morning to get to the office; but with the long hours of banking, the streets were usually empty when I left the house; and they were just as deserted when I returned home.

Even so, when I came here looking for apartment, I took the only one shown to me that had a large bay window. Barring rain clouds, the window lit up every corner of the living room in the morning. Light, in a city like London, is more precious than any stone.

Primrose Hill was a small, quiet bourgeois suburb of London, leafy and green without a chain store in sight. The buildings were painted in a variety of pastels ranging from persimmon-red to mint-green to lemon-yellow. Mine was painted in peach, and I'd planned to change it except I couldn't commit to a color.

I lay back on the couch and wondered how to pass the time before the delivery arrived. I fought to catch the remnants of Theo's scent on my arm. His scent was fading from my memory, and I couldn't help but think it was an allusion to him fading into my past.

"HELLO, BEN," I said opening the door.

"Hi, Audrey. I haven't seen you in awhile."

I was on a first name basis with three of the bike delivery guys. Ben was my favorite. He was blonde and had studied graphic design in school but delivered food to overworked under-social women to pay his rent.

"I've been traveling. Are you well?"

"Oh yes, in fact I signed my first client this week."

"That's great! An interesting one?"

"Yeah, totally. It's an online art market. Actually, it's a gallery in London that a friend's mum runs. They are looking to show for a global audience, so they're creating an art consortium online; and they need some branding work done."

"That's amazing. It's art related yet commercial so you can charge a nice rate, huh?"

"Exactly! It's a big gallery; and they're looking to expand to Milan, New York, and Paris in the next five years, so I hope I might be able to request a retainer."

"I'm so happy for you. What's the name of the gallery?"

"Maché."

"That's really awesome. I'm sure you're going make them very happy."

"Thanks, Audrey. Anyway, Guarav threw in an extra palak paneer and naan. I think he's nervous they're losing you as a customer."

"Thanks, Ben," I laughed out of embarrassment from being such a frequent customer while closing the door.

"See you soon, I hope," he said, turning in the entryway.

The mortification rose from my heart to my cheeks even before the door clicked into place. *I absolutely must start going out more,* I thought to myself.

I put the steaming paper bag on the kitchen table and grabbed my phone. It was seven o'clock in the evening here in London, meaning it was eight o'clock in Paris. Scrolling through my recent calls, I hoped that Gina wouldn't be out on Sunday night.

"Hi, you've reached Gina. I'm not available at the moment; but leave your name and number, and I'll call you right back."

I wondered why with today's technology we still all had voice mail, and I hung up at the beep.

Gina, dear— call me ASAP. xoxo, I texted.

I went to the kitchen and grabbed a fork. Opening the bag of comfort food, I took the TV off mute and tore into the hot curry and rice. My phone beeped at me from the table, and I checked it quickly hoping it would be her.

It was instead a message from Theo. *When are you coming to Istanbul?* A smiley face followed.

I put down the phone and rolled my eyes. I looked over at my computer. I'd already procrastinated for an entire two hours. My stomach churned, making me hyper-aware of what a letdown tonight had been. I instantly wanted to be back in Athens; but Istanbul — that was definitely off limits.

MORNINGS were always a gamble, and today was a losing hand. No matter how hard I tried to get myself out the door, there were things forgotten or misplaced. Shoes could not be found. Keys were lost behind the table. The worst was walking out the door, locking up the apartment, and getting into the car before realizing I'd forgotten my laptop. This stumbling minutia had already put me fifteen minutes behind schedule. With any more lost time, I would certainly run into traffic. It was already 7:00 a.m.

Running back to the house, my phone beeped at me. I pulled it out of my bag while clumsily searching for my keys to open the door.

It was Theo again.

I don't have time for this, I thought as I tossed the phone back in my bag. It was now Thursday; Theo and I had been sexting for three days. Messaging seemed to be everything I really needed as far as romance was concerned. The flirting was fun; but with Theo a few thousand kilometers away, it wasn't a drain on my energy or time — except for now at seven o'clock in the morning.

The front door opened, and I ran across the room for my laptop. I grabbed it and put it into my large black bag. My laptop this morning was the most valuable thing in my possession. It contained the cobbled-together presentation for National Motors that was scheduled for later in the afternoon. I still wasn't convinced we had a solid proposal, but Nick seemed pleased. I'd basically reconfigured our original idea by adding in other possible acquisition targets. It ticked all of Nick's boxes: conservative and low risk. Another career bullet dodged and I lived to keep my job another day, but I wasn't proud of what we were about to present.

I locked up the flat, and my phone beeped again. In my dash to the car, I checked to see who it was. It was another message from Theo, and I dropped it in my bag to be dealt with some other time.

Back in the car, I made my way to Regent's Park Road, and cleared my way through the Gloucester Avenue intersection. Delanccy was smooth, and I made a right onto Camden High Street. It was mostly clear, so I would make it in by 7:30 a.m. I needed another hour to format my research into something beautiful before Nick arrived. I didn't need any distractions.

"AUDREY, would you like to take the floor?" Nick said summoning me to the front of the room. National Motors had three people from their team in town, and we had four in the room. The "VIP Conference Room," as it was referred to internally, was located in the center of the twelfth floor of the bank and overlooked our second location across the street. I always thought it was a tragedy that such a well-financed banking institution didn't have rooms with better views, but I'd been spoiled working in New York where most conference rooms were designed to awe and impress.

I took my place in the front of the room with my PowerPoint presentation projected behind me on the wall. My presentation was thirty slides long, and it took me forty-five minutes to present it. The NMC team looked underwhelmed.

Angela Marks, National Motors' Vice President of Global Product Development, was the first to speak. "Thanks for coming up with this new angle on such short notice, but I'm still not convinced European hybrid technology is worth the investment. We might as well look at technology that's already compatible with the gas engines we produce today in the U.S."

I looked over at Nick. He was visibly at a loss for words, although I couldn't conceive that he was surprised. We had come at this solution from every which way, and it obviously still didn't fix the client's problem. If we didn't salvage this fast, our days with this client were numbered.

I decided to go for it.

"We've been trying to fit technology into your company that, obviously, doesn't make sense anymore; but it is what you asked for." I glanced over at Nick — who'd flushed a sudden red — but looked away before he could stop me with his eyes.

"Today there is evidence consumers are leap-frogging hybrid vehicles and going straight into electrics," I continued. The room stood silent, and a few eyes rolled. "Is there an electric strategy on the table?"

Michael Gruner, National Motors' Vice President of

Business Development, broke the awkward silence just as I found myself tempted to run out of the room to write my resignation letter. "It's come up, but there are other players in the market that are far more advanced than we are.

"Are you interested in developing the technology in the long run?" I said, trying to keep the conversation afloat. Nick leaned forward onto the table and tried to interject to stop me, but Michael had already started to respond.

"We have a problem with our board of directors. They've already agreed to support hybrid technology, but they are split on electric."

National Motors had too much oil interest represented on its board. It was hardly a secret. Of all the American car companies, it was held behind the most when it came to research and development because of it. I was sure it would cost the company in the end.

"Okay, that's clear enough," Nick said, trying to rescue the conversation. I understood his apprehension. Many of National Motors' board members also consulted with the bank for their other companies as well.

Nick was overweight by a few pounds; but when he wore his suit jacket, it was harder to tell. He had a blond mop of hair on the top of his head that was always a little too long and never in place, and his face was round and rosy. He was quintessentially British; and when he was angry, he reddened at his cheeks. That was usually the only indication he was upset. His cheeks were a lively crimson by this point.

"No, she's not wrong," Michael said, turning his attention back to me. "I'd like to know what you're proposing. This has been an ongoing debate internally too."

"We don't have anything to propose at this point," Nick said.

"But we could work something up," I added. "There are some boutique suppliers we've been keeping an eye on, both in the U.S. and in Europe."

"Look," Michael said, "we aren't anywhere close to being able to pull the trigger on an investment into electric; but if something exceptional came up, I think we could consider it."

Nick brought the conversation to a close with pointed frustration. "We'll work up some options in the coming days," he finished, shooting me a death look.

The meeting closed, and Nick asked me into his office before I could escape.

"I THINK that went really well," I said, trying to hedge his anger.

"Are you out of your fucking mind?" Nick threw his heap of papers onto his desk, scattering them senselessly. He stomped around the room as I looked on until he gathered enough composure to speak in full sentences. "That spun completely out of control. This is one of the bank's largest clients, and you made us look unprofessional. Not to mention the repercussions that will come from members of their board once the bullet points of this meeting get out."

"The longer we stayed on hybrid technology, that was inevitable; and you know it. At least we have a chance here to reinvent ourselves and our reputation."

"You are really something. I hope you don't think I'm going to protect you here. When this tanks, I have my own ass to cover. You better come up with something fucking amazing, Audrey. I'm talking pots of gold, unicorns, and rainbows. I don't want to have to look at you until you have it."

I spun around to leave. How the hell was this my fault? I'd just saved us a few more weeks with this client; and had it been up to me, I would have gone with an electric pitch weeks ago.

Rage surged through my body. *Fuck this. I'm the fucking hero here. Nick should be kissing my feet.*

I knew that was only partly true. I'd bought us time but potentially burned my most important bridge in the bank in doing so. I was starting to feel myself unraveling. Maybe it had been the weekend in Athens, but something felt different. Maybe it was all the work I'd put in this week.

I went back to my office and slammed the door. *Now what?* I wondered. I'd become so buried in my preparation for today; I didn't even know where to begin looking for solutions.

My phone lit up with an incoming message from Nir. It was a half-naked photo of us changing in the park. David must have taken it, but the memory was fuzzy. I continued on to read the messages Theo had sent earlier in the morning, and I found myself missing him. It seemed unfair to deny myself the pleasure of Theo for David's sake when David didn't actually benefit in any way from my restraint. Maybe he wouldn't even care?

I messaged Theo back and then opened my browser to begin searching for news on electric automotive technology. This would have to be an extremely quick study. Well into my fourth article, I noticed an ad for my Athens hotel in the corner of the screen. Clearly, the remarketing algorithms hadn't moved on yet from my trip to Greece. And then I wondered, *had I?*

I opened another window and indulgently looked at flights. With rage and defiance still streaming through my veins, I booked a ticket out for the next night.

I would arrive just in time for a late dinner on Friday — in Istanbul.

THEO

MALIK STOOD at the front of the room leading the video call with the London office. Under the conference room table, I held my phone and traced over the message she'd sent: "Want to have dinner tomorrow?"

She'd sent it an hour ago, and I needed to respond, but I was still processing it. As part of our sexting, of course, I'd told her to visit. It was a line to fuel more flirty banter. I hadn't suspected she'd actually come.

Where would she stay? Was I hosting her at my place for the weekend? I'd need to clean up. Did she think that I had time for this? I found it concerning that she was pushing a relationship forward so quickly. Thinking about it, anxiety began to raise my shoulders; but I started typing anyway.

"Sure! Great." I sent it quickly before I could overthink it anymore than I already had.

Malik called out my name from across the room. "Are you cool if we hire out the backend?" The eyes of the room fell on me. I hadn't a clue what he was talking about.

I cocked my head to the side as if I was considering the enquiry. Those in the meeting must have been discussing the ordering platform. "Sure, whatever will get it done the fastest," I replied, hoping I'd answered the right question.

When the meeting concluded, I returned to my office and shut the door. What were we doing? I was elated she was coming yet slightly apprehensive. Would this become complicated, or was she out to have a good time? *Do women jump on planes to see men they hardly know?* Then again, is it normal for men to invite them? Audrey had seemed reserved. I never thought she'd agree to it.

I'd need to think of an itinerary worthy of her visit. Maybe I'd show her my aunt's place in the countryside. Would that be sharing too much?

Cluelessness made me almost want to call David to find out more about his ex, but judiciousness prevailed — probably best not to stir that up.

Racking my brain, I remembered Mitch, our mutual friend that I'd seen briefly at the wedding reception while talking to Audrey. He'd worked in banking too before leaving to start a meditation coaching business. Maybe he'd be able to tell me more about her? I picked my phone back up and searched for his contact. David and I were still collaborating on a huge deal, and I didn't want any trouble over a woman I'd just met.

Just when I thought the call would go to voicemail,

Mitch picked up. We exchanged pleasantries and regret at not having been able to see each other in New York lately, and then I got down to business.

"I wanted to ask you something quickly."

"Excellent, hardly anyone calls me for financial advice anymore."

"Well, it isn't exactly financial advice," I admitted.

"Oh, now I'm even more intrigued."

"Tell me about Audrey Gardner, David's ex."

"Audrey! Yes, of course. Good banker — terrible girlfriend."

"Really? What does that mean?"

"Look man, I'm going to be completely frank with you," he started. "She's not worth the trouble. I'd let it go."

"Why?" I said hoping my skepticism wasn't obvious.

"I know she looks harmless, but she royally fucked David."

"How? I've never heard the full story. Just snippets from David."

"She's dangerously ambitious. A great banker, like I said, but merciless." I sat in silence waiting for him to divulge more. After a moment, he continued, "She worked on an initial public offering that David ended up buying into."

"Is that legal?"

"Well, she didn't actually sell it; but she was a part of the underwriting team. The problem was they overhyped the offering, and it ended up being a junk stock. When the crisis hit, David's firm almost went under because of it; but she made a shitload of money for the bank and for herself."

"No way."

"I'm totally serious. David lost his job, but she — with her insane bonus — quit and left New York. Believe me, a woman like that could do you real damage, so I'd stay away. Not to mention David's history with her."

My shoulders slumped. "Thanks for the heads up, man. Maybe I'll let it go," I added, hating the disappointment in my voice.

"Wise man."

Mitch and I continued to catch up for a few more minutes. He told me about his powerful meditation retreats and invited me to join the next time I found myself in New York.

"Of course," I said, knowing full well that time was not something I ever had in Manhattan.

I hung up the phone and sat back in my chair. I did have a lot to lose here, and I certainly wasn't about to let a deal hunter ruin me regardless of how sexy she might be. However, Audrey hadn't seemed at all like the callous person Mitch described. I'd found her relaxed and elegant. She'd been kind and generous in her manner of conversation. Maybe my lust for her had clouded my judgment? Or worse . . . *was it part of her game?*

The weight of the disappointment sat heavily on my shoulders while I contemplated how much I'd come to care for her without realizing it. It wouldn't be easy to give her up now. Especially since the time we'd spent together had been so great — so easy.

Maybe this call was divine intervention. I didn't have the capacity to invest anything into a potential relationship, so it would be prudent to keep some distance from Audrey.

Looking out at the clear night sky to the east, I

thought of Napoleon. *She may be a femme fatal, but the Turks can never be conquered.*

My phone buzzed. Audrey had replied. *Pick me up at the Regency Hotel — Bosporus at nine o'clock.*

Where could I take her now that my family's place was too risky? Azra appeared at my door to tell me she was leaving. "Good night," I told her.

I'd find a nice enough place to take Audrey somewhere in the city. There were plenty of options to choose from near her hotel. She'd gracefully arranged for her own accommodation — it was up to me to decide if she'd actually sleep there.

AUDREY

THE WARM WIND blew through my window while Theo's driver, who'd been waiting for me at the airport, sped us off to my hotel. My flight had been an easy one, but the manic dash out of London had been chaotic and fraught with obstacles. My assistant had walked me to my car rattling off calls still left to be made, meetings that needed to be rescheduled, and dinners requiring postponement. Even as I'd caught the Heathrow Express from Paddington Station, the doors had closed pinching the corner of my weekend bag. I was able to pry my bag loose, but the jam in the door led to a ten-minute suspension of service while station officials investigated the disturbance. The passengers in my car glared at me for the delay.

That was the culmination of a long, difficult week

which led to tears swelling up at the corner of my eyes. My boss seemed to no longer find any value in my ideas, and I was losing my excitement for chasing deals. Nick was still upset that I'd spoken out against his position in the client meeting; and while I understood why he was angry, I'm not sure how I could've done things any differently without sacrificing my integrity in front of our client. My hours were still long and tiring. How much longer would I be able to work at this exhausting pace?

On the plane my extreme fatigue manifested itself in disruptive thoughts. What was I doing flying to see a guy I barely knew in a country where I had no friends, family, or contacts? This would be a routine weekend for Gina, but maybe I was fooling myself that I could pull this off without over-investing myself. Theo's attention was clearly focused on work, as with most consultants; and the playboy lifestyle suited them much better than relationships.

I wondered what Theo was thinking. As a playboy, he wouldn't be looking for much — just a good time; but, of course, I didn't really know him. That made me nervous.

In any case, I'd arrived; and my shoulders were slightly less tense thinking of my imminent date with Theo than when I'd left London.

Istanbul so far looked as I'd imagined it, although the trees and parks lent it a slightly greener cast than expected. The driver took a road that ran along the periphery of the city near the water. Out the window I caught flashing glimpses of the majestic, blue Sea of Marmara between the buildings we passed as the driver and I made small talk to the end of our ability.

It was just before seven-thirty in the evening when we turned into the gates of the hotel. I looked at the clock in the dashboard of the car and noted that I had thirty minutes to get ready before Theo was picking me up. I had booked a hotel because I preferred to have my own place to escape to, and it also helped to keep some distance. I wanted to make sure that it was crystal clear I was here to have fun and not on the hunt for a boyfriend.

As the sun started to fall, the sky became a deep blue. The car pulled into the circle drive of the Regency Hotel, and I looked up at the exterior. The hotel was only three stories high and imposed its grandeur though design rather than dimensions. A golden light shone upon the darkening arched windows and white facade. In the light of pending dusk, it glowed.

The trees were rustling when I stepped out of the black luxury sedan. It wasn't just any car actually. It was a Volta: the most exclusive electric car available. Hailed as the epitome of German engineering, it didn't disappoint. Never having ridden in one, I'd been elated when the driver put my bag into its trunk at the airport. The car was gorgeous. I was touched, unexpectedly, that Theo hadn't spared any expense.

As the driver fought with the valet over my bag, I tried to brush the wrinkles out of my white blouse. My stomach spasmed with nervousness. *What will become of this weekend,* I wondered. I worried that I was turning into my mother. Had I been foolish to come here on a whim?

The wind blew a strand of my hair into my mouth as the valet struggled to take the bag from the driver's grip and hand it off to a bellboy. The excess of attention paid to my small weekender was amusing, and it made me smile.

Walking into the lobby, my stilettos clicked upon the slick floor, which was covered in shiny white marble with golden mosaic trim. The reflections from the chandelier hanging above bounced off the marble and followed me as I walked to the front desk.

"Hello, I have a reservation under Audrey Gardner."

"Ms. Gardner, it's our pleasure to welcome you to Regency Bosporus. Did you have a nice trip?"

"Indeed, thank you."

The man behind the counter took my passport and typed intently on his keyboard. The ice-cold granite top of the front desk chilled my skin when I rested my arms on it. I distracted myself by looking toward the back of the hotel — the terrace overlooking the strait tempted me with its evening sleepiness. Darkness would soon overtake the city.

"We have you booked into a Palace room, but we've upgraded you to a suite. Both have views on the Bosporus, but the suite has a separate living room and a double Jacuzzi tub." With all the travel I undertook for my job, I had elite status that came with upgrade perks for most hotels and airlines; still, I always enjoyed the thrill that came from receiving one unexpectedly.

My mind at once slipped back to Athens, remembering Theo carrying me in his arms from the living room to the bedroom of the suite I'd had there. I thought of his stomach's warmth on my inner thighs while my legs gripped around his torso. A smile coiled at the sides of my mouth.

"That's lovely. Thank you."

I TOOK A QUICK shower while my mind tossed back and forth between complete confidence and utter trepidation. I wondered what Theo was thinking about as he drove toward the hotel to pick me up. Perhaps, I'd been too bold in coming here. My hand trembled while I tried in vain to paint perfect lines of eyeliner. Hunger crept at my stomach, or was it nerves?

My phone chimed while I finished adding a touch of crimson lipstick. It was a text from Theo. He was early and waiting in the lobby. Was he early by accident, or was he eager to see me again? Maybe he was here to tell me he couldn't see me. Did he have a local girlfriend he'd not told me about?

I shook off my paranoia. David really had done a number on me. Grabbing my bag, I slid on my heels as a second text from Theo rang now from inside my purse: *If you have flats, wear them.*

I sat on the white-upholstered bench near the entryway of the suite. *How peculiar.*

Surveying myself in the reflection of the elevator mirror, the ambient lighting gave me a renewed wave of confidence. I was wearing a fitted black dress with a skirt that went down nearly to my knees, but the open back was the dress' greatest feature. Low maintenance was my modus operandi, but for a little flare I'd added two long, gold necklaces. The chains featured small clear crystals every few inches. I liked them because they were simple and elegant, and they always made me think of Gina since she'd given them to me as a gift. I wondered how the crisis at her gallery in Paris was unfolding. I wished there were more I could do to help.

I thought of Theo waiting for me downstairs and tried to imagine how he'd look. Images of his dark chiseled abs waving over me in Athens flashed in my mind like the faint recollections of a dream, but his face was more elusive. I struggled to remember the precise brown of his eyes. His smile, however, was seared in my brain; and thinking of it, my face brightened in the mirrored walls of the elevator. My palms were sweaty, and I used them to smooth down my dress as the elevator came to a jolting rest on the ground floor.

When the doors opened, I stepped out into the lobby; but where was Theo? Distress pinged at my heart. I'd been hoping to make an entrance, and now I'd have sit somewhere and wait for him. Casually and as confidently as possible, I scanned the room. Couples on vacation wore varying shades of pastels that starkly contrasted with the men in dark suits huddled over side tables scribbling notes and tapping away on tablets.

In the distance two men talked near the back terrace of the hotel. One was short, slim, and a bit older. He was dressed casually. The other flashed a wide smile. He was tall, fit, and had to lean over slightly to speak to the older man. It was Theo; I had recognized his smile before I recognized the man.

I walked over as confidently as I could to join them. Halfway across the shiny lobby floor, I caught Theo's eye; and he stopped speaking. Then he returned to the other man, shook his hand, and started toward me.

He was even hotter than my hazy memory had afforded him. He looked elegant in a white. buttoned-up shirt with a spread collar — the upper buttons undone exposed the soft tanned skin at the top of his chest. Over his shirt, he had on a black sport coat — also unbuttoned.

He was wearing dark jeans that hugged his legs perfectly. He sported casual, dark-grey, suede loafers that complemented the laid-back tenor of a city located on the sea. As he came closer, I zeroed in on the features of his face. His intense, chocolate eyes pierced me and stole half a breath from my chest. Now with him only a few yards away, my knees weakened.

"Hello," he said as we closed the distance between us. I instinctively held out my hand to shake his. *What was I doing?* This wasn't work. It was awkward seeing my one-night stand again, but I concealed my self-doubt in formality.

He took my hand and shook it firmly. It was a cold greeting considering the night we'd spent together. Yet, he too seemed slightly uncomfortable. "Welcome to Istanbul." he said.

"Thanks," I replied while looking around him unsure if I should make eye contact or not. He started toward the front entrance without me.

"Did you have a good flight?" he asked, a full two paces ahead. What was wrong with him? This was a mistake. I missed the warm Theo I'd last seen in Athens.

"Wait," I called after him. He turned around, but why was he being so distant? Was he uncomfortable that I'd come?

I reached into my bag unsure if I should give him what I'd brought. Maybe the kind guy I'd been texting with was actually a jerk in person. It was too late. I'd already summoned his attention.

"Here," I said, handing him the gift-wrapped box.

"What's this?" he asked. His stern lips arched into the hint of a smile.

"Just a little something from London."

Theo thumbed the small card where I'd written: *It's our secret.* His face scrunched with bafflement until he unwrapped the box and took off the lid. "What are they?" he asked.

"Cinnamon-flavored sugar sticks . . . for your coffee."

The wide smile that had captured me in Athens finally returned to his face as he placed the box down on the table just beside us. Wrapping his hand around my wrist, his stature melted; and he pulled me into him. He drew in a slow breath and kissed me lightly on the lips: an *amuse-bouche* that calmed my butterflies. As he pulled away, I could feel a fleeting, calm comfort finally between us. Taking my hand in his, he whispered, "I'm bringing you to one of my favorite places. I hope you're ready for an adventure."

He turned me toward the entrance and put his arm around my shoulders. My eyes closed as I lingered in the shadow of his scent: an aquatic blend of citrus and the sea. My elevated heartbeat confirmed that adventure was exactly why I'd come.

TWO VALETS stood at attention in front of both the driver-side and passenger-side doors waiting for us at the entrance of the hotel. Theo opened the passenger-side door for me himself; and as I slid into my seat, the hem of my dress crept up my leg. I let it linger outside the car a moment longer than needed.

Settling inside, I realized it was another Volta. The previous one had a grey interior with black, matte features; but this one was entirely black.

Theo took his place on the driver's side, and the valet

attending him closed the door. "Does everyone in Istanbul drive a Volta?" I asked.

"One day, I hope so," he replied, shooting me a side-eye.

The sun had just set, but the final rays of blood-orange light were still painting the horizon where it had slipped out of sight some minutes ago. In its wake, the half-moon appeared dimly against a darkening sky. The water of the Bosporus shimmered quietly in shades of blue and grey; as Theo drove, we made small talk. It seemed odd to start with such banal subjects after a week of innuendo and sexting.

Driving north up the coast, my mind flittered back to work. Could there be an opportunity with Volta for National Motors? I brushed it off as unlikely; but still, I would look into it tomorrow. I wondered how the technology could integrate into National Motors' product strategy; and furthermore, what could incentivize a potential deal?

"Theo, why do you drive a Volta?"

His brow furrowed, and then he took his eyes off the road to question me with his eyes. It was a simple question. I was just trying to make conversation, but I wondered if I'd said something unwise. I cursed myself for making myself look unsophisticated.

"It's an incredible piece of engineering, and it makes me feel better about my footprint on the environment."

I relaxed at hearing his simple answer. I was overthinking our interactions; I needed to stop. "So, you overspend on cars to appease your conscience?

"Basically," he acknowledged with a smile. Theo turned on his left turn signal, and we veered off the small, two-laned, coastal road and headed up into the hills. "Are you keen on getting one?" he asked.

"No, just curious." My gaze drifted around the sleekly designed interior. "Well maybe, one day."

Wisps of cypress and pine drifted in and out of the car as we pressed on farther into the hills.

"Where are we going," I asked. "Should I be nervous?"

Theo laughed. "You couldn't possibly be in better hands here in Istanbul."

I trusted him. I must have if I'd come here, but I didn't understand why. We barely knew each other. Theo's smile put me back at ease, and my attention was seduced back out the window by the magnificent scenery.

Curving along the face of a bluff, small houses revealed themselves less and less the higher we climbed. The dense forest grew even more congested as we ascended — the orange, terra-cotta rooftops giving way to intensc strokes of deep, natural green.

Theo extended his hand, palm up; and I slid mine into his. An intimate gesture — and yet — maybe just the comfort of an easy friendship. I was fairly sure he was also just in this for fun, but I appreciated that he was generous about it. He was more open and engaged than most of the consultant types I knew. In fact, it was hard to put him in a box. He seemed to be more of a mad, adventurous type without limits. Most consultants I knew were more reserved and self-conscious: insecure overachievers. It was the exact profile that both banks and consultancy firms recruited to fuel their company growth. I fit neatly in the box, but Theo didn't, and my own anxieties were countered by his self-assurance.

We drove another half hour, and houses nearly

disappeared completely making way for abundant pine forest. I was starting to wonder how we'd get back home. "Aren't you worried about getting stranded?"

"Not at all. This car can go five hundred kilometers on a single charge. Volta batteries have a longer range than any other electric model out there."

Theo turned onto a small gravel road. It was tiny and blended unnoticed into the forest. The sky above was now growing very dark. This was the strangest beginning to a second date I'd ever had. Or was it actually our first? I struggled to put a label on what this was.

"I should tell you, I'm not a fan of camping."

"Look at me, Audrey," Theo said peering over at me with a sparkle in his eye. "Do I look like I camp?" He had a point. He was too manicured.

His beard was trimmed short and perfectly edged along his jaw. Theo dressed simply in sober dark colors, but he always looked expensive. The long fingers that wrapped around the steering wheel were soft and smooth. I put the thought of sleeping in a tent out of my mind.

We continued down the path another two minutes until we reached a tiny house perched on the softly sloping hillside. It was actually more of a quaint cottage.

Tucked behind a thicket of cypress and pine trees, the house was two-stories tall, painted white, and had an older, Mediterranean-tiled roof that was darker than the terra-cotta roofs that tiled the hills of Istanbul's suburbs. *Where were we?* There was nothing modern about the little place.

"Here we are," Theo said, putting the car into park and releasing his seatbelt. I looked at him slightly unsure. He stepped out of the car and was already opening my door while I was still hesitantly unlatching my safety restraint. The confusion must have been plain on my face.

"Trust me," he said, extending his hand once again.

Taking it, I stepped out of the car as gracefully as possible.

"What is this place?"

"Istanbul's best kept secret." I looked at him unconvinced. "You'll see," he said confidently. Climbing the three small stairs that led to the front terrace, he opened the front door and peeked in.

The door was especially charming with its hand-carved floral motif that at one time must have been painted in turquoise since remnants of the color still streaked the grain of the wood. A set of brass handles in the middle helped to open the door; and a heavy floor bolt, also brass, lent the entryway an air of authority.

Theo held the front door open while I caught up; and stepping through, I entered into a slice of Turkish antiquity. The ceiling was decorated in wooden panels that extended out from the center like the rays of the sun. The walls were painted white and basked in the cutout light that permeated from a large, brass Damascus lantern hanging at the center of the ceiling. Layered and aging oriental carpets covered the creaky wood floor that peaked out from under the gaps, and tired-looking Ottoman lamps were placed in the corners to chase away the shadows. There were five small, wooden tables with simple matching chairs.

An older woman who was probably in her seventies greeted Theo. He leaned down to her, and she kissed his cheeks before lifting her hands to cradle his face. In Turkish, Theo introduced me, although I didn't understand a word.

In addition to English, I also spoke a little French and Spanish, which helped me to get by in most of the countries I visited. I could never escape the wave of insecurity that washed over me when I arrived in a country where I couldn't easily communicate.

Theo continued to speak with her for a minute and then beckoned me outside through the back door. "I want to show you something."

Out the back was a small, grass-covered hill illuminated by the white moonlight. It contrasted sharply with the dark of the pines that stood at attention slightly off to the left.

Theo was already starting up the hill while I was still taking it all in, so I had to run slightly to catch up. My feet slipped in the grass, and I was grateful to have worn my flats.

When I'd finally caught up, I slipped in another patch of wet grass; and the momentum of my running made me crash into the back of Theo's legs.

We were completely intertwined when I began a string of apologies, but Theo stifled them with an easy kiss that helped me to relax. It felt comforting to be so close to him.

I hoped that he didn't think I was crazy for having flown all the way to see him. As his kisses intensified, I concluded that, even if he did, it wasn't keeping him from having a good time. Our breath quickened between each kiss as my cheeks began to flush. Theo carefully rolled out from our entanglement and helped me back to my feet. "Maybe we should take this a little slower," he said.

I looked up and nodded in agreement.

We continued up the hill a few dozen more yards to the very top. As we reached the crest, the grey sea, illuminated by the bright moon, unfolded before us in one hundred and eighty degrees.

"Wow," I exclaimed in surprise. "What is this?"

"The Black Sea." I looked at Theo, completely forgoing the view, and reveled in his presence. His wide smile reappeared across his face; softening his eyes, he wrapped his arms around me while turning me to improve my view of the silky, dark horizon that stretched out before us.

We were all alone. The nearest house had been the one we'd just come from, and there were no lights to be seen in any direction except the large, yellow moon that hung in the sky.

My body searched for even more closeness, but I stifled the longing. This was an affair to appease a physical need not an emotional one. I wondered why he'd brought me all the way out here. Dinner in Istanbul would have been just as nice, so why all of the romance if we both knew this couldn't go anywhere?

The deep expanse of water continued to swirl in front of us, silently breathing as if asleep under the watchful eye of the moon. Kicking off my shoes, I broke away from Theo's grasp and headed down the embankment to the water — a spontaneous excuse to cut the mounting suspense.

I carefully placed my feet as I ran to avoid tripping in the damp earth. Black dirt made way to the light sand at the edge of the tide where my legs plunged into the water.

"We're going to be late for dinner!" Theo yelled after me. I didn't bother to turn around. I didn't care. I knew if I stayed desire would pull Theo into the water with me.

The Black Sea. I'd never seen it before — never had

felt it on my skin nor smelt it. Countless things I'd never done.

I turned around to see Theo taking off his shoes and folding his socks neatly on top of them. It was unlike me to do something so silly, but I wanted to show him that I could be adventurous too.

He bent over to roll up his jeans and stumbled as his center of gravity struggled to find its balance. I laughed ungraciously at the spectacle, and Theo looked up with frustration. He stepped forward to join me in the water and grabbed my hand.

"Happy?"

I looked up at him and smiled. He smiled back with his large grin and wrapped his arm around me, pulling me in closer.

Small waves lapped at our ankles. "How do you know about this place?"

"It used to belong to my grandmother."

I continued to watch the horizon. "I thought your grandparents lived in Munich."

"They do now," he said as a larger wave came crashing around our legs. The impact was unexpectedly strong, and I stumbled falling into the sea and shrieked. Theo picked me up by my arms to lift me out of the retreating current.

I was completely soaked from my waist down, and my dress was stuck tightly to my butt and my legs. All that effort in my hotel room to appear elegant and sexy had been washed away in the tide.

We walked back up to the grass that lined the sandy edge of the shore, and I saw that Theo's jeans were now wet up to his knees. I knew my dress would dry relatively quickly, but Theo's jeans would be wet all night.

"I kind of hate you now," he said, stating the somewhat obvious.

I sat in the grass hoping I'd be able to maneuver my wet panties off without him noticing but couldn't manage it. "We are responsible for our own decisions."

"Is that right?" He sat beside me and did his best to squeeze the saltwater from his jeans. Realizing the futility of his task, he gave up and turned his attention back to me. "What about the irresponsible ones?" A smile broke across my lips, and he lifted his hand to my hair to kiss me. Our kiss tasted of salt and solace.

My dress was clingy and cold in the stark night air. Theo put his hand around my knee and, slowly but deliberately, slid his way up my smooth, wet skin, stroking as he reached higher and higher. He was inches away from the tension that was building between my legs when he grazed the soft flesh of my inner thigh.

I was desperate to take my dress off and slink into the warmth of Theo's powerful form, but we hadn't even made it to dinner yet. He growled softly at the back of his throat and stole another kiss before standing and offering me his arm. "Come on, let's go. I think you deserve to be fed for coming all the way," he said, adding a wink.

WE SAT at one of the small tables in the rear of the house; my back was to the window, and Theo sat directly across from me. There was only one other seating of two middle-aged men who were engaged in a heated discussion near the doorway.

I looked at Theo, and he smiled back at me. I thought of my parents; they'd both be beside themselves with worry if they knew where I was at this very moment. I loved that. My father wasn't a fan of traveling; and while my mother lived the life of luxury vagrancy, Turkey would still be outside her range of comfortable destinations — let alone this nameless house in the middle of nowhere.

Theo reached across the table. I'd mistakenly thought he was aiming for my hand; but instead, he touched the two long, gold necklaces that hung around my neck.

"Are these special?"

"Gina gave them to me last year on my birthday. An artist friend of hers in France made them."

"They suit you," he said, wrapping them around his fingers and insisting I lean in closer to him. We were dangerously close for such a family style restaurant, but I was dying for him to kiss me.

The elderly woman brought out a feast of colorful dishes which made Theo release me.

"So how is Gina, by the way?" Theo's gaze was fixed on my lips, but he was behaving himself.

"She's in a bit of a bind. Her gallery is over-leveraged, and she's not sure how to save it. It's going to be hard to sell her way out of the problem." Theo nodded and peppered me with more questions about the gallery which I didn't have the answers too. "It's a shame because she has great taste and shows really great pieces," I said.

There were so many plates that we had to pull over the table next to us to accommodate them. I didn't recognize a single one, and I had to ask Theo about nearly all of them.

"This is home-style Black Sea cuisine. I thought you might like it. This one is like collard greens," he said, pointing to a ceramic bowl. "And this is like cornbread.

This style of cooking reminds me of the food I ate when I lived in South Carolina."

"What? You never mentioned that. When did you live in the U.S.?"

"A few years ago. I was posted there for awhile."

"As a consultant?"

Theo hesitated, "More or less."

He obviously didn't want to disclose. It was annoying. Consultants were annoying. They pretend their jobs are so important and secretive, but we all knew the real work was done by bankers like me. On the totem pole of finance, management consultants, in my opinion, lingered near the bottom.

I remembered what Theo had confessed just before I fell into the water and picked the conversation back up. "Wait, so this used to be your grandparents' place?"

Theo surveyed the room and then leaned in closer to the table. "That's right. It was where my father grew up. My grandmother started a restaurant here to earn a living for the family."

"What did your grandfather do?"

Theo's face turned overcast. "He was an academic — an economics professor at a university in Istanbul." I focused on his eyes. There was more he was keeping to himself.

I reached my arm across the table and took his hand. "Tell me."

He looked up at me from under his heavy eyelids. "There was a period of instability in the sixties and seventies following a series of coups here."

I'd googled Turkish history while waiting to board my flight at Heathrow, and I was now grateful to have the intellectual scaffolding to frame our conversation.

"The military and Kemalism versus the far-right conservative Islamists." I was proud to know the story, but I noted my insensitivity.

"So you know your history." His eyes widened, and he winked at me before continuing. "That's the easiest way to put it; but, of course, it was far more complicated in reality."

"Aren't most things?"

"True." He pulled his hand back and continued, "Anyway, as my grandfather had been a professor, he was left without a job when the universities faltered in the sixties. That's when my grandmother turned the house into a restaurant. A couple years later, though, my grandfather disappeared one night. His profession hadn't been forgotten by the far-right movement." Theo carried on quickly, "He returned a couple weeks later, badly beaten. Probably tortured, but he never admitted it for my grandmother's sake. They left for Germany a couple months later before Turkey collapsed into full chaos."

"Wow, that's incredible."

"Yeah, they were very lucky. The worst of the violence came just after and scorched the country for years."

"And this place? What happened?"

"When they left, they gave the house to my grandmother's sister, Dilay. She decided to keep it open as a restaurant."

When the woman came back with a dessert that looked like baklava, Theo grabbed her hand and said, "Dilay still runs it just as my grandmother did." She smiled and leaned down to give Theo a kiss on his forehead before turning back for the kitchen.

"That's really lovely." I paused to let him work out his thoughts. "So why have you come back here if history has been so cruel to your family?"

"It wasn't always like that here. It really is a beautiful country. There is more to it than my family's tragedy, and I'm here to remember that."

WE WALKED onto the small front porch and down the short staircase to the parking area. I reached to open the door; but Theo hooked an arm around my waist and rested my back against the car, pulling me into a slow kiss.

My lips parted as my body retreated for air. The evening of dinner and discovery had been sweet, but this was really why I'd come. Theo was what I wanted. He dropped his hands down to my hips, gripping them and willing them closer to his body. My dress had nearly dried, but it was still stiff and sticky from the salt.

He was already poised, and his erection was pressing exactly where I wanted it to be. The space between my legs felt tight as he held me in an urgent kiss.

Our polite dance around each other had lasted too long, yet we were still so far from my hotel. This was going to be a long ride home. He buried his face in my neck, nibbling and biting at me as if he'd lost all sense of propriety.

Dilay's voice cried out in the distance. I pushed Theo off, and he turned around to face his great-aunt who was waving his wallet on the porch. My cheeks flushed.

"Oops," he laughed. "I'll be right back." He walked back up to the old house to get his wallet and gave Dilay a hug. She yelled something more at him and lightly hit the back of his head as he'd turned to return to the car. I liked her. She had spunk. Although, I doubted she was very keen on me after witnessing our little scene. I felt like a flushed, desperate teenager.

Theo returned looking slightly sheepish as well.

"Did you get in trouble?"

"Totally." I tried to imagine him younger, growing up in Munich: tall and awkwardly boyish. He was so adorable.

Theo took the key from his pocket and walked around to the driver's side door. I eagerly followed him. "Can I drive? I've never driven one of these."

Theo turned to face me biting the corner of his cheek while his eyes narrowed against mine. "Actually, I've never driven an electric," I added, to tug at his heart.

"Really? Among all of your banker friends, surely one of them must drive a Volta."

The truth was I had no idea. My bosses at the bank didn't spend much time in the parking garage, so I wasn't aware of what they drove. "Not that I know of. Let me drive yours. Please?" The plea in my eye told him I'd make it up to him later.

"Jump in," he said, handing me the key card. Clicking the button to unlock the car, I realized that I had no idea how to open the door: there weren't any door handles.

"Touch the panel with your finger," he said with a laugh.

I did, and a thin handle disengaged. "Clever," I said marveling at the ingenuity.

"Come on, are you going to drive or just talk about it?" he joked.

We both climbed in, and Theo gave me a quick

tutorial in how the car operated. The designers had thought of every need that could possibly arise. I could see how this would become a popular car, even if much of the world would be slow to curb dependence on older fuel technologies. I scrambled to fix the mental notes to my memory for tomorrow's research.

Theo showed me how to turn it on. There was a button above near the roof for that; and quite frankly, it was a little disappointing: the car was completely silent. I looked over at Theo, and my brow furrowed. "Is it on?"

"Yes, of course. It's ready to go," he confirmed. Every car I'd ever driven had the tell-tale start-up-rev of the engine. Was this really as powerful of a car as everyone had hyped it up to be?

I put the car in reverse and then paused to look at Theo. I took his hand in mine quickly. "Hey, thanks for bringing me here." I wanted him to know what he'd shared tonight wasn't lost on me. I was a little uncomfortable with the overtures of romance, but this place was obviously important to him. Maybe he just wanted to share it with someone, and I'd been the only one that came along for the ride?

He squeezed my hand and smiled while turning his head toward the rear to make sure I wasn't about to hit something. Backing the car out into the drive, we dipped as the car transitioned onto the tiny gravel road. The shift into drive was completely smooth; but as soon as I went to accelerate, the car lurched forward.

"Slower!" Theo exclaimed, grabbing the dashboard. "She's more powerful than you think." It took a while to get used to the energy the car put at my disposal; but after a few initial hiccups, I got the hang of it. We arrived at the main road that had brought us down from the bluffs, and the car suddenly sank down further.

"What's going on?" I worriedly asked Theo.

"It's adjusting the clearance now that we've left the gravel road."

Incredible. It was like driving a computer. The paved road gave way to the curvy route that went back up into the hills, but the car handled the tight curves like a sports car — just as Theo had said.

Theo relaxed more into his seat when he seemed confident that I wasn't going to crash his beloved car. We drove in silence for a few minutes until he asked about my family. I told him about my younger brother in San Francisco, my father in Nashville, and recounted the detailed history of the day my mother left us when I was six to explore the riches and comforts that other men in more cosmopolitan cities had to offer her. This had made it difficult for all of us to love her; but with heavy doses of therapy, we'd all managed to maintain a distant and fragile relationship with her — well, except for my father, of course.

In their divorce settlement she'd been granted full ownership of one of their investment properties, an investment building in downtown Dallas. Ever intent on proving a point none of us understood, she sold it in the late eighties for forty thousand dollars to pay for an extended vacation in the south of Spain. That same building was sold two years ago for fifty million.

Dad had been devastated when my mother left. While always fully aware of her faults, she lent his life a certain amount of excitement. I suppose he always knew there was a risk that the very thing he loved about her would ultimately hurt him; however, when it comes to love, we often underestimate downside risk.

Theo was just as surprised as anyone who has ever heard the story, and he spent a few minutes rationalizing my mother's decisions until he arrived where we all eventually did — baffled acceptance.

Resigned to the unexplainable, he shifted his focus and placed his hand on my thigh as I drove. My leg tensed in response.

"You sure are presumptuous," I said teasingly.

"I can afford to be." His words lingered in the air, and I was unsure how to take them. "You're here in my city, I must be doing something right," he added. His phone beeped, and in the center console a text message in German appeared. Theo dismissed it.

"You don't seem to be complaining," I replied with a smile. I suppose he was justified in feeling flattered.

His fingertips stroked my leg again as they had on the beach, circling at his leisure. A tautness between my thighs answered his unrelenting touch.

The haloed light of Istanbul started to emerge beyond the hills. "I think you should drive the rest. I haven't a clue where we're going." Truer words had never been spoken.

"Sure. There is a small inlet here off the shoulder where you can pull over." I stopped the car as Theo had suggested and pressed the button above me to stop the car. We each got out and walked around the back to exchange places.

"Wait," he said as I crossed him. He grabbed my arm and lifted me onto the trunk of the car, pushing his body between my hungry legs. His hands reached behind me as he pulled me into a burning kiss. My legs, still sticky from the salty seawater, wrapped around his waist pulled him in even closer.

His scent intoxicated me. His breath flushed at my neck as he brushed the hair from my shoulders. Desperation was overtaking him. Our eyes locked, and I was sure I wouldn't be able to stop whatever was coming next. Headlights appeared at the distant curve in the road, and Theo jerked back abruptly.

"We can't." He stepped back. "Don't forget, this isn't the West," he said, slightly defeated as he lifted me off the trunk.

"I wasn't the one forgetting," I clarified.

A smile crept at the corners of his mouth. "Come on." He nodded his head to the side. "Let's get moving, before we end up in prison."

Back in the car with Theo driving, we spoke more about our childhoods as we drove along the darkened, two-lane road. Mine seemed a breeze compared to the endless racism he'd faced at school. I was starting to understand why he'd left Europe. Yet, this wasn't exactly his home either.

Silence filled the car when we both came to the end of our desire to converse. The lighted glow of the city was getting closer, but we were still outside of it. I placed my hand on his leg to fill the gap in conversation. His jeans were tight. His mind may have made him stop, but his erection was still defying him. My hand rubbed against the roughness of his bulging jeans, and he had to adjust himself in his seat. As my fingers grew warm from the friction, I wished that we'd already returned to the city. The anticipation of what was coming left me restless.

More text messages appeared in his dashboard, but he

continued to dismiss them one after the other. He was growing frustrated though. Something was up.

Theo turned the car into the circle drive of the hotel. Palm trees stood at attention like soldiers as we passed under them. The shadows cast by the moon waved over the car like a flickering silent film.

His phone began ringing through the car's speaker system, and Theo answered in German. While I couldn't make out the conversation, it was clear that the woman was calling with urgency.

As Theo continued the call with the car parked in front of the entrance, I got out and sat at one of the benches near the valet stand. It was awkward listening to private conversations, especially ones I couldn't follow. When he'd finally finished, Theo got out of the car and walked over to sit next to me.

"I have to go. There's been an emergency at work," he explained. My heart sank into my chest.

"Do you want to use the office in my suite and then spend the night?" I asked, trying to save our time together.

"I really do have to go into the office. It's going to be a long night."

What kind of emergency could possibly be important enough to ruin the rest of this night? He was a consultant, not an emergency room doctor. Maybe he was using work as an excuse to escape.

Theo said goodbye to me in the lobby of the hotel. I was sure that the concierge had been eavesdropping on every word of our conversation. I felt like a fool.

Who did Theo think he was? The burden of disillusionment was heavy in my chest. I couldn't imagine a situation at work where I'd be called away in the middle of the night, and I worked more than anyone — certainly more than our consultants. My mind began unwinding all of the possibilities for why he'd left.

Obviously, he just wasn't into this nearly as much as I thought — and maybe I'd accidentally put too much of myself into it. All of the texting and seduction was trivial if he could just run off at the slightest problem.

Slowly, I was coming to grips with the notion that I didn't need this drama in my life. I'd felt underappreciated in enough relationships. I didn't need another one to add to the pile.

THEO

MY ENTIRE BODY was straining to be with her. I drove out of the hotel's circle drive wondering if my career was worth the personal sacrifices I was making. Feeling awful for having left Audrey at her hotel alone, I vowed to make it up to her the next day before she returned to London.

I'd gone into tonight slightly apprehensive. I wasn't entirely sure what she was doing here; but since she'd already booked her tickets, I had decided that it would be poor form to cancel on her.

My departure from her hotel had been unavoidable. A fatal accident had occurred an hour earlier just outside of London, and the press was swarming for statements. The passenger, a woman, had been killed; but the driver, Brady Spence had survived.

Brady Spence was an actor famous for a recent string of successful, young-adult romance films. He had become very popular with the tabloids, and it was inevitable the paparazzi and gossip magazines would be hounding us relentlessly to get information about the company's safety technology. The timing couldn't have been worse in every respect.

I rang Anna in London as soon as I got back in the car. She was half German and British, a perfect mix of her father's German rigor and her mother's posher English elegance.

Over the phone, Anna read me the statement she'd cobbled together in response while I drove back to the office.

"I like it," I said. "It's a good balance of compassion without accepting blame."

"Exactly, we don't know the conditions of the accident. He might have been drinking. More will come out in the investigation," she acknowledged.

"Did you clear it with legal?

"Yes, in fact, Richard in New York helped with some of the input."

"I think you should run it by someone in the London office as well," I suggested. "Just in case there is a nuance in British or European law that Richard isn't aware of."

Anna and our head of operations agreed to split the media calls that were rapidly piling up. The investigation would take days, but we needed to address the tragedy and buy more time for the circumstances of the accident to come out.

I spent the next three hours rolling calls to lawyers and

investigators. Europe was already asleep, but the media in the U.S. was pushing the story into their evening coverage.

Anna called again in the dead of night. My eyes were tired, but my pulse was rapid from all the apprehension. Over in London, her voice sounded weary, "Theo, the police plan to take Brady into their custody once he's released from the hospital. I've just learned of it from a contact at *Red Confidential Magazine*."

I couldn't contain the sigh of relief as I lay back into my chair. "Has your contact heard why?"

"No, not yet, but I bet we will have more information tomorrow," Anna said. "Also, they've asked for an interview with the founder, not the head of operations."

"Well, tell them what we always tell them: the CEO is not available for comment."

"Okay, but you might want to get some sleep tonight. You may need the energy tomorrow. Also, is there anyway you can make it to London just in case you are needed for meetings?"

"I was meant to be in New York later this week, but maybe I can rearrange things."

"I think it could be useful for you to be here," Anna insisted.

We said goodnight, and I rested my head on the desk. I was so tired; I wasn't even sure I'd make it home.

Audrey had given me a key to her room in case I finished up quickly and wanted to return. It was already three o'clock in the morning as I drove through Istanbul on my way home, and I was genuinely torn between my bed and hers.

Realizing I'd pass her hotel first as I drove along the coastal road to get to my neighborhood, I instinctively turned the car into the drive of the hotel. She'd already be fast asleep, and even though Mitch had told me to be wary about trusting her . . . I didn't feel like sleeping alone.

I'D BEEN AWAKE for a good fifteen minutes, alternating my thoughts between Audrey and work, when she began to stir next to me. The truth was I'd been anxious to get up and back to the office, but something left me tethered to the place in her bed. When I'd crawled in next to her early in the morning, she woke slightly but not enough to speak in sentences. Instead, I'd wrapped my arm around her warm body and fell asleep instantly.

We both had work to do, and we'd agreed the night before that I would come back around three o'clock to pick her up for a touristy afternoon. As I shut the door to her hotel room, I caught a glimpse of her emerging from underneath the covers. It had taken a lot of self-control to keep from rushing back to take her. Ultimately though, I wanted our first time in Istanbul to be more special.

I stopped at home for a run with Laika followed by a quick shower. I brought her into the office with me to appease my sense of guilt. A true lover of cars, her head hung out the window the entire drive into work, fetching endless laughs from pedestrians.

Upon our arrival at the office, Laika made her methodical patrol through the empty cubicles looking for crumbs dropped during the week. Her route culminated with a stop in the kitchen; and then, finally, she joined me in my office, curling herself into one of the brown leather guest chairs for a nap.

I rather liked the quiet calm of being at the office on Saturdays. It reminded me of the serenity that inevitably comes following a difficult week, and there was no question that right now things were stormy.

"Hey," Malik said, his voice distant against the ceaseless background noise of the production plant. "Sorry in advance, my signal is a bit spotty out here." The plant in Gebze was a little over an hour away from our office in Istanbul; and Malik knew the commute better than anyone. Once we'd identified our manufacturing issues in the Turkish plant, I'd insisted he leave Berlin and join me in Istanbul for a year or two. He was a great fixer.

Malik started off by asking how we were managing the situation in London. The morning shows and newspapers were heavily covering the accident. Anna, along with our head of operations, had spent the night at the office rolling Skype interviews. I'd noticed this morning that she'd worn the same dress for an interview in London as she had during a patched video interview with a New York media outlet the night before.

At this point we were focused on hedging against whatever outcome the authorities would draw from their investigation. I filled Malik in on our response so far; but in case this would all blow over, I didn't want to lose sight of our other pressing internal priorities.

"I wanted to let you know the Model II pre-order event is set for a week from this coming Thursday," I said, filling him in on my progress. "The team in London has already started leaking it to the press, and we should see a crescendo of media coverage starting Monday."

"Given the trouble in London, don't you worry about having to delay the event?" he asked.

"No," I replied confidently, which was a lie. "How are you guys doing on the scaling problem?"

"Well, we are shipping one hundred and twenty thousand units a year out of Gebze. At this rate, it will take us two years to fulfill current orders on the Model I; but we are getting more orders every day."

"Malik, I'm worried that once the novelty of early adoption wears off, we will lose to competitors who are able to scale and fulfill demand faster than we do. Next year, I want to begin shipping two hundred and forty thousand annually."

"But that's double."

"I know; but if we don't find a way to hit those higher numbers, this company isn't going to take off." Depending on which way the investigation went in London this weekend, the company might fold anyway; but it was unproductive to distract myself with thoughts like that.

"There's no way the Gebze plant can be adapted to accommodate those numbers. We'll need a second plant to meet that goal on the Model I alone. Depending on how many orders come in for the Model II, we might need a third." Laika opened an eye and looked straight at me as if she understood the seriousness of the situation. "Here in Turkey, there aren't many old factories to choose from. We could look elsewhere in Europe."

"What about building one from scratch?"

"Conservatively, I'd say that would take three years from start to finish. Either scenario would be extremely cash intensive. You know, if we need cash, I think the Japanese are still interested in licensing our technology."

"I'd sell my soul first." Malik knew better, and I wasn't in the mood to be tested right now.

When I finished the call, I watched Laika nesting in her chair looking for a more comfortable position. She finally settled on her back with her belly facing the ceiling. "Maybe you're right," I told her. "Maybe it's time to let it go." I knew that wasn't an option, but I'd be lying if I said I never thought about it. The pressure of this job was endlessly intense, and I struggled to remember it was just work.

In truth — it wasn't just a job though — it was my life. I'd invested everything into this.

AUDREY

I GATHERED my laptop, mobile, and sunscreen and headed for the pool. I had five hours until Theo would pick me up for a condensed afternoon of tourism. This was hardly enough time to get everything done, but I was hopeful to make some progress.

The outdoor pool was surprisingly quiet, and I had my pick of private cabanas to choose from. I selected one that looked out onto the strait with the distant mountains hazy in the soft mid-morning light.

The pool that lay between my cabana and the Bosporus was tiled in an elegant blue, blending into the sea just beyond. I was tempted to jump in for a swim, but there was work to be done first.

A server arrived, and I stood to order a champagne cocktail while he arranged the towels on my chair. A breakfast of coffee, scrambled eggs, and toast was also promised to be on the way. Sitting back down, I threw a pillow on my lap and opened my computer to Google.

As I'd imagined, there weren't many companies investing in the space. There was Tesla in California leading the Americans and a few other large, established manufacturers doing their part to under-invest in the technology. And then, there was Volta.

I did some very light due diligence on all of them, but Volta was already emerging as the most interesting candidate. Obviously, I was somewhat biased having driven one the previous night. The company was three years old, although their proprietary electric technology had been in development long before that.

The research company that created the technology had been purchased by Volta early on. In fact, the majority of Volta's early financing was used to buy out that technology and all of the patents that came with it.

Both companies had been created by the same man, Aydin Demir, a German engineer. From what I could tell, he was a bit of a cowboy: unafraid to invest himself into extremely risky ventures but also very demanding and difficult to work with. He kept tight control over the operations of his company and had already sent a few partnerships packing.

I knew the type: thinning hair slicked back, cigar clenched between yellowed teeth, sitting at the head of the table barking orders. *Sounds like a picnic,* I thought to myself.

I tried to find a profile on the guy, but he appeared to be somewhat reclusive. It was his right-hand guy, Philipp

Konig, who took all the glory in the press. The Internet was rampant with rumors though; some saying that Mr. Demir's fortune had originated in oil. If I'd been the founder of an electric automobile company that I'd financed with oil money, maybe I would keep a low profile too.

"Ms. Gardner."

"Yes?" I said, too engrossed in my research to look up.

"Your order, Miss." I closed my computer and looked up at the server holding a wooden lap tray. I put my computer on the empty lounger next to me in the cabana, and the server placed my breakfast over my legs. This was easy to get used to, but I knew it was fleetingly temporary.

Flipping through other examples of young, successful startup founders in my mind as I ate breakfast, I couldn't find a parallel example. There were countless interviews featured Konig, Volta's Chief Operating Officer; and clicking through a few of them, a story emerged of a company intent on disrupting the auto industry. *Probably doesn't make a very good partner for National Motors,* I thought to myself.

Behind me, the hotel staff was putting the finishing touches to a wedding set-up. The occasional white flower petal would defiantly blow in my direction, and I thought of the couple that would be committing their lives in a few short hours. Were they blissful or merely resigned to each other? In either case, they'd picked a beautiful venue.

My own parents had thrown a massive wedding, as if big statements proved some guarantee of an idyllic life together. Tens of thousands were being invested in this couple's future success. *Good luck to them,* I thought, knowing full well their chance for lifelong happiness was remote.

I put my breakfast tray to the side; and sitting freely in my chair, I realized that a stiffness had been building up in my shoulders. An industry disrupter would be an obvious enemy to my client, an established giant in automotive. Yet, what if they could somehow be the answer to each other's problems? If I could identify that link, our issue might be solved.

The waiter came by to take the tray away, and I ordered another cocktail. It helped take the sting out of working on yet another weekend. As Gina would say, indulgence should be an everyday affair. Somewhere along the way, I'd adopted that motto of hers fully. It was the rest of them that I struggled to integrate into my rules of conduct.

An hour more of research revealed that production was a major stumbling block for Volta. Secondly, their product offering underwhelmed most analysts.

National Motors' issues were of a different, more established nature. The company, for example, struggled to sell efficiently what it produced.

Volta's management, finance, and communications teams were all based in London; but it kept engineering and development in Berlin. Philipp, the face of the company, was based in London. Perfect.

I stood triumphantly; and as discretely as possible, I adjusted the bottom of my swimsuit that had buried itself in my butt while I'd been working. I made my way to the pool for a fifteen-minute swim. I hadn't yet come to the end of the issue, but I'd made progress, and progress was always worth a bit of a reward.

I SPENT the rest of the afternoon preparing my pitch that would ultimately serve three purposes. First, I needed to convince Nick of the partnership idea; and as we weren't on the best of terms, that was the most crucial thing at this point. Second, if Nick came around on the deal, we'd need to sell it to the client. Last, we'd have to convince Volta on the idea. I was sure I could pull off the first two; but Volta was an attractive, up-and-coming startup, so we'd surely have competition for its attention.

This wasn't the first time I was hunting a deal without a precedent paving the way. Sometimes, these risky deals were glorious successes; and sometimes, they were definitely not. I was due a promotion at the bank and so was Nick; if I could pull something big like this off, it would seal the deal on my ascent up the ladder. It might even garner praise from the executive level — perhaps even catching the attention of the bank's president, Alex Thorne. On the other hand, if we didn't close something big soon, it could mean that both Nick and I would be in the market for a new job before the end of the year.

The deal that had left my ex gaping like a fish out of water, for example, had not been a raving success. Ultimately, that's why I'd left New York. When my boyfriend's firm nearly collapsed and I was the reason why, outsiders reveled in the gossip. I grew tired of providing explanations that didn't land. People preferred to believe the very worst: that I'd played David to get revenge.

I looked one last time at the water, its surface glistening like the tiled mirror of a disco ball. Back home, the Thames was surely doing the same, though maybe a little more grey than the striking blue that shimmered in front of me here. Grabbing my stuff, I headed reluctantly back to the indecent air-conditioning of the hotel.

Halfway through the garden, a bellboy was walking in my direction. "Ms. Gardner."

"Yes?"

"You received a call."

"Thank you," I said, taking the sealed envelope from his white-gloved fingers. I continued through the lobby and into the elevator assuming it was a message from Theo saying he was running late. He was, after all, one of only a few people who knew I was here.

Prior to getting on the plane, I'd also sent off a text message to Nir, my friend in New York, and Gina who, I was mostly sure, would be in Paris this weekend. Jet-setting for a fling was standard fare for Nir and Gina so I'd confided in them with ease. This also served as insurance: if I went missing in Turkey, someone would know where to look for me.

I tossed my canvas pool bag on the bed and opened the white envelope. It wasn't from Theo. Nick, my boss, had called the hotel looking for me. How did he know I was here?

My phone, on silent, had been in my bag all afternoon. I dug it out and flipped to my recent calls to dial his mobile. I'd missed thirteen calls from him this afternoon. I paused to fabricate an explanation but stopped myself. I didn't owe anyone a justification for how I spent my weekends. Nevertheless, my stomach ached as I dialed his number. Some of it was nerves, but I'd also not had anything to eat since breakfast four and a half hours ago.

Nick picked up the call yelling into the phone. He was upset to not find me in the office this afternoon when he'd stopped in. After he'd gotten most of it out, I started a conversation.

"Yes, I'm in Istanbul, but I'm working. I've developed a pitch for National Motors, and I think it's a solid one." Silence. "How did you find me in Turkey, anyway?"

"Your assistant was quick to confess," Nick explained. My lips pouted in disappointment in front of the gilded full-length mirror that stood at a slight angle from the parquet floor of the living room.

Nick asked for more details regarding the pitch I'd developed; and in my bikini with my laptop perched over my knees, I laid out the entire thing over the phone. This was definitely not how I'd planned to sell him my idea. He obviously wasn't in the mood to receive it right now. "I don't hate it, but what about other options?" Nick asked when I'd finished.

"I looked into everyone in the space. Volta is the only one that doesn't have a large strategic partner. This could be a huge opportunity for our client. I have a pitch deck built in PowerPoint. I can send it to you."

"Send me what you have then. When are you back in the office?"

"I fly back tomorrow night — in the office Monday."

"Fine, I'll send you my comments tonight by email. For the record, I'm more than a little concerned with this wave of erratic behavior, Audrey. Going off *piste* in meetings, disappearing from London. You need to snap out of it."

I stayed silent on the line without the slightest desire to appease his concerns. I worked for him, but I didn't report to the bank on my personal life.

THEO

I PULLED UP to the hotel with seconds to spare and found Audrey in the lobby sitting in an armchair. She was dressed in tight, dark-blue jeans, wedges, and a thin, airy, black tank top. We exchanged a kiss, casual and friendly as if I hadn't woken up this morning with the back of her body pressing into me. "Busy day?" I asked.

She sighed with an air of fatigue; but if she was tired, she put on a good show. "Very. I spent the entire time at the pool working. You?" She didn't seem to hold her frustration from last night against me.

"Same. Except I didn't have the luxury of working at the pool." We walked out to the car, and I followed her a half-step behind. Her ass looked hot in jeans; she was slight but filled them perfectly with her tight, round cheeks. Watching them shift as she walked was already turning me on. My desire to grab them and take her back upstairs required incredible restraint, and I had to look away. It was going to be a long afternoon.

So far, it had been somewhat difficult to get closer to her given all the interruptions. It had been easier in Athens when we'd slipped away amidst the attention-diverting festivities of the wedding reception.

The valet handed back my keys to the car, which he hadn't bothered to move; and I held the door open for Audrey as she got in. "I'm not driving?" she teased.

I shut her door and walked around to the driver's side and got in. "No, you're not," I said starting the car.

"So where are we going then?"

"We're going to head to the Old City. I'm taking you to the Grand Bazaar." Her face lit up at the suggested itinerary. The market had over four thousand shops and was built during the Ottoman Empire in the fourteen hundreds. I knew she'd love it.

Arriving at the ancient walled city, I pulled into a small parking garage I'd identified during my many visits to the Bazaar with friends and family who'd come here to vacation over the last two years. It was a tiny place near the top of a hill that fit only a handful of cars. I liked the guy who ran the place, and I trusted him to look after the car. Audrey and I walked down the inclined road to the market. It was a Saturday; and as we got closer, the streets became more congested with the foot traffic of Istanbul's early summer tourists.

We arrived at the main gate, and Audrey's eyes widened with eagerness. "You've heard of this place before, right?"

"Of course, but I wasn't expecting it to be so big — and crowded for that matter."

"So the Bazaar is organized by the type of goods sold. Carpets have one section, gold another. Antiques you'll find toward the center, and textiles in another part. Is there anything in particular you want to see?"

"All of it," she said, her body bouncing as we stood near the entrance. "But first, I need something to eat. I'm starving."

"Ah, me too," I said, realizing I'd not eaten a thing all day.

We entered the market, and I led her to a narrow side street that housed a small grill house I liked. Sitting at one of the wood tables lined up along the length of the alleyway, I ordered a marinated beef dish and some dolmas to share. It was an oasis of calm in one of the most chaotic scenes of Istanbul. Dried peppers hung above us; and smoke wafted across from the hot, sizzling grill. The distant hum from the noisy bazaar around us created a muffled tune behind our easy conversation.

We exchanged anecdotes to pass the time — one upping each other to compete for the prize of most outlandish work experience. When we'd finished our belated lunch, I suggested we wander without a specific itinerary.

We started our route by passing shop after shop of gold jewelry, carpets, and then textiles. Carpets seemed to capture her attention the most, and I explained to her the art of buying a carpet, as best as I remembered it from my grandfather.

Aside from the occasional carpet, Audrey never stopped long enough to inspect anything in detail. She was more of a passerby, taking in the richness of color and stimulation — one of many romanticized tourists in from Europe for the weekend — escaping her own capital city for the wonder and adventure of the Orient. I followed a body width behind her through the covered streets.

Her ponytail swished slightly to the rhythm of her ass as she walked — the movement unnoticeable to everyone in the crowd except for me. She glided through the congested market lanes and her tourist comrades with grace and ease, sticking out slightly to the eye in her chic ensemble and remarkable curves. I had to fight not to stare at her; it was punishing. And, I was sure she knew it, too.

Audrey was drawing me in like a seasoned seductress, yet her manner was unhurried which made me question whether it was by deliberate design or casual accident. Was she really as calculating as Mitch had described, or was she oblivious to her beguiling power? I couldn't put my finger on it.

She clearly wasn't a local; and the merchants hounded her incessantly. I stayed close behind hoping my presence would bring some reprieve. Audrey was kind to the sellers but firm; and when she'd tire of bantering in broken English, she simply walked on with a trail of pleas and "bargains" in her wake. Nevertheless, I was there to stop them in Turkish if they got a little too close. The unremitting chaos of the market could turn even the bravest vacationer mad, and we still had a long night ahead of us.

The time passed quickly. Already five thirty in the afternoon, we would soon be running late to dinner and more importantly to the sunset. I grabbed her hand from behind, turning her around to me as two merchants continued trying to sell to her back.

"What do you think? Should we get going?"

She beamed at me with wonder in her eyes. "Oh sure, I think I've seen enough."

I pulled her back down the small street in the direction we'd just come, leaving the sellers in a haze of despondency. I was sure they'd identify new prey by the time the crowd closed in behind us.

We turned left out of the street onto another and eventually found ourselves traversing another section of gold sellers. Audrey dropped my hand and turned her attention to a shop we'd passed. It was full of necklaces with circular airy pendants that hung from thin gold chains. They looked nothing like what one usually found in the bazaar; they were light and modern. I asked the merchant who made them, and he replied that his daughter handcrafted them at home. I repeated the information to Audrey in English.

"How old is his daughter?"

I translated the question to the merchant who replied in English. "She's sixteen."

Audrey looked up and smiled. "She's incredibly talented. How did she learn to do this?"

"My wife taught her, but my daughter thought her mother's designs were old-fashioned," he said, handing her a pendant that clearly was an older work from another part of the booth. "So my daughter makes her own style."

"She does beautiful work." Audrey handed back the one the man's wife had crafted but kept the daughter's necklace in her hand.

The man looked at me. "You should buy one for your girlfriend," he said.

I was about to reply, but Audrey beat me to it. "Oh no, sorry. No, we're just friends," she said. "Good friends." She looked up at me and smiled before returning her attention to the vendor.

"These would easily sell in London or Paris. How much are they?"

Was that what she thought? Were we really just friends? I could tell my brow had furrowed. The demotion wasn't sitting well with me. And I was surprised by my dislike of the label. Perhaps my concern over Audrey's expectations was unfounded. *Maybe I should be more concerned over my own?*

"This one you have is a hundred and fifty Turkish lira," he said. She looked at me inquisitively, and I told her it was the equivalent of fifty U.S. dollars.

I started to negotiate with the man in Turkish, but Audrey held out her hand to stop me. "No, it's absolutely worth that. I don't like to haggle with artists." She reached into her bag to search for her wallet.

"No, please. Let me," I said handing the seller the lira.

Audrey smiled graciously and then looked back at the man. She held out the pendant she'd been holding in her hand. "I can have this very one?"

"Of course." The merchant reached into his wallet and inserted the money. "Wait," he commanded. He flipped through his wallet until he came to a photo and handed it to Audrey. "This is her. This is my daughter. And my wife. Together."

Audrey told the man his family was beautiful and then put the gold chain over her head to wear the necklace. We continued a few more steps down the street, and I grabbed her hand again to get her attention. Pulling her close, I told her the necklace was to remember our weekend together.

The truth was I liked having her around; and if she lived in Istanbul, I'd pursue her; but she didn't. I did, however, want her to remember her stay here. I was selfish in that regard. I wanted her to think of me — to desire me — even if we couldn't be together.

"That's very sweet." She rose on her toes to my cheek whispering, "Though I don't need gold to remember this weekend."

"But it will help." I could feel the stares from locals walking nearby. I released her from my grasp and added more space between us, but my mind was already fantasizing.

I looked at my watch. "It's already six o'clock. We have an hour before we are due to leave for dinner. Are you keen to go back to the hotel first?"

Audrey looked up at me, and her smile answered my question.

AUDREY

I OPENED the closet in my room to remember what I'd hastily stuffed in my bag yesterday morning. I pulled an elegant, midnight-blue strapless dress out from the rack. I hoped that it wouldn't be too much. Would it look like I was trying too hard? It wasn't too revealing, but I loved how it showed off my shoulders. The way it silhouetted my body was worth the outrageous price I'd paid for it at Selfridges in London.

I pulled my ponytail out and shook my hair. It had served me well during the sun-drenched urban afternoon but with a strapless dress I wanted the locks draping my shoulders. Knocking over a plant trying to find the hairdryer, I lost two minutes as I scurried to clean it up.

Finally, blowing out the afternoon fatigue from my hair, I was ready.

Once down in the lobby, I saw Theo sitting near the entrance to the back terrace. He had on the same dark-red jeans and white-buttoned shirt he'd been wearing during our afternoon tour, but he'd added the light grey blazer I'd noticed in the back of his car. I saw he was talking to the same man I'd seen him with the night before when I'd entered the lobby. *Who was this guy?*

Theo saw me and interrupted his conversation by standing up and holding out his hand. I walked over to take it. "Audrey, this is Erol. He's brought our ride for the night."

"Lovely to meet you, Erol." I looked to Theo, "You want to change cars? Why?"

The two exchanged keys. "We're not taking a car." I looked at him puzzled, but he only indulged me in a smile. The more time I spent with him, the more mysterious he became.

Tucking the new set of keys into his pocket, Theo said goodbye to his friend and led me out down to the back terrace by the pool. The energy of the terrace now was completely different from when I'd been working there some hours earlier. The pool was still and quiet, but the wedding that had been set up in the garden earlier in the day was now in full swing. And it was huge — so much so that it was spilling over into every corner of the hotel grounds. There must have been five or six hundred people drinking, dancing, and celebrating.

Theo walked us up to a high-top table and plucked both a glass of champagne and a glass of sparkling water from the tray of a passing server. Handing me the glass of champagne, he toasted in the air. "Cheers . . . to our second wedding together."

I leaned over to him. "Are we wedding crashing?"

"Yep." He put his half-finished glass on the table and took mine out of my hand. "Dance with me."

I looked at him with wide eyes. I'd never crashed a wedding before, and I didn't feel comfortable doing so now. Theo, on the other hand, was unfazed.

He led us onto the dance floor and pulled me into him tightly. It felt good to be so close to him, and I thought back to our dance the previous weekend at David's wedding in Athens. There it had been hotter and more intense because of the sweltering heat; but even so, the energy between us now ran just as high.

I was tense as we danced and looked around to see if we were on the verge of being thrown out. "Relax, Audrey. This is Turkey."

"What does that mean?"

"Here, weddings are large. The families invite everyone they know; sometimes an entire village shows up. It's just the way it is. No one is going to know we're not on the guest list," he said whispering into my ear as we danced.

My eyes narrowed as I tried to determine whether he was telling the truth or making this up. I suppose it didn't matter. I pressed in closer to his body and let the song wash over us. Theo spun me out a few times making the skirt of my dress twirl around my thighs. He was so confident. I loved that about him, but sometimes I hated it. Why was it so much easier for men to be confident?

At work it was no different. My male coworkers spewed confidence and bad ideas, which was partially why I now had to develop a new deal on the fly for my client.

"I'm happy you came to Istanbul," he whispered, his forehead touching mine.

"It's crazy isn't it? I don't usually do these things."

"No?" he asked pulling back slightly. "Well, I'm glad you decided to this weekend."

I stared up into his smiling eyes. "Me too," I confessed.

The song ended, and Theo bent down and kissed me. "Are you ready?"

"Ready for what?"

With my hand firmly in his, he guided us from the dance floor out toward the lip of the terrace overlooking the Bosporus. He was purposefully not answering my question. At the edge of the water, not far from the dock, he crossed behind me and wrapped his arms around the front of my chest.

"It is so beautiful here," I said unable to keep the thought to myself.

Theo squeezed his arms slightly hugging me into him. "It is. I never grow tired of the city's beauty." We lingered there staring into the water and out to the Anatolian side of the Bosporus. He gestured out to the water with a nod of his head.

He let me go and turned off to the right. "Come."

I followed him over to the boat landing. There was a large, tacky yacht tied to the dock. Covered in pink and white balloons, I was sure it was a part of the wedding festivities. I continued after Theo and saw there was a classic, small, mahogany Riva bobbing just behind the gaudy fiberglass yacht. Theo took the keys from his pocket and turned around with a smile.

"This is our ride?" I couldn't believe it.

"What do you say? The water is the best place to watch the sunset," Theo said.

"Yes, absolutely!" Rivas were a thing for the French Riviera or Venice; new ones cost nearly a million dollars; and used, mid-range models rang up at around half a million dollars. I knew that much from the summer vacations spent in the south of France with David, my ex, and his family. I was surprised to see one in Istanbul, but I was beyond thrilled. Their elegance was unparalleled. They were objects for movies and royalty, not for real life.

This one had a deep-navy-blue hull, and the deck was a beautiful, polished mahogany. The upholstery was white leather. It was absolutely stunning. Slipping off my heels on the dock, I searched for an explanation. "How did you find one here to rent? Are they common?" I hadn't seen any since I'd arrived, and I'd spent a full day watching the water as I worked.

Theo was already in the boat and reaching for my hand to help me step in. "It's not a rental." I looked up at him bewildered. "It's mine."

What? A wave crashed up on the boat as he said it; and my front foot slipped as I was stepping in, tossing me on top of Theo. He caught me laughing. He was clearly amused, but I wasn't. I picked my shoes up off the floor and tucked them somewhere safe. "Are you okay?" he asked.

"Yes, I'm fine. Thanks."

He shot me an enormous smile and turned his attention to the front of the boat. Something wasn't adding up. There was no way a consultant could afford a boat like this.

Maybe he was lying to me about his family? Maybe he

was born with a silver spoon in his mouth after all. But why had he told me the contrary? Was he just messing with me or, worse, trying to impress me with things that didn't belong to him?

Theo maneuvered the boat away from the dock as I made my way to him at the front. A fisherman sat on a dock next to the hotel, and Theo called out to him in Turkish. They seemed to be joking with each other. Watching his casual and friendly exchange, I realized how kind he was with others — even strangers.

I sat in the leather seat next to him and angled myself so I could see him and the water ahead of us. I pushed all my questions about his unexplainable wealth out of my mind. What did it matter? I was having fun, and I'd be gone in less than twenty-four hours. His secrets were his own to keep. At the end of the day, they didn't concern me — I was just along for a ride.

We headed south, away from the Black Sea toward the Old City we'd just come from.

The sea air brushed against my cheeks as we made our way down the expansive channel. I had to pull my hair back into a ponytail so I could more easily see the houses we passed on the shore. As we drove by landmarks he recognized, Theo played the role of tour guide filling me in on the history of the country, its inhabitants, rulers, and religions.

"What are those?" I asked curiously pointing across to one of the old mansions along the European shore of the strait.

"Lovely, aren't they? It's a *yali* — the waterfront houses of the nobility. Most of them were built in the nineteenth century. Some of them cost more than one hundred million dollars today."

"No!" My eyes widened, and I searched his face to see if he was joking.

But Theo maintained his authority on the information. "Yeah, I'm not kidding."

"That's insane!"

We spent a half hour cruising until we entered the open water of the Sea of Marmara. The sun was bright as it trailed on the horizon, and the glare from its reflection on the water was blinding even with sunglasses on. I turned to look at Theo to save my eyes. He drove the boat in a semi-circle so we pointed east.

We weren't far from shore — maybe eight hundred meters. Theo let the boat drift and walked toward the back. The water was a soft aqua-blue in the light of the impending sunset, and the clouds above cast off shades of orange and sapphire.

I crawled onto the small, flat sun lounge at the stern. Theo stayed near the helm but came to sit on the circular bench at the back of the cockpit. He was more relaxed compared to the previous night. Drifting in the boat, it was easy to mistake our night together for some holiday vacation. The salty wind that blew by was nothing like the chilled wind of London now in late spring.

Sliding his arm across the small barrier between us, he put his hand in my hair and pulled out my ponytail. Shaking it out, I rolled onto my stomach to look at him. My breasts hung in my dress, grazing the top of the upholstered deck that I was stretched out on. Theo, with his arm still outreached, leaned even further to cup them. I loved the way they became electrified at his touch.

Emboldened, he pinched them: my panties growing damp with each flick of his finger. I rolled onto my back to watch the colors change in the sky.

He followed me by crawling over the back of the bench and onto the platform where I lay. There was a fair amount of boat traffic; I was sure he wouldn't try anything here. His eyes narrowed at the sight of my breasts spilling out the sides of my dress. He ran his fingers along the curve of the one closest to him. My nipples were still hard — both from the sweet torture he'd inflicted and from the breeze that rolled off the sea. I was tempted to ask him to take us back to the hotel. He stretched out next to me and continued to drag his fingers along my frame. He was thinking about something — calculating.

He rotated onto his back and looked up at the sky. "It'll be getting dark soon," he said stating the obvious. I lifted myself onto my elbows and looked at the horizon, but I became distracted when I saw he was extremely aroused. His tight, burgundy jeans did little to conceal his provocation.

Reaching down, I ran my hand along his length. "Do we have somewhere to be?"

He looked over at me. "Indeed, we do."

It took an enormous amount of restraint not to lift my dress and slide myself on top of him. However, I didn't want to put on a show for the traffic that was moving in and out of the strait. I decided to seek answers instead.

"How long have you had this boat?" I asked. After all, maybe it had been passed down to him; or maybe it wasn't really his — maybe it actually belonged to a client, and he'd been joking with me earlier.

Theo turned back onto his chest and crawled over the lounger toward the helm. "Come here, Audrey," he beckoned, dodging the question.

"No, I don't want to come with you. Why don't you

answer my question?" Theo shuddered, and his face grew cold. My boldness surprised even me.

"I . . . well, I . . . "

"Well what?" I said, raising my voice. "In Athens you were so open and kind; but here in Istanbul, it's like you're dodging me and hiding in shadows all the time. Why?"

I wanted to know why he'd left me last night and why there were so many the secrets. Why did he drive a fancy boat?

Theo closed his eyes and inhaled. I'd ruined our moment, but I didn't care. I needed to know more about this man that I'd come a long way to visit. "Is it me? You just don't want to share with me?" Theo bit down on his lip, but my questions were coming faster than he could answer them. "It's fine, Theo. I get it. I can just go back to London if you're uncomfortable."

"No, it's not that," he said, sitting down in one of the cockpit chairs. I could tell he was weighing what to say — choosing his words.

"Audrey, I . . . "

"Look, just take me back to the hotel," I finally offered.

Theo stood. His look of bewilderment changed to anger. "I don't want you to leave." He rushed over to me and took my hand in his. "Audrey, I'm really touched that you've come. I don't want you to go."

The man I'd fallen for a week ago was standing in front of me asking that I give him something . . . time, maybe. At once he kissed me with his searching hands. His touch was insistent and starved, and I forgot why I'd cared so much about the truth.

He pushed the strap of my dress down from my

shoulder to extend a kiss that became something more insatiable. I looked up to the sky, my lips parted, surrendering to it.

Theo drew me to the front of the cockpit and slid open a black door concealed in the dashboard. I hesitated, but he pulled me into the small cabin beneath the deck. It was large enough to sleep two, and there was a white-upholstered lounge couch that went around the walls of the cabin. It was tiny, and I had to bend down slightly to walk. Diving onto the couch, Theo clearly struggled more to move around underneath the deck. I was still getting my bearings when he grabbed my hips and pulled me to his lap.

"This is cozy," I gasped between kisses.

He pulled back and confessed. "There's actually a bed, but I'm too desperate to set it up." He directed my hips while I rode him through his pants, trying to release the tension that boiled inside me.

He threw me off his lap, and I landed on the lounge at the other side of the cabin. He lunged at me, ravenous. I tried to catch his eyes but couldn't.

Grabbing for my thong, he pulled it off. I'd worn it with the intent of teasing him with it later, but he robbed me of the opportunity. He lifted my dress to my waist and opened the zip at the back, releasing my breasts. Leaning back, he took in the disheveled scene while I was still catching up to what was happening. Undoing a couple of buttons at the top of his shirt, he slid it over his head. He was back on top of me before the shirt even hit the floor.

"Shouldn't we get to dinner?"

"I have something else in store for you first." His fingers were circling me below as he spoke. With his other hand he began attacking the belt buckle that restrained him. Then, neglecting me, he stood as best he could to release himself. His stiffened cock was exactly as I'd remembered it: long with a distinct swollen head. He quickly rolled on a condom.

He returned to me and began licking the soft wet flesh between my legs. I held him there for a few minutes before begging him to enter me.

"I'm really close," I confessed. My legs began to tighten and extend, searching for the pleasure to take hold. Grabbing the sides of my ribcage, he lifted me from the couch and lowered me on his lap. I collapsed over him in relief. I'd fantasized of Theo since we'd left each other in Athens, and my body had ached to experience his carnal talents again.

Our bodies rolled in unison while the world buckled all around us. His eyes closed as he concentrated on his pleasure. I was unable to quell my explosion as he continued to grind me on his lap. As I came in his arms, I became lost in the euphoria.

In sharing the physical release, I unexpectedly surrendered a little piece of my soul too. Theo stared into my eyes watching attentively as I finished — taking everything I gave him in that moment.

Catching one of my nipples in his mouth, his breathing too became labored. His pattern slowed and became irregular: he was extremely close. Releasing my breast and gasping for breath, he lifted me over and over again until he burst inside of me. While he might not have been able to tell what I wanted to hear: the truth, he'd reached into the depths of himself to give me everything he did have to ransom.

We remained there for a minute, clinging to each other

— intimate and yet semi-strangers. His face was buried in my chest, and I let him linger there while he gathered himself.

"Are you okay?"

I smiled. "Of course."

"I'm sorry, that was rather unexpected."

"Really?" I said suspiciously.

"I promise. I just wanted to show you the sunset."

Stars pricked in my eyes, and I lay there silently waiting for them to dissipate. Theo was there with a towel to rescue me.

"There is a bathroom here," he said, pointing to a small-concealed room. "I'm going to go up and start driving toward dinner. We were meant to be on our way thirty minutes ago." He bit his lower lip and smiled, eyes sweeping my body a final time.

When I joined Theo back above at the helm, he'd already fully redressed; one would have never known the indiscretions that had just taken place between us. I liked the idea of our sexy secret, and I nuzzled myself under his arm. *Don't fall for him, Audrey,* I told myself. But deep down, I knew it was already too late. This would undoubtedly be painful to unwind from later, and I still had another night here in Turkey. I'd pay for my missteps later, per usual.

The sun had fully fallen in our absence, and the canvas of the western sky bled an intense pink. The edges of the clouds glowed electric. Every outrageous sunset seems more unique than those that precede it; but even so, I was sure this one was the most beautiful. I worked to commit the moment into my memory.

THEO

WITH THE SUNSET TO OUR BACKS, we drove toward the Bosporus. The sea shimmered like grey satin as we crossed over her. Audrey sat in the seat next to me; and occasionally, I'd reach my arm around to hold her. I thought about explaining myself a little more. Certainly she'd calculated that Rivas didn't go along with consultant salaries, but maybe it was still too early. After what Mitch had told me, I wanted to get to know her even better first. Furthermore, I was starting to fall for Audrey; and I didn't want to be disappointed if she treated me differently once she found out who I really was — as it so often happened.

Since we were already late for dinner, I decided to

show off the speed of my luxury toy to make up for our time below the deck. Entering into the strait though, I reduced our speed to give her the opportunity to take in the sights once more. The water was calm, rippling in silence while we moved swiftly above.

In the distance I could see the island. I loved coming to this place. I pulled the boat up to a tiny dock; and an attendant descended the steep, stone stairway to help me tether the boat to the isolated isle. I looked up; and my friend, a server at the restaurant, peered over the edge of the balcony to welcome us.

With the boat secured in place, I stepped out and turned around to Audrey. "Welcome to my second favorite place in Istanbul," I said, extending my arm for her to use while she stepped onto the tired, salt-worn, stone stairway.

"If you keep ticking off your favorites, I might run out of reasons to return," she said jokingly.

"I highly doubt that," I returned with confidence. I was starting to hope that this wouldn't be her last visit.

When we'd finished dinner, I piloted the Riva to a dock on the European side of the strait and helped Audrey navigate the bobbing, wooden platform and creaky stairs until we reached the sturdier cement platform. All throughout dinner, Audrey had been quiet and introspective. I hoped she wasn't upset about our small spat on the boat — nor about what'd happened after. I was resolved to share more of what I could with her.

"Thank you," she whispered.

"Of, course," I said, walking ahead to meet my driver in the small parking lot. He was there with my car.

We exchanged handshakes, and I switched keys with

the driver before reaching the passenger-side door to open it for Audrey.

"I have a surprise for you."

"Another? You have so many secrets," she said.

"Don't we all?"

I started the car and peeled out of the parking lot making a left onto the coastal road. Turning inland to head back into the hills, I rolled our windows down to take in the piney aroma of the Istanbul suburbs.

Audrey looked over at me, and I could feel them coming — questions.

AUDREY

WE PULLED INTO THE DRIVE OF A HOUSE, and Theo turned off the car. At one point I'd thought about trying to set the record straight over his secrecy, but I reminded myself that the weekend was nearly over. Knowing I didn't really have the right to ask such questions of him, I still couldn't help but feel that I couldn't enjoy his company completely while there were so many queries waiting for answers.

Stepping out, I looked up at the large two-story house. It was starting to get really late.

Theo walked around the car and grabbed me by the hand. "Come," he beckoned. Walking to the front door, he pulled out another small set of keys from his pocket.

"This your house?"

He answered me with a wink and opened the door; but we were immediately pushed back out by a massive, barking, mass of fur.

"You have a dog?"

"I do. Isn't she beautiful?"

"She's . . . enthusiastic."

We walked through the main door which opened into an expansive living room. The space was a marvel of architecture with a high ceiling and straight vertical lines that focused the eye directly out to the dark evening water in the distance. To the right was a large American-style open kitchen with an island in the center. Everything was decorated in shades of blue and grey . . . like the night sea.

"Wow, your house is beautiful," I said involuntary admitting my surprise. Consultant salaries must go a lot further in Istanbul than they did in London. I added the house to my running list of things that just weren't adding up. "Did you build it?"

"Yes and no. It was half-started when I found it. The owner was selling, so I purchased it and brought in my own architect."

The space inside was decorated sparsely. "Did you do all of this by yourself?" I asked gesturing around the room.

"Is it obvious?" As I walked toward him, Theo laughed and tucked the mail that was on the counter under a magazine. What was he hiding? A separation perhaps? My eyes narrowed on the counter. "Laika and I don't really need much. I did a better job on my office," he added unnecessarily.

There was only one lonely sofa in the living room. He

didn't even have a dining room table; he lived like a student, albeit a well-off one.

It was here that I grasped my earliest sense of his loneliness. But how could he be lonely when he was so outgoing and friendly with everyone? Maybe he worked too much and actually spent a lot of time alone with his dog?

"I move around a lot and spend most of my time in other countries, so I haven't really gotten around to furnishing this place," he said looking around the room with his hands on his hips.

"Are these your parents?" I asked, picking up a photo frame from a solitary console table on the far wall.

"Yes, that was taken just after they'd married."

Placing the photo back on the table, I looked up at him, unsure of what to say. "You're mother was really beautiful."

He smiled and took my hand leading me through the living room out to the back yard. Theo picked up a gnarled tennis ball, throwing it across the lawn. Laika was already running for it before it'd even been released from his hand.

Theo reached into his pocket and checked his buzzing phone. He was addicted to his mobile. I was only going to be here a few hours more, why couldn't he pry himself away from work?

I kicked off my heels and sank my feet into the manicured grass, standing just behind Theo. I didn't dare get between Laika and her ball or between Laika and Theo for that matter.

The backyard featured a large pool, the underwater light casting a subtle, blue-aquatic hue throughout the center of the yard.

Laika had caught her ball mid-air and was now running at full speed for Theo.

"She's really good," I cheered.

Theo was clearly in love. "She's the best," he boasted.

The game continued for a few more minutes, and I circled the perimeter of the lawn taking in the inky view from every possible angle. The lights from the city and the two bridges illuminated just enough to tease my eye.

"You don't have a dog?" Theo asked as I slowly made my way back to his side of the lawn.

"No, they don't exactly go along with banking hours."

"That's true, but they're easy to make time for once you have one."

"I don't dislike them. I've just never found it convenient for my lifestyle," I admitted.

Laika came bounding back down the lawn and dropped her slimy treasure at my feet. I looked at Theo for direction, but he gave me nothing more than a smile. *Be cool, Audrey,* I thought to myself. I picked up the slithery mess and tossed it as far as I could. Laika was off and running.

She returned the ball directly to Theo without even giving me a glance. If I was to charm Theo, it was clear I'd need to work on Laika first.

"Have you had her long?" I asked while he launched the ball again.

"Almost two years," he said. "I went to Bodrum on holiday a couple summers ago, and she came up to me on the beach. We played together during the afternoon; but when dusk fell and I returned to my room, she followed me. After that, I couldn't leave her there."

"She picked you."

"I like to think so. Together, we keep each other

company." He looked at her and smiled. "Ok, lady," Theo said, asking for his dog's attention. "That's enough for tonight, don't you think?" Laika looked back at him clearly disappointed before looking over at me for help.

"Maybe just one more," I said, stepping over and taking the ball from Theo's hand. Laika bolted at full speed down the lawn, and I threw the ball again as far as I could. It was probably obvious to both of us: Laika wasn't the only one I was trying to win over.

WE WALKED BACK INTO THE HOUSE, but my feet were grassy. "Is there a bathroom?"

"Yes, of course, over here." Theo walked me back toward the entrance revealing an entire section of the house I hadn't seen when I came in. "Here you go," he said, opening the door and flipping on the light.

Walking into the bathroom, I could see that just beyond was a guest bedroom. His house was enormous, and I hadn't even seen the second floor yet. The first floor alone was at least three times the size of my London apartment.

With clean feet, I stepped back into the living room to find Laika half-asleep on her corner bed and Theo at the island in the kitchen checking his phone.

"I think you thoroughly exhausted her."

"I have that affect on women," he said, setting down his phone and grabbing a bottle of champagne he'd taken out of the refrigerator.

"I thought you didn't drink?"

Theo popped open the bottle with the grace of an

experienced hand, making me slightly suspicious. "I don't, but if I'm going to try it, I want it to be with you."

Handing me a full glass, he lifted his own. "What are we drinking to?" I asked.

"To firsts — may we never run out of them."

I raised my glass to his and smiled. *What was that supposed to mean?* I watched him take a small sip of champagne. For a playboy, his intentions were rather unclear.

I looked beyond to the black shimmering water. Peaks of light from the illuminated city calmly waved on the reflective surface of the sea. The other side of the city, the Asian side, was unmoving and silent.

The expansive, darkened sky loomed above the hazy layer of civilization. The stars were slowly revealing themselves; Aires was clearer in the sky than I'd ever seen him before.

Theo met me at the window, whispering in my ear. "I like breaking rules with you, Audrey."

THEO

I LIFTED AN ARM AND PRESSED my hand into the window. The skin at her neck was flushed and warm. She turned under my arm to face me.

"Prove how much you like breaking rules," she said, obviously wanting to play.

I plucked the glass of champagne out of her grip, setting it on a side table. Taking her in my arms, she kissed me slowly and gently. The champagne tasted sweet on her tongue.

"I'm glad you came to visit," I confided. Mitch's warnings were hardly believable now that I was coming to know her.

I'd broken many of my own rules in taking her to

Dilay's place, sharing my boat, and bringing her now to my home. Against my best intentions, I just couldn't help myself with her.

"It was certainly worth it," she said in-between kisses.

I took her by the hand and led her up the staircase at the other end of the room. It was a ploy to get her upstairs — obvious maybe — but effective.

We arrived at the second floor, and from there she could see two hundred and seventy degrees. "If you look hard enough on a clear day, you can see all the way to the Black Sea," I whispered.

Wrapping my hands around her open back, my fingers slid into her dress. My breath was heavy at her neck, and I could see the wisps of short, loose hair fluttering as I exhaled. The tension was thick. She was waiting for me to make my next move. She wanted to be seduced, that's why she'd flown here.

I slid my hands down from her waist to trace the curve of her bottom. "I've been thinking of you all week, Audrey," I confessed. I lowered my lips to her shoulder. "You can't know how much I've thought about taking you in this very room."

I spoke softly of my frustrated, solitary fantasies as she listened silently. I was sure she was imagining me pleasuring myself alone, anticipating her arrival.

"Where do you have these . . . fantasies?" she asked, confirming my suspicions.

I nodded toward the bed and kissed her slowly. "There."

She smiled coming out of the kiss, clearly amused I was sharing this much with her. "And sometimes there," I continued, shifting my gaze from her eyes over to the deep-blue velvet armchair in the corner of the room.

My agenda became clear. I pressed my body into hers, and she braced herself with her hands at my waist, taking the opportunity to explore my stomach.

Sliding my hands up her back, I took in the taut muscles under my fingertips. I walked her over to the furniture in the corner. Turning her around and bending her over the arm of the chair, I lifted the bottom of her dress until it rested over her lower back.

The black lace of her thong framed her cheeks perfectly: two beautiful arcs and beneath them — paradise. I tried to burn the image into my brain for the fantasies I'd be left with after she'd be gone. I was more attracted to her than anyone I'd ever been with before. Audrey was a drug.

I couldn't get enough of her body, but she also challenged me intellectually. This wasn't typical of the women I usually dated, and I was surprised by how much I liked it. But I was still cautious and treaded carefully — struggling to determine just how dangerous she could be.

Taking her backside into my hands, my thumbs caught in the subtle line between her ass and her thigh, lingering there for a split second enjoying the change in texture and heat. A faint line of perspiration there dampened my fingers. I cupped the lower part of her butt cheek. Her body writhed under my touch to tell me I was going too slowly. I was torturing her, but I couldn't stop.

Her necklace fell out from her cleavage and brushed against the chair. I thought about our afternoon at the market; Audrey was tough to figure out. We were both playing cool, but we were obviously drawn to each other. I wondered if she was still just in this for the fun. *Was I?*

Taking the sides of her hips in my hands, I gripped them while wanting to use her splayed body to exact my own pleasure. My thumb hooked into the black lace and snapped it gently against the top of her ass.

I reached between her legs from behind, taking her in my hand. She was already beginning to soak through the bottom of her panties as she ground into my palm.

"I want it, Theo."

"Not yet."

My middle finger began running light circles around her clit from behind; and she responded by widening her stance, giving me fuller access. I stayed there awhile playing her. She widened her legs further, rocking her pelvis into my hand as her breath deepened and slowed.

I curled my arm around the front of her waist and pulled her up into the air at my side, roughly, carrying her to the bed.

Laying her on her back, I grabbed her damp panties and fumbled to get them off. Impatiently, I ripped them apart and threw them to the floor. Plunging two fingers deeply into her, I covered her clit with my mouth. Her complaints ceased, and she bunched the comforter over her head in her fists. Her legs tightened and extended, telling me she was close. I wanted to feel her clench around me as she came.

With my free hand I tore off my jeans, and I stroked myself twice to measure my hardness. I reached into the nightstand; and ripping apart the condom wrapper, I slid it down my shaft as quickly as possible.

Slowly entering her, my body became awash in her warmth, the pleasure extending all the way up to my head. "More," she begged, curling her legs around me. She was becoming greedy, but in that moment I was willing to give her everything she wanted.

I thrust deeper, and her breath deepened once again.

She succumbed loudly — a triumphant mix of pain and pleasure in each small cry while she tightened herself around my swollen dick.

Her heated fragrance smelled of gardenia and musk; and under my light kisses, she tasted of salt. When her eyes opened, she gifted me a smile. I descended under the sheets, licking and exploring the newly fallen light dew that now covered her intimate skin. I was eager to finish myself; but first, I wanted to taste her.

Her words became sporadic; and finally, she fell silent —while the quickness of her breath told me she was taking pleasure a second time.

I entered her again quickly, and my ass tightened holding back my own orgasm while she finished roiling in hers. Her face was flushed and her brow furrowed. The roots of my pleasure took hold between my legs before shooting twinges of inclination down the backs of my thighs. When the surge ascended, I came fiercely, giving her everything I had in one blinding, suspended moment. I collapsed onto the bed and scooped her into my arms desperately — I needed her close.

While I couldn't afford complicated right now — as hard as I tried — there was something deeper happening that I wasn't able to stop or control. I was sliding down a slippery slope, but I'd never felt more alive — more complete.

Not another word was uttered, and we fell asleep in gratified silence.

AUDREY

I WOKE TO AN EMPTY BED but with a sweet smell curling through the air. Theo had busied himself in his massive kitchen preparing breakfast. By the time I made it down the stairs, he had laid it on a large table in the backyard. The sky had become overcast during the night; and stepping out onto the patio, I was grateful for the relaxing, breezy morning.

Theo joined me on the patio also in bare feet; he was wearing jeans and a grey t-shirt. Given the only thing I had with me was my dress from the previous night, I'd grabbed a t-shirt from his walk-in closet and coupled it with a pair of sweatpants I'd rolled down at the waist so that they'd stay on.

"Nice outfit," he said before kissing me and handing me a frothy cappuccino.

"I hope you don't mind me pillaging your wardrobe?"

"Not at all, it suits you. Come have a seat. Breakfast is ready."

The food he'd prepared was rather elaborate: pancakes, eggs, toast, jam, and fruit; I was impressed.

Picking through breakfast, we discussed American and British politics to avoid going too personal this early in the morning. We'd both finished eating when I stood up and walked down to the pool. I slid off the rolled sweatpants and sat at the edge, putting my legs into the water. Theo came and joined me in a chair nearby.

"You must do just fine as a consultant," I said trying to bait him.

"I do okay. But also, real estate prices here aren't what they are in London obviously."

"Still, this looks like a great neighborhood. Your house is beautiful, and the view is incredible."

He smiled but wouldn't reveal anymore. How was it possible that a consultant made more than I did? Maybe he was actually a partner in his firm? That was the only explanation I could come up with. It was disappointing on some level. Normally, I loved making more than the men I slept with. I was used to picking up the checks on my dates because I couldn't stand the feeling of owing a man something when he paid for my dinner. I'd always known this was an allergic reaction to my mother's lifestyle.

My mother had squandered her assets and hung off men to survive — I lived in fear of succumbing to a similar fate. My grandmother had raised me to be financially independent, and there was nothing I feared more than my career collapsing and having to rely on a man to help me.

Financial autonomy meant not having to stay in bad relationships; and ever since my breakup in New York, I was more grateful for this wisdom than ever.

I looked up at Theo as the sun poked out from behind a cloud, making me squint to see him. I imagined it was now around noon. "I should get back to the hotel and check out. My flight is at four o'clock."

"Of course, I'll drive you to the airport."

"No, you don't need to. I can take a taxi, really. I could use the time to put some order to my project this week."

"Fine, but then I'll send you back with Kaden, my driver."

"Who is he by the way — who does he work for?"

"He was a friend of the family, and I hired him to help his family out. In reality, he mostly helps me out."

"Okay, I'll take that deal then." I was grateful to have some space this afternoon. Hanging out with Theo was great; but it was intense, and I wasn't sure I wanted to spend too much time with him. It was meant to be a light affair after all.

I stood from the pool and shook out my legs.

"So when do I get to see you again?" he asked. The question hit me like a bolt of lightening. "I'm meant to come up to London at the end of this week for meetings. Will you be around?"

"Really? How come?" I asked, dodging the question. This seemed like a strange move for him to make.

"It has to do with a problem at work. I expect I'll have work dinners Thursday and Friday, but we can plan to see each other on the weekend if you'd like, or I can even fly us somewhere. We could go to Paris, for example."

If I wanted to go to Paris, I could fly myself. Did he think I needed a man to travel? My body tensed. "I'm not sure I can leave London, but maybe we could stay there for the weekend."

He smiled with his huge, white grin. "I'll confirm things on my side this week and let you know."

I realized that I too was smiling, and my body was calm. Happy. I was going to see him again. I didn't want to jinx what we had going on so I relaxed, resolved to not mistake this for more than it was. Most men I knew had a track record of overpromising and underdelivering.

THEO

IT WAS SUNDAY NIGHT AROUND DINNERTIME when Anna called to give me the news. Brady Spence had been arrested for driving under the influence of an impressive list of bad decisions. The investigation found that he'd had an incredibly high blood alcohol limit and had also taken cocaine and some MDMA. They'd also found an eight ball hidden beneath one of the front floor mats.

"Look, I hate to call this good news given the circumstances, but this is good news," Anna said. "I don't think you need to worry about coming to London at this point."

"Is the investigation closed?"

"No, but no one is asking about the possibility of

faulty safety technology anymore. In fact, the investigator you spoke with Friday night called me this morning. They believe the reaction of the computer system minimized a potentially worse accident. It was the driver that turned the car erroneously to the right taking them off the highway. The car rolled once, and the fatality likely would have been prevented if the passenger had been wearing her seat belt. There will probably be a few more interviews to give to media, but I'll book them for someone else."

"Okay, thanks Anna. You've out performed us all this weekend. I'm not sure what I'd do without you."

"It's my pleasure; or well, you know what I mean."

We hung up the phone, and I looked over at Laika. I collapsed on my large, ashen couch; and she didn't miss a beat jumping on top of me. She wanted to play. Walking out to the backyard, I threw a ball into the pool. Laika immediately leapt in the water for it, and I dove in after her. She was a great swimmer, and I'd taught her how to swim toward the stairs when she felt tired and wanted to get out. That made me feel more comfortable about her playing in the backyard without me. I floated in the pool looking up at the ruby-orange sky while Laika tried furiously to get a game on.

There was no question now. I had to go to New York next week instead of London. Audrey would be landing soon if not already, but I couldn't call to tell her tonight. In case plans would change, I'd wait a couple days to be sure.

Would she think I was playing with her if I cancelled so soon? My heart stung over the idea of having to wait even longer to see her. She'd only just left, but I already missed her. In the wake of her absence, the house and backyard seemed silent and empty.

Laika swam up and batted at my shoulder. I'd indulge her by playing for a minute, but then we'd have to get back to work.

AUDREY

NICK AND I STARED NERVOUSLY at the conference room phone. Our counterparts were already five minutes late. I tried not to read too much into it.

After returning to London, Nick and I succeeded in getting National Motors on board with approaching Volta. I'd set up this call between Nick, the Chief Operating Officer of Volta, and myself. It was meant to be a delicate approach; we didn't want to overstate our interest in Volta.

When they finally joined us on the line, it was a friendly get-to-know-you call. We learned a bit more about their challenges at this early stage of their growth, and I then spent the rest of the week outlining how our client would make a good partner with a healthy dose of what my client would require in return.

It was now Wednesday, and a late-afternoon meeting was scheduled in London for us to flesh out more of what a sweetheart deal might look like between the two companies. Nick had already called me to his office twice today to go over our strategy. In a little less than three days, he'd become this deal's greatest champion despite its high risk. I suppose when grasping at straws, a person will champion whatever might save his or her neck.

The deal was not a standard transaction. In fact, it looked more like a partnership for a tech startup than anything else; but the terms were straightforward. National Motors would give Volta access to two antiquated manufacturing facilities it'd already planned to divest. In addition, it would invest some cash into Volta in exchange for a three percent stake in the company.

Most importantly, this could potentially be one of the largest deals of the year. The trades would be eager to cover it if it came together. A media win was nearly guaranteed, and that would give my client's share price a nice lift. It was a win-win.

National Motors was having a quarterly board meeting in two weeks to vote on the proposal, so we had that much time to pull a deal together; but we were only meeting Philipp, the Chief Operating Officer for Volta, face-to-face for the first time this afternoon. The deal was still somewhat of a long shot, but Nick seemed confident that we were within striking range. I, personally, had never seen a deal like this close in such a short amount of time, so I had to defer to his experience.

The president of Roland Capital in New York, Alex Thorne, had already telephoned Nick to pledge whatever resources we needed to seal the deal. Everyone in the bank was watching us closely.

Looking around my office for anything I may have forgotten, I folded my laptop and tucked it in my bag. I dug through my purse to find my lip-gloss. It wasn't lost on me that I was competing in an industry dominated by men. My gender often left me sidelined; but looking pulled together was an asset in an *if you can't beat them, join them* sort of way. I wasn't proud of it, but I was too busy to adopt a more privileged stance on the issue.

I walked over to the office door and closed it to peer into the mirror I'd stuck on the back ages ago. Even after smoothing a light layer of dusty-rose gloss on my lips, I looked tired. A little blush, powder, and mascara later, it was as good as it was going to get. I grabbed my bag and headed over to Nick's office so we could walk over together.

On my way down the hallway, Theo texted to say hello; but I didn't have time for him right now. I'd reply later, although my stomach flipped knowing that he was thinking of me. It had been hard to keep him off my mind, and I'd been worried the feeling might not have been mutual.

Philipp Konig was already waiting in the conference room when we walked in. There were three people he'd brought with him: two women and a man, which made the gender equation equal. I was sure it was a first in this building.

Philipp stood to introduce his colleagues. He was tall, blond, and smiling with confidence. The slight German accent immediately made me think of Theo, but I couldn't afford the distraction.

Nick opened the meeting by outlining point by point

what we were looking to do, and Philipp responded by pointing out where Volta would be interested. However, he was careful to set the tone by letting us know that Aydin Demir, the owner, kept a tight rein on his independence and ownership. This guy sounded like a real, reclusive piece of work. If the owner was a pain-in-the-ass, it could very well kill my deal.

If that wasn't bad enough, Volta was insisting on a much higher cash contribution than my team had been able to justify. "We'll have to work on the cash piece obviously. I can send over more information to help with the valuation. We're already engaged with that in New York," Philipp said before listing the banks they were working with as underwriters for their forthcoming initial public offering. I cringed as he finished. I knew David was now working at one of them in New York, Kleinman.

How had our bank not been involved in this, I wondered. Roland Capital Group, my investment bank, was at the center of most large I.P.O.s. I was surprised that the New York office wasn't already part of the underwriting.

Philipp continued, "We are meeting with underwriters in New York at the end of the week. Our CEO, Aydin, might also be there for the meeting if you want to have a sidebar just after."

"It'll depend if our client agrees on the points we've discussed — the valuation being a critical piece of that obviously," Nick clarified.

Philipp had just given more of himself away than he realized. Volta was actually hungry for this deal or at least one like it.

WALKING INTO MY OFFICE, I saw a box had been delivered while I was in the meeting. I picked it up and inspected it. I wasn't expecting anything. It was probably more real estate investment spam. Somehow, I'd been put on some terrible list that frequently tried to sell me on so-called luxury investment properties in Spain. As if I had anytime to visit my hypothetical second home in Majorca.

I dropped the package in the corner behind my desk and logged into my computer. It was seven o'clock in the evening, and I'd been saddled with the task of developing the final briefing that would be sent to the client later tonight so they'd have it first thing in the morning.

Theo sent me a few more messages saying that he needed to talk. Afraid of what that might mean, I buried myself in work and planned to get back to him when I got home.

Following a few hours of work, my eyes were blurring into a PowerPoint haze when my phone rang — it was Theo. I picked it up relishing the distraction, and I also needed to tell him I might not be able to see him in London after all this weekend. Following a minute or so of routine flirtation, Theo broke his news first.

"Hey, how come you never reply to my messages?

Oops. He'd noticed. "Theo, I've been really busy, I just haven't had time. But make no mistake, I was delighted to hear from you."

The quiet on the other end of the line grew uncomfortable, and I searched for something else to say but came up empty.

"That's fine and all, but Audrey, I'd appreciate it if you'd reply," Theo said finally breaking the silence. "I might have something really important to tell you."

"I'll make more of an effort to get back in real time. So what's your news?" I asked, rather excited to hear what he was so anxious to tell me.

"I'm really sorry, but it doesn't look like I'm coming to London after all."

"Oh, I see," I replied fighting away the bitter taste of disappointment. "It's fine, I'll be in the office working most of the weekend anyway."

"I'm really sorry. I have to go to New York instead," he revealed. My breath halted for a split second.

While I'd been working on the final pitch, I suspected that Nick had agreed with the National Motors' team that we should meet in New York next Monday.

I knew Nick was already scheduled to meet with his bosses in New York which had him on edge. He was desperate to arrive with good news to share with his higher-ups. Being called into meetings to the headquarters office could either mean great or incredibly bad news.

But should I tell Theo that I might also be there? At the end of the day, if I went, I'd be in New York for potentially one of the largest deals I'd ever worked on. There was a lot riding on the outcome of my meetings. Seeing him would introduce a distraction, and I didn't need that.

More concerning was that maybe this was Theo's way of backing out of our date. I decided it was best to let him do so gracefully. "No worries, weekends are infinitely supplied. If this one doesn't work then maybe there'll be another," I added.

The truth was I felt a little crushed. I was starting to really care about Theo, and I'd thought he felt the same about me. *Maybe I'd been too brash in flying to Istanbul to see him.*

Afraid he would find it creepy for me to be in the same city on the other side of the Atlantic at the same time, I kept my potential travel plans to New York a secret. I'd made a huge move in going to Istanbul, and I really needed him to make an equal one before I could invest anymore in this affair. If that was even what this was.

He sighed into the phone. "Of course. We'll see each other another weekend." I noted he didn't suggest one in particular. I felt an indisputable twinge of disappointment. Yet, on the other hand, I'm not sure what I had been expecting either.

After my return to London from Istanbul, I'd deleted my Tinder account. It was a stupid thing to do, but I'd done it while still awash in the soft euphoria of the weekend. Now in the cruel light of Theo's phone call, I vowed to reinstall it as soon as I went home. This wasn't the first time a man had backpedaled on me, and I refused to feel wounded.

I hung up and called out to my assistant to see if the sushi order she'd made earlier had come in. It was going to be a long night, and I'd be ineffective and asleep if I ordered what I really wanted: Indian cuisine.

I turned my attention back to the computer and dug into the terms we'd discussed with Philipp and his team.

Gina texted me while I stuffed yellowtail sashimi and a bowl of rice into my mouth. I chatted with her on messenger while I inhaled the rest of my dinner. She was excited over meeting the London gallery people who were interested to invest in her Paris shop. I was happy for her.

She also was aghast over Brady Spence's car accident and wondered if I'd heard about it. *Had I heard about it?* The crash controversy was threatening to kill my deal. We exchanged a string of emojis to end the conversation; and with no rice left to pick at, I tossed my bowl in the trash and returned to my pitch deck.

LOOKING AT THE CORNER of my computer screen, I saw it was already one thirty in the morning. I'd just sent the final deck off, and I was expected back at the office in six hours. I slumped back in my chair and sighed. The adrenaline from the day subsided, and fatigue began to overtake me. It had been an excruciatingly long day.

I looked at the small box I'd tossed in the corner earlier in the afternoon and accepted that the day was over. I had nothing left to give. I'd open the sales package, toss it in the trash, and go home.

With the end of a pair of scissors, I cut through the clear tape and pried open the cardboard flaps with both hands. Inside, a white card sat on a dark grey box with unmistakable white letters across the top: *Amore*. The Italian lingerie brand was on the unfulfilled Christmas lists of most of my girlfriends. *Amore's* signature packaging was the lingerie version of Tiffany's little blue box.

I placed the sealed white card down on the desk and carefully opened the package. Grey tissue paper leapt from the container as I muddled through to discover three beautiful pairs of black lace panties — each one slightly different from the other.

I opened the card for clues. This certainly was the most effective real estate sales pitch I'd received yet.

If I replace what I broke, can I see you again? — T

I couldn't hold back the smile that spread throughout my body, but talk about mixed signals. Why had he cancelled our weekend then? My heart yearned for a complicated explanation and hoped that he missed me. With him so far away, I wouldn't be getting answers anytime soon; but for now I was happy enough with the ambiguity. I tucked the box under my arm; and leaving my computer docked on my desk, I grabbed my bag to go home. That was enough turmoil for one day.

THEO

THE ACCELERATION from take-off pressed my body deep into the broad leather seat. The plane dipped sharply in favor of my side of the aircraft; the pilot was adjusting his trajectory bound for New York. It was a flight I'd taken countless times.

Out to the east, I had a perfect view of the two bridges that connect Europe and Asia. Their pathways through the detached landscape glowed brightly yellow against the black water of the Bosporus. I thought of my flight and the reason I was on it. If global commerce and finance were the new bridges of the modern world, I was a small, moving piece in that complicated network.

My grandparents, part of a generation of Turkish

refugees, sought a better life than the one they'd inherited; I was the optimistic outcome of the new future they'd built for their children in Germany.

The lights were still dimmed from take-off as we made our way higher into the sky. Music from my youth streamed through my earbuds making me especially dreamy and optimistic. I lived a good life — a fast life.

Song after song cycled by until I found myself in the middle of a personal fantasy — with Audrey. She was sitting across from me at dinner — her eyes sparkling in the flickering light of a candle. Half-glasses of wine and water constructed a crystal barrier between us. We were laughing — happy — both friends and new lovers.

I tried to quell the distraction and tap back into the flow of ideas that I'd been brainstorming for work, but I couldn't shake her from my mind. The red of her lips contrasted starkly with the white of her smile. I let go of the guilt and settled into the Audrey-fantasy. If only she wasn't in London.

White light came streaming in the cabin with brash cruelty as the steward prepared first class for its dinner service. I closed my eyes again, but my daydream was gone — a fleeting thought that'd be forgotten in a matter of minutes.

I missed her easy banter, her smile, the feeling of her breath against my chest as she succumbed to pleasure. I hoped she didn't think I'd cancelled our weekend on a whim, but I began obsessing about the possibility anyway. Stuck at thirty thousand feet, there was nothing I could do. I'd call her tomorrow to let her know I was thinking of her.

The future of this company was riding on the outcome of the forthcoming week. I'd start with tomorrow's meeting of the underwriters for the initial public offering. Later, I'd meet with potential partners; and Thursday was the launch event for the Model II pre-orders.

I'd never over-scheduled a week like this in my life, but things were happening fast, and this was the only way to get everything done. It would be a week to remember — if I could pull it all off.

We still had yet to reconcile the share price with our underwriters, and we needed to make sure our pre-order sales event would make a huge splash in the market. If the event were successful, it would help us justify a higher company valuation, meaning more cash to outfit new production plants to ramp up our manufacturing.

I'd sacrificed so much to get at this juncture: broken relationships, endless working hours, not to mention the wealth I'd invested. Success at this point wasn't optional.

The steward came by placing a grey polyester napkin over my tray table, and I browsed the movie options on my screen. I considered an easy rom-com but opted for the latest superhero remake instead. Superpowers were exactly what I was going for this week. If I allowed myself to daydream about Audrey all the way to New York, there was no telling what kind of trouble I'd get into.

AUDREY

I GAVE MY ROLLER BAG A BIG PULL while my butt held open the heavy door to my hotel room. The bellboys downstairs had all been busy when I checked in, so I'd found my way to my room all by myself. It was little trouble since I already knew the place like the back of my hand. I'd opted to stay further uptown from the financial district so I could sleep close to my old stomping grounds of the Lower East Side.

Even as waves of restoration had poured over the island, this little enclave still held onto its aura of historical grunginess. It was here that I'd spent my first three years out of undergrad finding my way in the bubble of Manhattan. When I'd bought my apartment, the Lower East Side was still one of the roughest areas of the borough; but by the time I'd left, the neighborhood had become one of the hottest in town. I'd made a killing on the apartment when I sold it.

The Elizabeth Hotel in the Bowery was one of my favorite hotels in the city, and it was conveniently located a couple blocks south of my former apartment. I'd taken many meetings here in the opulent lobby of this hotel. It felt, in someway, like a second home.

My body lumbered with the fatigue induced from too much travel and not enough sleep. My breath was short and shallow, and my eyes were tearing at the corners from exhaustion.

Opening my suitcase, I grabbed my bag of liquids and made my way to the bathroom in my black strapless and one of my new lace thongs courtesy of Theo. It felt refreshing to wash off the grime of the trip. Passing a full-length mirror, I stopped to take in my figure and turned to show off my backside. It was true: just wearing *Amore* lingerie seemed to lift everything up to its rightful place.

The softly-spoken room was decorated with a nod to New York at the turn of the previous century but with taste, modernity, and convenience. The small living room was set into the northwest corner of the suite and featured unremarkable brown leather couches. My absolute favorite piece in the room, however, was the viridian-green velvet armchair. It stuck out being the only vividly colored piece in the suite, as if it had arrived there by accident.

On the side table next to the armchair was an iced bottle of champagne and two glasses. Clearly, management had mistaken my booking for one of a more romantic nature.

Thinking of Theo opening the bottle of champagne in his house, I wondered why he'd broken off his visit to London. He was impossible to figure out: one minute crafting meaningful gestures to make me feel special and another using the mask of his work to flee.

Makeup-free and with a wet face, I made my way to the large, loft-style steel casement windows. They were one of my favorite features of the hotel. My room was on the twelfth floor; and with virtually no large towers nearby, I was able to see a few blocks to the west.

As much as I'd tried to find some place better, it was impossible to deny the magical charm of New York City. She was a living dichotomy of excessive success and broken dreams; but if you were lucky enough to have her smile upon you, there was no greater feeling than basking in the warmth of her glittering spotlight.

As I watched the ceaseless pace of the city flow through its streets, alive with cars streaming down the avenue and people scurrying along the sidewalks, the comfort of being home gave way quickly to the insecurity of feeling like an outsider. In a place where someone is only as valuable as his or her last deal, I wondered if my city had forgotten me.

The paint had hardly dried in my former office when the guy who'd been internally promoted to my position moved in. The space that I once filled in my industry, in restaurants, in the hearts of my local friends, and in the beds of my broken relationships had been replaced, no doubt, many times over by others.

Theo was no different. While we were obviously attracted to each other, he also lived lightly. Always on the move, he hadn't even bothered to furnish his house; and I feared that he similarly underinvested in relationships. If we'd never see each other again, he'd be seeing someone else in a matter of weeks — maybe days.

I threw on some clothes and went downstairs to my favorite restaurant. It wasn't anything special, but I liked how the staff always recognized me when I popped by.

Stepping into the chic diner, my emotions were mixed — this had been a place David and I often came to together. I stood at the hostess stand for a minute before a woman came up to seat me. She was new. I'd never seen her before.

"Is this your first time dining with us?" she asked while walking me to my table. I sighed in response. I didn't have the energy to explain that I'd probably logged more hours here than she had.

"No," I replied simply.

While waiting for my late night fare, I imagined how the next day would unfold. The executives at National Motors had agreed to a pre-meeting with Nick and me downtown in their offices at ten o'clock. At two o'clock in the afternoon, we were scheduled to meet at the offices of Maven Birche, one of Volta's underwriting banks. Thankfully, it wasn't at Kleinman; but just thinking about the possibility of running into my ex, David, at work made my stomach turn nervously.

He was now happily married, but I still wasn't sure how I felt about his quick recovery after we broke up.

When my food arrived, I surveyed the other couples seated around me as I ate. It was just a regular, casual Sunday night for them. They'd come to the restaurant because one of them had suggested ordering in and watching a movie, but their partner countered with the suggestion of walking over to the diner at the Elizabeth Hotel. I sometimes wanted that — an easy, predictable

Sunday night with my lover — flings didn't offer such comforts. I fantasized about Theo walking in and sitting down at the other side of the booth, apologizing for being late because he had a hard time hailing a cab. He would ask if I'd chosen a movie for us to see.

After finishing and paying the check, I sat at the table for an extra moment wondering if Theo might ever become more than a fling. But that was impossible. *Stop with the fantasies, Audrey.*

As my romantic illusions came to an end, my eye wandered to catch another couple that had appeared at the entrance. It was David and Delia. I guess he hadn't bothered to create new traditions with his wife — he'd simply recycled ours? This was a cruel sort of karma. I stood to go say hello; but as the hostess took them to a table near the front window, I could see they were arguing.

Maybe it was best if I didn't say hello. I left out the back entrance that led directly into the lobby of the hotel and hoped they hadn't seen me.

Back in my room, I curled on my side under the fluffy hotel comforter. My thoughts lingered on Theo for a few minutes more. I wanted him to be there next to me in bed. With my eyelids sufficiently burdened by sleep, I closed them one final time as the memory flashed of the first time I saw him: a beautiful stranger.

I MET NICK IN THE LOBBY of National Motor's downtown offices. His tie was crooked and his body tense. We exchanged good mornings, and I asked how his meetings in the city had gone the Friday before.

"Audrey, we need this deal to come through," he said, stammering while his eyes scanned the lobby.

"I take it didn't go so well?"

"Alex Thorne told me that the National Motors' team was taking meetings last week in London while they were there to meet with us." Alex, the president of our bank, was a neurosis-filled, arrogant jerk; but those meetings were a bad sign. If he sensed that Nick and I weren't performing, we could be fired before the week's end. The ball already seemed to be in motion. We needed to stop it immediately.

"Who are they talking to?"

"Kleinman." *Ouch!* "Horowitz and Goldwyn," he continued. My stomach twisted with nausea. It was embarrassing enough to lose a client, but to hand them over to my ex's firm — no way. There was now infinitely more riding on this deal than the obvious upside of the transaction.

I grabbed Nick's elbow as he paced around the sitting area. He looked at me surprised. The English aren't much for touching, but I felt the situation merited my boldness. "Nick, we are going to get this. I don't know how, but we're going to pull it off."

He stared me straight in the eye before returning his obsessive gaze back to the polished lobby floor. "I certainly hope that you are right."

I felt for Nick. I needed a successful deal to save my job and my reputation, but Nick had a whole other list of reasons to succeed. I'd suffered in my breakup, but his wife of fifteen years had just left him. His children now lived on the other side of the city, and his finances were no doubt a heavier burden than ever.

"We don't have any other choice but for me to be

right. We are not walking into this next meeting as the bankers on the verge of losing their clients. We are storming in as the heroes who are saving these executives' asses."

Nick looked up from the floor and managed a feeble smile. He was in the fight, but he didn't have much left in him. I'd have to convey the momentum and importance of the deal for both of us. It had been a full two years since I secured a significant deal. If I didn't do something big soon to make a name for myself, I'd surely get lost in the tide. I closed my eyes briefly, took in a huge breath, held it for three seconds, and let it out. *You can do this, Audrey.*

The building's security officer called us over to his desk and gave us our temporary credentials. An assistant from National Motors led us to the elevators and placed us in the conference room. My eye immediately focused on the plates of buttery croissants at the center of the table, but my performance in high-pressure situations was always better on a slightly empty stomach. I saw the bottles of water at the end of the room and opted for one of those before plugging in my equipment and setting up the presentation.

Michael Gruner was the first one to enter the room. He ran business development for National Motors and was cheery enough; but once we'd all sat down, he didn't hesitate to cut straight to the point regarding his reservations about a partnership with a company like Volta.

"It's an incredibly high-risk move. We've been around for a hundred years, and the reason we've succeeded for this long is that we have a steady hand when it comes to our investments."

I understood completely where he was coming from. He worked in a risk-averse culture. I could feel it just walking down the bare, sober-grey hallways. While newer automotive companies were paving a way for themselves in the market through bold communication and marketing, National Motors was still selecting moves from a playbook that was written to sell to my grandparents' generation. And while it'd tweaked its strategy along the way to reach younger customers with shifting consumption priorities, National Motors never seemed to be leading the conversation.

I did my best to convey our understanding of their predicament but made it clear in our casual conversation that today's executives weren't competing in the same market as those who'd come before. While Michael seemed to get it, he complained that it was harder to convince the leadership above him. The eternal struggle — as long as a person is receiving a paycheck, there is always someone higher with more authority. In that sense maybe Aydin Demir, the mysterious CEO of Volta, had chosen the glorified path after all: he ran the company under his own hand with free rein to do as he pleased. *Maybe it was time for me to step out on my own and create my own advisory firm?*

"Look, I'm also not sure we can get to their valuation," Michael said, placing his battle flag in the ground. "The model is contingent on a variety of assumptions that seem a bit indulgent."

He opened the briefing we'd prepared. "For example, here Volta places a lot of faith in the new model it's releasing, saying that the company expects a hundred thousand orders in the next six months; but so far in the trades, there isn't any indication that Volta will sell that many pre-orders. In fact, analysts are concerned that this type of selling process doesn't even apply to automotive. Crowdfunded startups maybe — but not large ticket items like cars. Do they think they're a tech company?"

"I believe that's exactly what they think," I added to clarify. It made me think of when I'd explained the concept of crowdfunded pre-order fashion to Theo in Athens. "A lot of tech companies are doing this in some form these days. It offers access to a more flexible source of capital."

At that moment Angela Marks, the other executive we'd met in London, entered the room with National Motors' head of legal and their Chief Financial Officer. They took seats on either side of Michael. Their CFO reached for a chocolate croissant, and my stomach clenched with hunger.

"Well, we could delay committing until after the pre-order event, but time is becoming a major issue now. It would be good if we could have a deal outlined, so you can start getting support among your board members ahead of the meeting next week," Nick suggested.

"I know," sighed Michael. He was difficult to read. On one hand, he'd seemed excited about the technology when we were all in London; but now he was clearly skittish. I wondered if it was Volta or us that made him that way all of a sudden.

"There isn't much time to lobby the board as it is," he confirmed. "Also, I've been thinking that we're not asking enough of Volta on the technology side of this agreement. I think it should put something more valuable on the table to justify the higher cash contribution."

I doubted that Volta would agree to share its

technology with National Motors. Even as a partner, my client was still a competitor.

"I think we could definitely ask for more in the area of technology transfer," Angela agreed.

"The terms as they are now seem a little weak," Nick chimed in. "The entire premise of the deal is built around you gaining insights into electric car manufacturing. The deal as it's currently structured gives you friend-status to a hot, up-and-coming competitor; but it lacks the tangible engineering piece that is critical to your long-term success."

I bit down on the inside of my cheek. The truth was that we'd pushed Volta on this; but Philipp Konig, Volta's Chief Operating Officer who we'd be negotiating with in the meeting later this afternoon, had refused the request on the grounds that Aydin Demir, his boss, would never go for it.

I was skeptical about exciting our client by promising something it might not be able to have. One way or another, maybe I could get Volta to move on it.

"They seem cash-hungry, and technology sharing will cost them little in financial terms," Nick finished. The three executives nodded at each other in agreement.

The five of us ticked through the remaining items in the presentation. It was important that our team be united in what we'd be asking from Volta later in the afternoon. In reality, National Motors had plenty of cash on hand to spend. It was one of the largest second-tier car companies in the U.S.; and following a dismal decade of one fiscal crisis after another, management had successfully restructured the company. The resulting surplus cash was salted away for rainy days and acquisitions.

This was an important deal for National Motors; but

in the context of its operations, the investment wasn't a watershed amount of money.

We wrapped up and agreed to meet in the lobby of Maven Birche at one forty-five in the afternoon. I packed up my computer quickly, as Nick and I said goodbye to our clients. Waiting for an assistant to walk us to the elevators, I couldn't get out of there fast enough.

"I'm dying to get a bite to eat," I told Nick.

"It's a little early for lunch, but we do have two hours to kill."

"Let's call it a working lunch. I'll eat, and you can work on refining our talking points for our next meeting."

"You know, I've seen you propose better deals," he replied jokingly. He was clearly feeling better than when we'd met in the lobby an hour ago. Realizing that, my shoulders relaxed a little; but there was still a long day ahead for both of us.

WITH OUR GAME PLAN for the day set, Nick picked up the check at the restaurant; and we set out for Maven Birche's offices. As the lead underwriter for Volta's initial public offering, Maven Birche had volunteered to host our meeting in its building.

The success of this meeting would be determined by the likeliness of National Motors and Volta reaching across the table to negotiate the finer points of their potential sweetheart deal. If the two companies walked away from that table uninterested, Nick and I would be screwed.

We were the first to arrive at the bank's offices that

were housed in an enormous, iconic glass skyscraper on Liberty Street in the financial district. Sitting on the black leather sofas that made up a small waiting area, I checked my watch. We'd come ten minutes early.

Nick looked over at me. "Nervous?"

I looked up from my phone. "Should I be?" I went back to typing a quick message to Theo, who'd inundated my phone with messages earlier in the morning. He was probably trying to make up for cancelling on me, but I really was too busy to deal with that right now. I'd call him later tonight when things calmed down to let him know I was in town.

After hitting send, I looked up at Nick. "We both know that on some level this is a Hail Mary. We've put all we have into this deal. I don't think we can regret anything at this point."

"Audrey, you are far too resigned when faced with the possibility of unemployment. I wish you were a little more stressed over this."

"Then, I take it back," I said with a wink. "You manage the pitch; I'll lead us in some yoga." I may have been joking; but in truth, I was beyond worried; I just couldn't let Nick see it.

At that moment, we saw the National Motors' team pull up to the outside corner of the building and make their way to the revolving door entrance. I reached to pick my bag up from the floor and saw that my hand was rattling with nerves.

Get it together, Audrey, I told myself before taking two deep breaths while walking toward our clients.

We shook hands with the National Motors' people and secured credentials for everyone. A concierge of sorts escorted us up to the thirtieth floor. I had actually never been to the Maven Birche offices before, but they looked nearly identical to any other investment bank I'd ever visited — sterile, expensive, and devoid of personality.

An open floor space, to our right as we walked down the hall, was filled with desks and analysts toiling away under the influence of their afternoon caffeine rush. At this hour they'd be waiting for their bosses to make the big decisions of the day so they could commit themselves to another ten hours of executing orders before they went home.

For a lucky few their dedication would pay off in a series of promotions; but for the rest — burnout would soon creep up on them. The traces of those who'd left would be paved over with the sweat and tears of those eager to join the illustrious firms of New York. As for me, I wondered if I'd climbed high enough yet. How high would be too high?

The hallway narrowed into a long pathway of offices before opening up to a large glass conference room in the distance. Sheer shades had been pulled down behind the glass wall, but the sun on the building across the street hinted at a spectacular view of the financial district.

As we entered the conference room, a nearby door swung open; and a stream of ten or so suits filed past us in the hallway. I knew that Volta was meeting with its underwriting banks prior to our meeting. These banks had scored one of the most significant I.P.O. clients of the year. Their work on the public offering would result in tens of millions of dollars in bank fees. I was jealous. Our smaller sweetheart deal would result in only a few million for my bank, Roland Capital.

One by one they paraded by us. Most were men around my age, young overachievers, peppered with the occasional senior banker to establish legacy, authority, and importance with their exciting new client. I smiled vacantly as they passed me, not recognizing a single one, until I laid eyes on the very last man. My heart stopped.

It took everything in my power to hold down the nausea that was stirring in my throat, heat rushing across my cheeks.

He grabbed me by the elbow and leaned close.

"Well, isn't this a surprise," David said, his eyes glowing under the stark florescent lighting. "I didn't know you were coming to New York."

I looked behind at Nick and excused myself by telling him I'd only be a second. I was almost rendered speechless. *David was working on Volta's I.P.O. deal?*

"What?" he said, brows raised. "A week or so ago, we partied in Athens; and now, you don't have anything to say to me?"

David seemed to be enjoying the encounter, but I was immediately concerned over what his involvement might mean for my deal. It was one thing for David and I to bury the hatchet in our personal lives; but when it came to our careers, the wounds were still raw.

Clearly, I couldn't do my job in New York without my personal life mucking it up. "I didn't expect to see you here," I mustered. "I didn't realize that you were still working in capital markets."

"I suppose you didn't."

I couldn't let this shake me. This next meeting was too important. "I have to go, David."

"Of course." He looked at me and looked back at the conference room he'd just exited. "So you're also working on Volta?" he deduced. "This is too good to be true. Are you getting ready to stab Theo in the back, as well?"

Why was he bringing up Theo? Did he know about Istanbul?

I opened my mouth to offer something to mollify his concealed threat. I didn't want him to try sabotaging my relationship with Volta, but I came up short. I hadn't a clue what to say to him, nor did I understand why he was bringing Theo into this. I cringed at the thought that David knew about our secret affair.

"We should catch up over a drink," he tossed over his shoulder while walking away. I continued the last few meters down the hall by myself, pretending I hadn't heard him. My being back in New York was none of his business, I assured myself. David would be well advised to focus on his new marriage and leave the past where it was, even if the wrench of his betrayal had never really left me. *Don't look back.*

Arriving at the conference room, I was reaching to open the door when I turned around. David was looking at me over his shoulder. I quickly refocused myself on the large windowed room. My heart was beating hard — I could feel it leaping in my chest as my slippery hands grasped the door handle. I closed my eyes, took a deep breath, and pushed my way into the room.

SIX YEARS AGO, I was the happiest I'd ever been in my life. A recent Wharton undergrad, I was living in New York and had more disposable income than I could dispose of. Financially, it was a very comfortable life; but from a work perspective I slaved away on five hours of sleep a night. Banking in New York wasn't for the faint of heart, and I had been proud to be making my own way.

It was in the middle of a Hampton's sunset, during my

first full summer, that I'd met David. A girlfriend of mine was overseeing the organization of a summer weekend party — a lavish affair in a mansion worthy of Jay Gatsby.

While sitting out on the beach watching the sky, two of my girlfriends struck up a flirty conversation with a group of guys who had passed us in the sand. As they continued their banter, David sat down next to me. We discussed the irony of expensive charity events, and I relaxed, weary of the gossip and politics that seemed to stifle most conversations in the Hamptons. He was twelve years older which always did it for me. Older men bore the success of their careers, making it easy for me to benchmark my own victories.

We'd been dating for three years when he proposed to me at the Guggenheim Museum on Fifth Avenue. Those three years had been a dream. David was kind and generous; and while we both worked ungodly hours, I cherished the time that we spent together on the weekends. We planned to marry six months after his lavish proposal; and in a year or two, we planned to start a family.

The breakup almost killed me.

Infidelity burns itself into the heart like a brand, and the swing between feeling inadequate and incensed never really leaves. I'd never gotten to the end of processing it; but then again, betrayal doesn't leave much to process. It just is what it is — you wake up one morning to discover that the one person you trusted more than anyone in the world has never really ever given himself over to you in return.

Today, I wasn't all that much different from the woman who woke up that day except — I'd vowed to never go through that kind of pain again.

THE GLASS DOOR CREAKED and caught loudly on its pivoting mechanism as I stumbled into the room. There were a dozen or so people around the table who all turned at the disruption. I avoided their eyes and looked quickly to the handle, as if I was inspecting what was wrong with the door.

Philipp Konig from Volta came to my rescue. We exchanged pleasantries, but I was hardly able to focus on what he was saying. "Aydin had to step out of our earlier meeting to deal with something urgent." *Volta's CEO was here?*

It had not been confirmed in our meeting agenda; and I was surprised that the founder would sit in on such a preliminary meeting; but then again, the micromanagement lived up to Aydin Demir's storied and controlling reputation.

"He should be back any minute, but I suggest we get started without him," Philipp explained. *Fine by me*, I thought. I was anxious to get through this and leave as soon as I could.

A technician came over to ask for my presentation, and I handed him my computer while telling him where to access the file on my desktop. I sat next to Nick who looked at me questioningly. I'd have to explain to him later that my ex was now also working for our client. I hoped that somehow this transaction would continue without any more hurdles.

Philipp began the meeting apologizing for the absence of his boss before giving the room a summary on what Volta had accomplished as of today. He also explained how a potential sweetheart deal with my client would fit into its longer-term strategy; scaling infrastructure by adding more production facilities was a priority in addition to accessing additional funding. Thankfully, I'd stressed that in the presentation I was about to stand up and give.

Then Philipp looked toward the glass door. "Ah, here we go," he said, rising out of his seat. It seemed the late participant had arrived. The entire table shifted its attention toward the door. Turning, my eyes locked on a pair of startled, deep, brown eyes. A cold wave of terror rocked through my body.

What the hell was Theo doing here?

My heartbeat began to race again, and Theo's eyes focused narrowly on me as he walked through the entryway. How could I have been so stupid? *Volta must have been Theo's client too!*

While he'd said that he was specializing on financial transactions, his access to Volta cars in Istanbul and his disappearance the night of the Brady Spence accident now made sense.

He was also too surprised to speak. That's when I realized . . . I was supposed to be in London, not sitting in front of him in a Manhattan conference room.

"Hello," he finally said to the room. "My apologies for the delay. I hope I didn't miss anything critical." Philipp joined Theo's side to introduce him individually to a couple of key participants.

Before I could catch my breath, they were standing at my side, and Philipp said, "This is Audrey Gardner. We met in London last week."

"Hello," I replied as dryly as I could manage while I stood up to shake Theo's hand.

"Audrey's representing National Motors' interests on behalf of Roland Capital Group," Philipp added. It was beyond unpleasant having someone else explain my resumé to the man I was sleeping with.

"It's nice to meet you," I said, slightly awkwardly. How were we supposed to play this? I'd have some serious explaining to do if it became known that I knew one of Volta's consultants — intimately.

Philipp continued his introduction. "Audrey, this is Aydin Demir, Volta's CEO and founder."

At his words, the world seemed to contract and tilt on its axis. My stomach fell to the floor; and my eyes widened with shock which was quickly obliterated by a prickling, fever-like rage.

Aydin Demir?

Theo had lied to me about everything. His job — *even his name? Fuck me.* I was sleeping with the CEO of my client's target.

I looked up at him, but I could only see the color red. My pulse pounded heavily in my temples and even louder in my ears.

"Audrey, are you okay?" Philipp's voice punched through the fog. "You seem a little . . . off color."

I choked out an assurance that I was fine, and left Theo's hand hanging as I turned around to find Nick. It was an awkward move. I should have stayed and pretended everything was normal, but I couldn't possibly play the actress now. My legs were shaking, and I worried I'd collapse in my heels.

It took an incredible amount of restraint not to run out the door as the implications of sleeping with a liar—and a deal partner—thrashed around inside my head. I'd only just recovered from running into David.

"Are you okay?" Nick asked.

"Yes, fine. Just nervous," I murmured.

"Well, pull it together," he returned under his breath. "We've reached the final innings of the game. There shouldn't be any more surprises."

If only he knew. "Let's hope not." I had to tell Nick, but it was impossible in this moment. I ran through the options to excuse myself and cast my gaze around the room. Theo was staring at me while talking to Philipp. His expression was cool, calculating.

I diverted my attention to the rest of the room. National Motors had seven people present — nine counting Nick and I. Volta had eight people including its legal and financial advisors. This was too big to lose. We, and our client, had a lot riding on this. I had to remember that.

Finally, with all parties present, we retook our seats around the long, mahogany table. Theo sat on the Volta side in the center — the power position. Michael Gruner, the head of Business Development from National Motors, was positioned directly across from Theo and gave an introduction on National Motors' interests.

Theo did the same for Volta, connecting with every gaze at the table but mine. I was furious — at him and at myself for being so foolish. How many times can a girl be so blatantly taken in by a liar? So, I really had been just a fling — so unimportant — it wasn't worth him telling me the truth about his life — or worse — he didn't trust me enough to tell me.

He looked angry over there on the other side of the table, but where did he get off being mad at me?

Nick passed out the term sheets that we'd developed.

"Audrey, could you take us through this?" I jolted in my seat, having completely forgotten about my presentation.

I looked back across the table at Theo who immediately looked away, his face cast in a heavy frown. He was angry with me and had no right to be. My eyes tapered, and I steeled my look. I couldn't let this be about us. I had a job to do, and no man was going to mess that up.

I stood from my chair and walked toward the front of the room; my wireless presentation remote was pinched between my thumb and index fingers as I tried to control my shaking hands.

It took thirty minutes for me to finish the presentation since we'd paused intermittently to discuss specific points. Michael and the rest of the National Motors' team insisted hard on more comprehensive technology transfer as we had discussed earlier in our morning meeting.

Volta was opposed; but their lawyer, a fast-talking guy by the name of Richard Traub, insisted they'd come back on this point after running the numbers themselves. Theo, for his part, stared fixedly at the papers in front of him, refusing to look up. He was letting Richard do all of the talking.

When my part was finished, I went back and sat down next to Nick. Both parties seemed more or less optimistic about the deal; but, of course, that was usually the case in face-to-face meetings. The hard part would come when the lawyers and financial advisors volleyed the red-lined agreement between themselves. Of course, if we ever got to that point, the ideal outcome was probable. For now, it was tentative at best.

I lifted my fingers to the table and slid them along the shiny, timbered surface a few inches. It reminded me of the mahogany deck on Theo's Riva — or, I guess it was *Aydin's* boat? My stomach churned again. Trust was everything to me, and Theo—or Aydin—had permanently ruptured mine.

The meeting concluded with a summary of next steps; each person jotting down their respective to-do list. My list was hefty enough, and it was hard keeping track of the progress made on each deal point. I was struggling to follow the discussion while my desperate inner thoughts dominated.

Theo wrapped it all up by saying that he was really excited about the potential partnership, flattering my client, and mentioning how difficult it was to find a large, established partner who valued the proliferation of electric automotive technology. My lips pursed slightly, but I made myself relax them. If only National Motors really was that kind of partner — we could have moved on a deal like this one — years ago. Now, with the technology uptake and growing momentum in the marketplace, it was going to cost National Motors a lot more than it could have; and Theo knew that well.

At the close of the meeting, I turned to Nick and recited our game plan for the afternoon. I needed to get out of there — fast. "You have that meeting with your friend, right? So, I'll see you at the restaurant at eight o'clock for dinner with our clients and some members of the Volta team?"

"Hey, slow down," he said, pulling me toward the back wall. "What on earth is going on with you?"

"Nothing, just anxious to get back to work."

His eyes sharpened. "Audrey, I'm not buying it." I

could tell he wanted to get back to tending our client, but he wasn't going to until I confessed. I swallowed my pride and decided that sharing something was safer than nothing.

"My ex, David Reed, is working for one of Volta's underwriters. That's who I ran into unexpectedly in the hallway." It was as good as I could do for now. I didn't even know where to begin with Theo, and I didn't want to launch into that confession until I was able to think it through first. "It threw me for a loop, but it's fine."

"It better be," he said. "You need to get it together."

I smiled at him stiffly. "Do you mind if I head out? It would be helpful if I could finish some of the items on my list before dinner." I could feel a pair of intense, brown eyes on me from across the room.

"Of course, good call. It will save us time if we can have a more productive conversation at dinner."

"That's why you allocate my bonuses so generously," I whispered with a smile, trying to cover up my desperation to leave.

I went over to the front of the room and unplugged my computer. Packing it in my bag, I could see Theo on the other side of the room shaking hands and making his goodbyes. Bag in hand, I slipped out while the rest of the participants continued to discuss among themselves.

At the elevator I aggressively called for the ground floor with my finger. Down the hall, the creaky glass door opened and shut with a squeal. It could have been anyone — but I knew it was him.

The elevator opened; and I leapt in, pressing the "close" button. Another wave of nausea crashed upwards from my stomach to my head making me dizzy. *Hurry, hurry!*

The doors slid closed, and the elevator began its long descent. I took in deep breaths all the way to the bottom.

Once back in the lobby, I made for the front door — my black heels clacking as I hurried across the shiny, polished floor. I'd just entered the revolving door when I heard his voice call out behind me. Ignoring him, I pushed completely through the door. Outside, I turned and started running.

THEO

I RUSHED TO CATCH UP WITH HER, but she was moving fast. I yelled out her name, but she didn't even pause. When I finally caught up, I placed myself in the way, blocking her as she tried to go around me.

"Hey, we need to talk," I told her, stating the obvious. I needed to know if she'd been manipulating me all along.

"Do we? I'm not sure we ever need to speak again."

"No, Audrey, come on." She was being unfair. *If she wasn't playing me, why did she lie about not being in London?*

"Were you ever going to tell me the truth or was this just some game you play?" She said it with a fierceness I'd never seen in her before. Her coldness shocked me, and it took me a beat to find my words. I'd assumed she'd been using *me*; but now seeing how upset she was, maybe she hadn't.

"Look, I'm just as surprised as you are. I should have told you about my company; but after you'd fixed on the consultant thing, I never found the right time to set the record straight."

"Theo," she said with authority before taking it back. "Wait — what is your name exactly?"

"Theo is my middle name. That's what all of my friends and family call me."

Audrey covered her eyes with her fingers, pushing up her eyebrows as she worked out the new information. "So, all our dinner dates were bad times to tell me? Lying in my bed, it just slipped your mind?" Her voice was low and was growing louder the longer we stood there on the sidewalk. "You flat out lied to me!" she yelled. "You said you were a consultant."

"Actually, I never told you I was a consultant. You assumed that, and I never corrected you." I paused. "But I should have, obviously."

"Are you fucking kidding me?" She gaped at me in astonishment, but I'd felt that detail was important to get across. She ducked away and passed by me. I had to hurry to catch up with her again.

"Hey!" I yelled when I'd managed to get back in front of her. People walking by were starting to watch. I didn't want to create a scene. "You're angry? What about me?" I asked, trying to lower my voice. "When I spoke to you last, you were supposedly in London this week. It's you who flat out lied to me."

She swallowed, hands fisted at her sides. "When you canceled our weekend in London, I thought you were also cutting off our affair." She dropped her chin and crossed her arms. "This is a big transaction for me, for my bank. I didn't want the disappointment of you letting me go to be a distraction in New York, so I didn't tell you."

"Is that all?"

"I also didn't want you to think I'd flown here just to see you like some crazy stalker."

"Well, in a way you did fly here to see me," I said, trying to lighten up the conversation. I reached my hand to lift her chin. "If I'd known you were here, I would have wanted to see you. I always want to see you, Audrey." She bit her lower lip and shook her head.

"Look, I just have to ask," I said stumbling to find my words. "It is a little strange that you show up all of a sudden in the middle of this deal."

She shook her head and pressed her shoulders back brusquely. "You think that I knew who you were the entire time?" she said startled.

"I don't know what to think, but I have a lot to be concerned about too."

"This entire deal is on your table because of me, Theo."

I grabbed her arm trying to snap her out of her anger. "Look, I know what you did to David when he was your boyfriend."

At that, her eyes widened. I shouldn't have said it. Not then. I tried my best to recover. "Audrey, we really need to talk about this."

"Fuck. You," she said walking away. "And you know what, he wasn't my boyfriend." She swung back around to face me. "He was my fiancé." She turned back around and continued to leave. I ran to catch up with her again.

When I did, I saw the tears. She was brushing them

from her cheeks as quickly as she could, but she couldn't hide them. She was upset, but I didn't want it to end like this. The prospect of losing her made me realize how much I wanted her in my life.

She stopped and took a deep breath but kept her eyes fixated on the cement of the sidewalk. "It's a conflict of interest for me to negotiate on behalf of my client and have a personal interest in your outcome," she explained. "We cannot communicate. We cannot see each other."

I reached out and lifted her chin while searching her green eyes to find a connection beyond her words, but she'd already shut me out.

"Regardless of how we got here, this deal is too important to both of us. Let's just focus on our work. That's the only thing that I care about right now."

Her words pierced like an arrow. I guess it wasn't very hard to see where any man stood in her life when her career was on the line. I suppose Mitch had warned me, but I never imagined I'd be caught in the web.

"Is that how you really feel?"

"It doesn't matter how I feel," she said flatly. "Goodbye, Theo." She turned and continued walking uptown. Her dark form slowly disappeared into the increasingly crowded sidewalk.

It was a completely different view of the very same person who, only a few days ago, had elegantly maneuvered through the crowds of the Grand Bazaar; now, she stormed through the sea of power suits on the sidewalk without the slightest need to seek out the comfort of my presence.

Here, she was at home; and I was the foreigner. I stood in place — powerless — not knowing what to do as I watched her walk off.

When I'd woken up this morning, I thought that today would be one of the best days of my life; but it was a little after four o'clock in the afternoon; and it was already up there with the worst.

AUDREY

AS I MADE MY WAY UP BROADWAY, my head was pounding the entire walk up the street; and I felt as if I was living a reoccurring a nightmare. I had been. I'd taken a similar walk the night I found out about David and his lies. Why had I come back here? What was wrong with me?

People crowded the sidewalks — all of them rushing with purpose but without direction. It seemed as if I was walking in slow motion against their daily hustle.

In the financial district, I took note of the bankers and traders that I passed — all of them following in the footsteps of those who'd come before them. We were all trying to impart our legacy on the world next to countless others doing the same. It was a model that had been forged many years before me and glorified only a few.

I had felt that my path through the desks and deals was different; but maybe I, too, was a nameless face among so many driven others — sacrificing everything for some kind of fleeting success. Somehow, Theo not only crushed the feelings I'd developed for him but also left me questioning the professional and personal choices I'd made.

When I reached Tribeca, I kicked off my heels to find relief in the pair of flats tucked in my bag for a previously anticipated afternoon of shopping; however, by the time I'd arrived in SoHo, tears were pricking my eyes and threatening to track down my cheeks.

I walked briskly past the shops and elaborately decorated storefronts. I was desperate to get to my hotel; but truly, I just wanted to go home — to London.

When I reached the Elizabeth Hotel, I was still steaming with pain; but the anger and frustration had subsided. In my room, I tore off my suit and silk shirt, throwing them over the back of the green velvet chair. My bra and panties were crumbled on the floor wherever I'd taken them off. I turned on the shower and looked in the mirror while I waited for the water to heat up. My face was puffy and pink — a real mess.

I collapsed my arms and face over the sink and started to cry. How could this have happened? As I chastised myself for being so stupid, the tears poured out even harder. Theo was a liar; they were all liars. For the first time in years, I'd started to really fall for someone; but in the end he was no different than those before him. *But why had he lied?* The answer was obvious. He thought that I was just another woman looking for a man with money.

How offensive.

I'd worked so hard to earn my own wealth precisely so I would never be forced into that position. And while my breakup with David had been devastating, this one somehow stung even more.

How could he believe that I'd somehow been manipulating him? I'd tried so hard to keep my professional life out of my personal one.

But what if I was I overvaluing what I'd felt for Theo just because it had been taken from me? I couldn't ignore the suspicion edging its way into my mind. Theo, after all, hadn't even trusted me enough to tell me about his company. Clearly, whatever we'd had — had never been real to begin with.

Worst of all, Theo believed what so many others suspected — that I was a cold and vengeful woman. If Theo truly thought I was capable of trying to destroy David, I couldn't understand why he'd let me into his life in the first place.

Because he never let you into his world, whispered a tiny voice within. *He never even told you who he was.*

I turned toward the shower and walked in. The door was still swinging shut when I collapsed to sit on the hexagon tiles. I rested my forehead on my knees and continued to cry. I cried for being foolish. I cried for the loss of a love that I'd never really had with David or really started with Theo. I cried because money and success were the only real things I had in my life; but again and again, they seemed to take the happiness in my life and twist it into something ugly.

None of it mattered, I told myself. Now that he was on the other side of the table from my client, there was no future for us anyway. It was a clear conflict of interest, and my professional life had already suffered enough unmerited disgrace. I wasn't about to invite any more.

I reminded myself that Theo was never meant to be anything more than fun. The water from the shower continued its endless flow over my body until it eventually stopped feeling like water. I abandoned myself to it completely.

ONCE I'D PULLED MYSELF TOGETHER and out of the shower, I grabbed a billowy bath towel and wrapped it around me. The tears were gone; there were no more to cry. I called room service to order a large bottle of Evian in a bucket of ice. I'd need to rehydrate if I was to be good for anything this afternoon, and the ice would help bring down the swelling around my eyes.

I forced myself to concentrate as I worked at my computer for two hours until I had barely enough time to get to the restaurant for dinner. I hurried to get ready and out the door, all the while wondering what to tell Nick. At Roland Capital, we had a policy that required disclosure of relationships with bosses, subordinates, clients, and vendors.

But what about the CEO of a target — probably should report it — but if the affair was over anyway?

I thought of National Motors' management team. What would they think of me dating the CEO of a target that I'd brought to them in the first place? There was no way around it. It would look horrible. And if I confessed to Nick, it would put him in a tough, ethical position.

I arrived at The Belmont, a beautiful, airy restaurant that spun its menu around sophisticated Southern cuisine.

I hadn't picked it, but I'd been delighted when I received the email confirming the location. Now, the thought of eating made me ill. I arrived with ten minutes to spare and headed directly to the bar. Philipp Konig from Volta was also early, so I took the stool right next to him.

"What are you having?" I asked.

"It's my signature drink: two parts bourbon and one part Amaro with a dash of orange bitters and an expressed orange peel."

"Yikes, that sounds strong."

"Maybe, but I bet you could use one."

"I think you're right." I gave him a tight smile and caught the bartender's eye, ordering a "Black Manhattan" as Philipp called it. "So how do you feel after today's meeting?" I inquired. In truth I was fishing to find out how the tenor of tonight's dinner was going to go.

"I think it might have legs, but Aydin of course will be difficult to convince," he admitted.

"Is he coming tonight?" Part of me hoped to see him, and the other prayed he wouldn't show up.

"No, he told me he had a lot of work. You know we're still keeping our eye on the Brady Spence investigation — just in case his defense tries to blame our technology. Aydin takes that very personally."

"I can see that."

"He might seem withdrawn, but Aydin is a passionate man. His life revolves around Volta." Philipp sighed heavily and took another sip of his drink. Mine arrived just in time, and I took a hefty sip before even bothering to raise my glass to meet Philipp's.

The dinner proceeded as most work meals do. The clients spoke as freely as they could in front of each other while Nick and I held our cards closer to our chest. The deal wasn't done; and even if the agreement came through, there wasn't any guarantee that National Motors wouldn't trade us in for one of the other banks it was taking meetings with. Our position at the table was still a precarious one.

As Nick signed for the check, Angela Marks made the suggestion that we stay in town to be available in case internal disputes arose before their board meeting next week. "You just never know what might come up. It could be useful to have you on this side of the pond."

I deferred to Nick. He was the one who made the staffing calls. "Certainly," he said. "Audrey will be here without question, and I should be able to swing it. I just have to check in with London."

With that, my fate was decided. I'd be in New York longer than I'd expected. It was painfully ironic since I couldn't wait to escape to the comfort of London even though I had a feeling no ocean would be big enough to keep my current problems at bay.

IT WAS NEARLY MIDNIGHT when I walked back into the lobby of the Elizabeth Hotel. I was glad the day was over, and the idea of collapsing into my bed was something I'd been fantasizing about for the last two hours.

The lobby was bathed in a warm, yellow light reminiscent of the old parlor rooms in the twenties. The couches and armchairs, in varying shades of red, cream, and brown, formed small enclaves within the room. People chatted quietly as I passed in silence.

I was making my way straight back toward the elevators when a voice called out my name. I recognized it instantly and froze. I let out a long exhale and turned around toward the lounge area.

"Hello, David."

He smiled. "I knew that if you were in New York you'd be staying here."

I was unhappy to see him, but I didn't walk away. "The site of our first date."

"So, you do remember," David said.

I didn't offer a reply but stared at him for a moment buying time while I sorted out his reason for showing up here.

There is a thin line between love and hate; and when we'd split, I found myself hating him as a way to put him in my past. However, the truth was that whenever I scratched the surface of that story, I still loved him on some level. Hate as an emotion is much easier to live with than lost love; and during these last three years, it had served me well.

That was why I'd gone to his wedding. I wanted closure. I desperately wanted to move on. *Why was he here and not home with his new wife?*

He gestured for me to sit by him on the sofa. I hesitated at first; but in my exhausted state, I obliged thinking that giving in would hurry along whatever was coming next. It was uncomfortable seeing him alone, so the sooner he left — the better.

"David, what are you doing here?"

"I wanted to see you. Is that too much to ask?"

"I think your wife might say so."

David bit his lip before taking a sip of his drink. "I thought we could talk about what happened between us. I wanted to apologize for my part."

"Apology accepted, but it's late. I'd like to get some sleep."

"You aren't sorry for what you put me through?" he shot back.

"What I put *you* through?" I was shocked but didn't want to rehash his cheating. I responded instead to his direct accusation. "No, you invested in a product. It would have been a conflict of interest for me to have advised you on that product."

"But you didn't stop me."

"How could I? That would have been a violation of protocol at the bank and very well could have sent us both to prison for insider trading."

"Come on. We both know you let me hang because you were mad at me."

"David, you are a sharp banker. You ran the risk on the investment and decided to go for it. That is not on me." I paused before continuing. "And why did you invite me to your wedding if you still resent me so much?"

David sat back in his armchair; his drink slipped slightly in his hand, and I worried he might drop it. His eyes were bloodshot.

"Well, you know, we share so many friends," he said breaking the silence. "I sort of thought maybe we could be one of those postmodern ex-couples — that stay friends."

I waited for more before acknowledging what he'd said.

"You know I'm sorry. I was a really shit partner; I can't deny that."

"What exactly are you sorry for?"

"I'm sorry that I cheated. I deserved you walking out when you did."

It was the first time I was hearing him admit to what he'd done, let alone apologize for it. Granted, I hadn't left him much of a chance after we'd broken up.

"And I'm sorry that I never said that sooner."

"Apology accepted. I think we can both move on now, right? You have a beautiful wife waiting for you, and I have . . . " I sighed. "A lot of work waiting for me."

He didn't say anything and continued to sit in his chair staring at me.

"Look, David, it's really late; and we both have early mornings. Let's put you in a car to go home." I stood and held out my hand.

"I miss you, Audrey," he said. It landed in my heart amidst ambivalence and regret. I missed him too on some level; but the David that I missed was a myth: someone who never existed. He hugged me before walking out to call a cab, and I probably lingered there a moment too long.

AFTER CATCHING A CAB DOWNTOWN, warm cappuccino in hand, I scanned through my phone and found two hundred emails unread and three missed calls. I opened my call log. The calls were all from Theo. I let out a long exhale as consciousness began to flood my mind with yesterday's events and disappointment. Why was he calling me when we both knew we had no future?

I walked into the office to find Nick grabbing up papers and his computer. I looked at my phone for the time. It was two minutes to nine o'clock.

"Where are you going?" I inquired.

"*We* are going over to National Motors' offices."

"Really, already?"

"Michael and the other executives want to pull out of the deal."

The coffee I was holding over his desk dropped and landed on the table with a small splatter. "You're kidding me," I said mopping up the drops of milk with a napkin.

"Audrey, if we lose this deal, it will cost me my job. And probably yours," he added.

My eyes rolled back as I closed them slowly. My stale bourbon-headache was still stinging at my temples. This was going to be a shit day, no doubt about it.

Nick and I took a cab to our client's offices and were welcomed grimly. Michael, the executive who'd been our focal point for most of our relationship with the client, pulled us into his office.

"I'm afraid I've only got bad news to share today," he started. As you know, we had a conference call to inform the board of our intent. Anthony Pierce, one of our board members, has been loudly campaigning against any electric deal and has intensified his crusade upon learning that we've been meeting with Volta."

Pierce was the board member who had a strong interest in oil; he was on the payroll of many traditional energy companies. He voiced his opinions aggressively in op-eds that were published in some of the largest U.S. publications, creating buzz and twenty-four hours of media flurry each time he did. He was our largest bottleneck to a deal.

"What is he saying?" Nick asked.

"He's framed his argument around the valuation, so he's picking apart the model, not the technology, to mask his bias. He's also threatened to write an opinion piece about Volta not being a sustainable model for the automotive industry."

I played out the chain of possible events this week. How could this guy openly sabotage a deal that benefited companies he sat on the boards of? Michael leaned back in his large, dark-brown leather chair and said, as if reading my mind, "He'd likely publish it first and take the slap on the wrist after."

"But on what grounds is he making his argument? What part of the model doesn't he agree with?" I asked, while bitterness swelled at the back of my throat. I'd created the model that underpinned this deal, and I was taking this a little personally. I needed to remain calm and sharp if I was to work through this.

"Our model uses the assumption, in Volta's favor, that we will see a huge increase in market demand for electric cars; however, that projection isn't yet proven."

That's why it's a projection, I thought to myself.

Michael continued, "No other electric car manufacturer has hit the numbers that we are expecting from Volta; and to Pierce's point, maybe, they are inflated. Right now, analysts are only expecting the pre-order event to sell five thousand cars at most."

"And the model estimates a hundred thousand pre-orders over the next six months," Nick confirmed.

Michael nodded, "If Volta only does five thousand orders on the opening day which would be bolstered from all of the publicity, it's probably unrealistic to think it can pull off a hundred thousand in only six months once the buzz dies down. Orders enter a queue for fulfillment; so any customer thinking about purchasing a Model II is incentivized to pay their deposit as early as possible — on the opening day of the pre-order event."

I liked Michael; he was rational and worked through a problem. Most of my clients in a similar situation would be screaming at us by this point.

"The valuation heavily assumes a strong reveal on the Model II," he continued. "To put that in perspective, we sell two and a half million cars a year. If they sell a hundred thousand cars in six months — that means that they, as a start up, will have sold eight percent of what we sell in the same amount of time. It's absurd."

"But not impossible," I added. "Look, I understand if you want to pump the breaks on the deal; but we are going to have solid answers by end-of-day Thursday. We shouldn't scrap everything we have now just because there is a squeaky door in your house. If the Model II reveal flops, then we go back to the drawing board. But what if it's a success? Your company will have the advantage of having been in the right place at the right time — negotiating a sweetheart deal with the company everyone will be wanting to get in bed with." The words came out of my mouth before I could digest their irony.

"There are other board members who have also become skittish. The trades are lukewarm about the offering coming Thursday, and a deal like this is unprecedented for us," Michael explained.

"Can you let the board know that you're taking Anthony's concern very seriously, and that you'll be watching Volta's performance on Thursday before making a decision to move forward?" Nick suggested. "We don't lose anything."

"The only risk is that Volta performs well; in that case, the deal could become more expensive." Michael let out a long sigh after he said it.

"But you can always walk away," Nick said to console him.

"It's true. I like this. We can give the board this update. It should appease Anthony and the others who now echo his concerns."

"In the meantime, we can seed that we're worried about the valuation. Perhaps Volta might consider what else it can pony up," I added.

THEO

WEDNESDAY NIGHT BLED QUICKLY into Thursday morning. Philipp and I had pulled an all-nighter, occasionally catching a few minutes of sleep between navigating tech crises with the digital team back in London. They'd created a payment network that supplied coverage for North America and Europe; but for the rest of the world, we'd designated a small team to take buyer information and work out payments locally.

At 3:00 a.m., a glitch occurred with the payment processors on the ordering page. There was no point hosting a launch if we couldn't sell the product we were launching.

Fueled by coffee and the occasional rolled cigarette

from the hidden stash in Philipp's desk drawer, my nerves were shaken and my limbs visibly trembled from the pressure.

My stomach was tied in knots for most of the night over the idea of having to postpone the sales event. I knew that if this happened, it would cost me dearly on the National Motors deal; and worst of all, a failure today could jeopardize the most important transaction underway: the initial public offering.

By six in the morning, the issue appeared to be resolved; and Philipp and I caught a half hour of sleep each. I was too exhausted to even digest the relief of having resolved the glitch — we were four hours away from the start of the pre-order.

I grabbed a quick shower before Philipp and I headed down to Times Square. We'd split up the list of interview requests. He'd take the morning shows, and I'd be taking the more business-focused media. At ten in the morning when the pre-order went live, Philipp would be in front of a national audience of four million people; and I'd be with Anna speaking to America's largest business-media outlet. The viewership of my show was only going to be around two hundred thousand people; however, they were more likely to be in our target market.

I was uneasy about it.

I'd always hated interviews, and I distrusted the media. When my parents were killed, the local papers had tried to make it seem as if it had been their fault. I'd been bullied into these interviews by my team; but if it was going to help boost sales, I was committed. Thankfully, the fact that I normally dodged the media had fueled the press' interest — an unexpected but welcome development.

I was feeling optimistic, but I was also sweating from the stress. If the pre-order event failed to generate enough orders, it would put us in a weak position both in negotiating the rest of the National Motors deal and in the talks over the initial public offering. Everything was riding on today's outcome.

Anna met me in the lobby, and we shared a car service uptown.

"Theo, don't be nervous," she said. "The media coverage has been more than we could have wished for, and there have been over a million hits on the pre-order's webpage from people looking for information."

"Right, but it takes a lot to get someone to lay down a two grand deposit for a car they won't see for years." Had this been a terrible idea? If it flopped, the failing would be remembered indefinitely.

"That's why we need to keep on message. A Volta is a status symbol: the aspirational purchase for the early adopter. It's not just any car."

I heard what she was saying, but it wasn't making much of a difference. I stared out the car window as people walked by on the sidewalks. Enormous buildings towered over them, leaving pedestrians bathed in grey shadows. *Where was Audrey?*

She hadn't replied to any of my texts, but I had a hard time believing that it was really over. I'd need to fix it somehow — show her how we could be together one day, if not right now. Knowing that she was just minutes away though made focusing a challenge, but I had to remember that today was just about my company.

SITTING IN THE GREENROOM at the television studio, a makeup artist was buffing my face with powder when Anna walked in with a copy of *The New York Times* in hand. Her expression was solemn.

"What is it?"

"Anthony Pierce wrote another op-ed."

"Fuck." Anthony had been a giant pain in my ass since the very beginning of my first company. He was nothing more than an outdated, political propagandist. Nevertheless, he was persuasive enough. "What did he say?"

"That Volta as a business is unsustainable. He also picks apart the technology, specifically the range and the burden on the power grid."

It was nothing new, but he'd obviously published it to coincide with our launch. I knew that he sat on National Motors' board. I'd have to deal with that later.

At ten o'clock the online ordering platform opened for business as I gave my first interview. The team in London hadn't slept in two days, but it was paying off. Within the first hour we received five thousand orders; that was what analysts had expected for the entire day. Anna leaked the information to the trades and anyone else who was keen on the story. She managed to get the *New York Times* to open a live news feed.

By noon the news went completely viral, and orders started pouring in. Judging from social media, many people were pre-ordering just to be able to brag they'd been one of the first to be a part of it.

We'd taken twenty-five thousand orders by one o'clock in the afternoon, averaging over eight thousand cars an hour. Interview requests streamed in from all over the world, but Anna and I agreed to keep a low profile.

The buzz was gaining momentum, and we didn't want to spoil it.

Anna's phone rang while we were discussing what to do next. "Hello?" Her face turned grey. "I'll have to get right back to you. Let me check."

Hanging up the phone, she said, "Theo, the site crashed. It's *The Times* asking for a comment."

My heart rate shot up, and I could feel my face burn with heat. "Get London on the phone, now!"

The digital team explained that the server had become overloaded. They hadn't expected so much traffic to the site. They were increasing space, but it would take twenty minutes. I ran the math in my head. That would cost us nearly three thousand cars sold. "Tell them to hurry. And get *The Times* back on the phone. Maybe they'll spin it into a story."

Anna nodded in agreement.

"Wait," I said. "Tell London to increase the space to accommodate twelve thousand orders an hour. Just in case." Anna's eyes popped. "You never know."

Once the story of our website crash leaked, traffic to the site tripled. By five o'clock in the afternoon, orders were up to nearly nine thousand orders an hour. The final tally a day and a half later would come in at two hundred and fifty thousand cars — pre-ordered.

We'd completely underestimated the "me-too" factor and the virality of the news item. The order numbers were two and a half times more than what we'd planned for in the first six months, but I felt vindicated. The production headaches could be sorted later.

No doubt Malik back in Istanbul was having a heart attack. We'd exceeded our manufacturing capacity and desperately needed to develop new factories in order to meet the orders within a reasonable time frame. We needed the National Motors deal now more than ever. I really wanted those old factories.

It was one o'clock in the morning when I texted Audrey. I was sure she'd followed the news of the day, so I didn't bother to report our results. I missed hearing her voice. Within seconds, the text was marked as received. *She's still awake.* I picked up my phone and dialed her number.

It had been incredibly hot watching her present at our meeting on Monday. There was no doubt about it; she really was good at her job — so good that I wished that she'd been on our side of the table.

"Hello," she said in a low voice. "You've had a spectacular day."

"It was very good, but not perfect."

Audrey laughed into the phone. "It's hard to imagine how it could have been any better, Theo. I know for sure that my job will be significantly more difficult next week."

"How could it be perfect if I didn't get to see you? And don't worry about the deal. It will all get sorted," I said, trying to reassure her.

The truth was — the deal that was on the table was a fair one. I didn't really have the patience to squeeze anything more out of National Motors although I did look forward to seeing its team across the negotiating table again. The power around the table would now be weighted on my side.

"Theo, you shouldn't be calling me like this."

"Come on, we're both adults. We can do whatever we please."

"That's not true, and you know it. You'll be watched now; and if you are seen with a banker from the other side, it would be more trouble than it's worth for both of us."

I felt ashamed for doubting Audrey's business ethics. She was professional and principled. But even as she pushed me away, I could sense that she didn't want to believe it was over. She wanted to see me too, so I pressed her.

"Where are you staying?"

"I'm not telling."

"Don't make me beg, Audrey. I'm too proud." She was close to caving. All I needed was to add a little more pressure. "Look, I won't come up. Just see me in the lobby for a nightcap."

Silence hung over the line suspending time. I'd stopped breathing. "Ok, just a drink to talk," she said. "About us, nothing work-related."

"Where are you staying?" I asked again.

"The Elizabeth Hotel in the Bowery."

"I'm only a few minutes away by car. I'll be there in ten."

I hung up the phone and bolted to the closet for a fresh shirt. The one I'd been wearing all day was tired and smelled of old sweat. Stopping in the bathroom, I jumped in the shower quickly and added a few sprays of cologne too.

In the car I ran the numbers from the day again in my head. Total cash raised today equaled five hundred million dollars. All things considered, it was the easiest round of fundraising I'd ever led. It was exactly what I needed to raise this summer, but the game had changed. With the huge demand, it was crucial that we deliver.

Volta would need that cash to bump up production,

and maybe I could use the momentum to raise even more in the I.P.O.

Philipp and I had changed our goal. We no longer needed five hundred million; we already had that. We needed a billion.

The National Motors deal and the initial public offering, slated for September, were still critical; but today would be a huge shot in the arm for our valuation. I looked forward to walking back into the banks downtown next week in a more powerful position, although I worried about where I stood with Audrey.

Going to see her now was an opportunity to save what we'd started. In accepting to see me, she hadn't completely shut the door; but she hadn't left much space for me to slip back through either.

ENTERING THE LOBBY of Audrey's hotel, my eyes were overwhelmed. Sofas and chairs crowded small, open areas to either side where men and women continued their blurred conversations in hushed corners. I really needed to take a page from Audrey's book. Her hotel was sexier than mine.

Ahead to the right, Audrey unfolded herself from a red armchair. She was wearing a simple black dress that went down beyond her knees, but it wasn't what was uncovered that teased me. It was how tightly it wrapped over everything else. Her silky silhouette walked straight for me as I took in every one of her curves. I loved watching her body move fluidly through a room.

She said hello, and I slid my hand over the tight black fabric that covered her hip. I couldn't help myself. She grabbed my hand and reminded me that I was here to talk — nothing more. Her hair was pulled tight into that high ponytail that swished when she walked. Her face was naked — exposed — but the sparkle in her eye was all she needed to look perfect.

Without a touch she led me to the bar and perched on a crimson velvet barstool. I didn't want to be here in public. The adrenaline of the day had made me hungrier for her than ever.

"Audrey, let's go upstairs."

She looked me straight in the eye. "You promised. If you mention it again, I will get up and walk away. Make no mistake, I am not playing a game."

Resigned, I ordered a sparkling water; and she chose a small pour of apple brandy when she saw the bottle of Calvados behind the bar.

"This is what you drink in the wee hours of the morning? Isn't it a bit strong?"

"This is what I drink when you show up in the lobby of my hotel."

"You're still mad at me?"

She took a small sip from her snifter glass. Her eyes closed as she swallowed. "You mean for all your lies?" She said it with spite on her tongue and washed it down with another sip of brandy. "Theo, you left me feeling like an idiot. If you had told me the truth, I could have excused myself from the deal."

"Would you really have taken yourself off such a large transaction? Wasn't it your idea in the first place?"

"Yes, but I'm not the only one at the bank working on it." She looked up at the bottles that made up the back wall of the bar. "I came up with the idea in Istanbul, but I suppose now that's obvious."

"I wish I'd known; I could have taken you on a factory tour," I said, attempting a joke.

She laughed lightly, indulging me. "Thankfully, you didn't."

We sat together at the bar for half an hour. Our knees danced together in an endless game of unrequited lust. It was clear that we wanted to be together, but Audrey wouldn't allow anything more than the slightest brush. She apologized for not telling me about being in New York.

For my part, I expressed my regret at not sharing the true nature of my work. The brief encounter at the bar was a way of pushing re-set on the paradigm of our knowing each other. "Where do we go from here?" I asked. "I don't just want to see you across a conference-room table. Florescent lighting washes me out."

She giggled, swallowing another sip of her brandy; but as she laughed, the fumes must have gone up into her nose. She bent over my lap coughing as she struggled to breathe again.

When she eventually recovered, I was disappointed to see that her expression had turned serious. Her eyes swept the room before returning to me. "Theo, as long as we're negotiating a transaction, I can't see you."

"And yet here you sit — coughing in my lap," I added. It was too easy.

"I make bad decisions when I'm tired."

"I'll be happy to remember that."

"Speaking of, we both could use some sleep. I'm going to go back up," she said asking for the check. Her glass was still half full.

"Aren't you going to finish what you started," I asked gesturing to her Calvados.

"Not tonight." The bartender handed her the check, and she signed it to her room while I continued my inspection of the curves that shifted underneath her fitted dress.

"So that's it?"

"Theo, I don't know what you want me to say. Can't we just suspend it? It's early; it's not like we're heavily invested in each other. I think it's best that we focus on the jobs we have to do." She was trying to hide her feelings from me, but her eyes told me everything I needed to know.

"You don't feel invested in this?" I said, leaning in closer to her. She immediately pulled back without uttering a word. I sighed as I got off the stool and extended my hand to help her. This woman was all business. "Come on, Audrey. We only live once. I think we should at least have some fun."

When Audrey flinched, I knew I'd said the wrong thing. "Theo, this is more than just fun for me." She turned giving me her back, took a couple steps, and turned right back around. "Please don't put me in a more difficult position than I'm already in. I need to close this deal." She reached back for my hand and squeezed it. "I have a lot riding on this too."

She walked me toward the entrance, but we were stopped by a sudden apparition. "Theo. Audrey. What a surprise to see you tonight. Together."

I held my breath, searching for the right reaction as David stood there, silently studying us both. Audrey had been right to be cautious.

"It's good to see you," I said, noting his rumpled shirt and disheveled hair. Hopefully, he'd been drinking enough to forget this meeting by the morning. If word got out of our affair, it could be a disaster for us both; and I was starting to realize that David was just unstable enough to do something stupid. Then a darker thought emerged. How did David know where Audrey was staying?

Audrey folded her arms across her chest.

"I think I'll excuse myself for the night." She turned toward the elevators, but David was quick to call after her.

"Aren't you still working for National Motors?" It was subtle, but the threat was clear. He must have been drinking quite a lot to behave this way in front of me. We were acquaintances, but I was also his client.

Audrey turned on her heel and walked back toward us.

"Theo and I were just catching up outside of work, that's all. In fact we were reminiscing about your wedding."

"I bet you were. I also bet your bosses would be delighted to know you're taking meetings with their target at two o'clock in the morning — at your hotel. But that's always been your style, right? The best business is done between the sheets?"

Audrey shook her head. Her eyes raged as her body tensed; I could tell she didn't want to validate his attack with a response. She steeled her look narrowly on him. "Go home, David," she said before turning and walking to the elevator bank.

David, snapping out of his strange spat, turned his attention back to me. "You know, just a little banter with the ex."

My smile was cool. "It goes without saying that your personal life can not interfere with the work you're doing for Volta. We might be friends, but I would hate to have to ask Kleinman for a change." David, face flushing, began to speak; but I cut him off before he could utter a word.

"And business aside — know this — if you do anything to hurt Audrey or affect her reputation . . . " I took a breath, and my gaze was unwavering ice as I stared him down.

Few people ever saw this side of me: the fighter, the kid with a bloodied nose who'd been pushed and punched one too many times. But David had shown his true colors, and I was only too happy to reveal mine. "You survived one scandal, David; but I could destroy you with a single phone call, and you know it."

I walked out to my car leaving David Reed intoxicated and alone in the lobby. No doubt Audrey was furious, but she'd kept a cool head.

Maybe it was best that she and I were no longer seeing each other. I would do everything I could to protect her, but I also needed to focus on what was best for my company. I'd come too far to lose myself to distractions now.

AUDREY

I STAGGERED THROUGH THE DOOR at exactly ten minutes after nine o'clock. Nick didn't say anything out aloud, but he most certainly noted my delay with his eyes.

"We're hosting a meeting here in two hours. Volta is coming to follow up on the open items from Monday. Are you up-to-date on the points?"

I was sure that the shame of running in late could be easily seen all over my face. I was tempted to justify myself by mentioning my late night meeting with none other than Volta's CEO, but I wasn't prepared to resign for the few, smug seconds that might bring.

"Of course. What are the executives at National

Motors saying about Volta's launch performance?" I asked, trying to show I was with him.

"You could say they have a new appreciation for the so-called startup. National Motors is set to pay a hundred million in exchange for a three percent stake."

"I think everyone has a new appreciation for Volta," I said. "That's a valuation of over three billion. Not bad . . . I mean, for Volta." Theo hadn't been able to help himself this morning when he texted me about all of the new interest flowing into his company. One of my client's competitors had reached out and was also interested in forming a partnership. While I could play off the revelation as him sharing his excitement, I knew very well that he was back-channeling to make sure we knew that Volta had options. He was playing me which was disappointing — and obviously — working. "I've heard they're being approached by other partners."

"Really, who told you?"

"I ran into someone on their I.P.O. team last night in the lobby of my hotel." That was partially accurate. "Of course, who knows if it's true or not," I added as insurance.

"Well, it's not surprising." Nick paused and placed both of his palms on his desk before looking up at me. "We might have to pay a lot more than National Motors committed to. Audrey, we need to close this as soon as possible before it becomes out of range for our client."

"Let's see what Volta's executives have to say. Maybe they'll surprise us?"

The two of us walked over to the conference room, and I was delighted to see that someone had brought in pastries. Since the meeting was now on our turf, I indulged in a small one.

Theo had seemed sincere the night before; and since I'd seen him, I was starting to feel that there still might be a chance for us. Maybe things would work out between us — if we settled this deal quickly and could move on with our lives.

I was at a loss on how to handle David though. I'd nearly slapped him in my lobby the night before, but I'd remained cool for Theo's sake. David could get nasty when he drank too much.

Nick and I were still talking about our strategy when Richard Traub, Volta's lead lawyer, entered the conference room. He was alone and explained that he'd been sent to negotiate on Theo's behalf. I was grateful and disappointed at the same time, reminding myself to be happy that Theo was staying true to my wishes. The alternative was recusing myself, and I really didn't want to do that. I couldn't fathom someone else coming in and taking over.

"I'm going to get straight to the point," Richard began. "Volta insists on a revisit of the valuation as a result of yesterday's overwhelming demand. For a three percent stake, the price has gone up to one hundred and twenty million.

I ran the math in my head. Theo was pushing a valuation of four billion. It was unheard of at their early stage of growth.

"Obviously, given the events yesterday that is still a great deal for your client." Richard looked down at his notes, and I shifted my gaze quickly to Nick.

"Regarding the technology sharing," Richard continued, "my client remains unwilling to compromise on this point." He pushed a piece of paper across the table to us. "This is the proposed licensing fee structure from Volta. I think you'll find that it's more than fair."

I glanced over the fee structure while quickly running the math. He was right. The fees were incredibly reasonable. Nick shot me a strange look. Obviously, something was off.

I wondered why Volta was all of a sudden becoming so accommodating. Surely my relationship with Theo—or ex-relationship — wasn't enough to explain this sudden generosity. My chest tightened at the thought he'd be willing to compromise his company for the sake of closing the deal quickly. But just as swiftly, I stifled the idea.

Theo was a businessman, and I couldn't forget that even if we had a future together months from now I would always come second to Volta.

"All other terms that were discussed Monday remain as they were, including the production and manufacturing real estate items," Richard finished.

"Okay, we'll run this by our client when we finish here," Nick explained, frowning. There had to be a catch. Maybe I'd missed something in the term sheet?

"There's just one more thing — off the record," Richard said, folding his hands in front of him on the conference room table. Nick and I glanced at each other, waiting for the sword to drop. Whatever it was, it had to be big.

"My client is concerned that this partnership will fail to be fruitful given the dissonance coming from one of National Motors' board members. Therefore, I would say that the likelihood of this sweetheart deal firming up is directly correlated to the likelihood of Mr. Pierce leaving his position."

My eyes widened in disbelief. I couldn't hide it; and Richard smiled, looking pleased at having successfully delivered his wild card.

It seemed Theo had his own agenda after all. The idea that he was trying to disrupt the composition of my client's board was shocking. It wasn't something that the executives at National Motors could even really control. Board member terms were set at two years, and Anthony still had six months left on his.

Could Anthony's op-ed be considered grounds for a conflict of interest or unethical behavior? There was no doubt that he was obstructive, but could a case be made that this prevented the board from functioning effectively? My mind was spinning out the possible tangents faster than I could keep up.

Admittedly, this was way above my paygrade and probably everyone at National Motors that we were collaborating with. Shareholders were the only ones that really held this kind of power. I started to wonder how to possibly influence them. Thankfully, Nick replied quickly, "You know very well that's not something that we can detail in our agreement."

"Sure, but let's say my client would like to know that National Motors is taking the concern into consideration — a gentleman's agreement, if you will." Richard sat back in his chair and smiled while looking back and forth between both of us.

I understood that Theo was upset about Pierce. We all were, in fact; but did he really think he could play National Motors' board members like chess pieces? It was audacious to the point of arrogance. And he knew very well that I would be the one who had to deal with the fallout.

I turned my attention to Nick. "Well, we'll see what we can do."

Richard stood to shake our hands. "Great. I expect to hear from you soon. I have a number of other interested parties to reply to," he added, grinning.

I SPENT THE REST OF THE DAY adjusting and firming up the terms for the agreement while Nick met with the National Motors' team at their offices. I'd sent over the updated terms at around five o'clock and went over to meet him at six thirty.

I'd expected Nick to be tired, but I found him in Michael Gruner's office practically bouncing in his seat. Both Michael and Nick relayed their successes of the day. They'd obviously been working alliances within the board and at the shareholder level.

"Audrey, you'll stay on here in New York until next Thursday when the board meets to discuss the Volta deal. I have to go back to London tonight, but I'll be back on Tuesday just in case more support is required."

Another week in New York — I was envious of Nick being able to go home. This city had worn me out, and I was afraid of the trouble that might come if I stayed any longer. I needed time alone to sort out my thoughts and feelings.

It was seven thirty when I caught a cab to return to my hotel. Walking into my room, I glanced at the crisp white bedding that the cleaning lady had smoothed into place at some point earlier in the day. The thought of climbing alone into the fresh, cold sheets was as far as my fantasies went for the night. My feet were tired and ached from my heels.

A large vase overflowing with light-pink peonies sat on the side table next to the viridian velvet armchair. A small card had been placed just in front of them on the table. There was nothing written on it except for my name.

I buried my nose in three or four of the flowers to breathe in their fragrance. Picking up the envelope, I tore it open as I walked toward the bathroom. Inside was a thin piece of card stock with *Aydin Demir* letterpressed at the top.

Be outside at 8:30 p.m.

I placed the card down on the edge of the bathtub and plugged the drain while turning on the water.

Sitting on the side of the tub, I sprinkled in the jasmine mint bath salt from the large glass jar and swished my feet around to dilute the salts into the water. The ink blurred from the small pools that had formed on the lip of the tub. *What to do about this?*

I felt my chest constricting. I knew I couldn't see him — not now. Continuing to swish my feet, I vowed to text him once I'd finished with the tub.

He knew better than to be seen with me especially after we'd run into David only last night. And besides, I didn't like being told where to be and when. I alone would decide where I'd be at eight thirty.

When I finished, I dried my feet and went to my bag to pick up my phone. Theo had texted again.

I won't take no for an answer, Audrey. 8:30.

I sat down on the edge of the bed and sighed heavily. If I didn't go, I could see exactly how the next days, weeks, and months would play out. My transaction would go through. Nick and I would be heroes at the bank. I'd get a great bonus, and National Motors would continue to be my client for years to come. I liked the picture that all of that painted.

I then thought about what might happen if I did go outside at eight thirty, but I couldn't see anything. There was no image created in my mind. It was all blank. It excited me a little in a rebellious way.

I thought of Gina and what she would do. It was one thirty in the morning in Paris. I wondered if she'd be awake. I decided to chance it; after all, it was a Friday night. Really, I was desperate to talk to someone.

Gina answered the phone groggily. She'd just fallen asleep when I called but insisted we keep talking.

"I have big news about the gallery," she explained.

The contacts she'd been speaking to in London were coming the following week to discuss a potential partnership. Gina was optimistic, but she always viewed the world through rose-colored glasses.

"But not only that, I've sold four pieces this week including the Simeti I'd planned to show at my art fair."

"Wow, that's incredible! Do you think it's enough to save the gallery?"

"We're still a couple hundred thousand off, but it's within striking range now. The sales have attracted some buzz."

I congratulated her on this latest development and explained the chaos that had erupted in New York.

"I knew Theo looked familiar," she exclaimed. "I'm sure I've seen him in the press."

That was unlikely, but I didn't correct her. Gina was wide-awake by the time I began to tell her about Theo and I running into David the night before.

"You know, I wouldn't worry about David. I'm sure

he's happy for you and Theo; or well, you know what I mean."

"Maybe, but something tells me to tread carefully."

"Don't lose sleep over that. Have fun; sort out the details later or never. Theo obviously cares for you. Give yourself a break, and go see him if that's what your heart is telling you to do."

AT EIGHT THIRTY on the dot, I walked out of the Elizabeth Hotel and onto the sidewalk. Unsure where this night was going, I'd put on my knee length tight black dress. It was one of those wardrobe staples that could work just as well at the beach as it could for a night out in Manhattan. I'd thrown this dress on the night before when I'd gone to see Theo in the lobby, but this time I paired it with stilettos and makeup. It was just enough to look elegant but restrained. I didn't want to encourage him — or at least that's what I told myself.

A driver and a Volta Model I sedan were waiting for me on the curb. I cringed at the small group of pedestrians admiring the car. I'd texted Theo back at the last minute telling him I'd go downstairs but only on the condition that whatever he was up to would be completely under the radar. So far, he was failing.

I slipped into the car as quickly as I could and dropped the side of my face into my hand. *What was I doing?*

The driver and I exchanged greetings; but when I asked him where we were going, he declined to share any information. He only said that we'd be driving for about thirty minutes.

I relaxed into the back of my seat, resigned to whatever would be coming next. There would be a price to pay for this — I just hoped that it wouldn't be too expensive.

I woke up when the driver shut his door and walked around to open mine. The compounded exhaustion from the last week was catching up with me. Thankfully, the weekend had arrived; and I was expecting less excitement over the next two days.

I blinked away the lingering sleepiness, reached for my purse, and climbed out of the car. To my right, the sound of trees rustled in the summer breeze. I looked up at them and realized that we'd pulled up next to Central Park. *What were we doing all the way up here?*

The driver motioned for me to walk toward the entrance of the building that stood in front of us. I looked up at its gothic structure. *The Winona?*

The building was a real estate legend in New York City. Built in the late eighteen hundreds, it was a large, residential palace that towered over the west side of the park. As one of the city's most exclusive addresses, it was notoriously difficult to buy property in the building; therefore, the eighty apartments that made up the monstrous structure were primarily occupied by celebrities and the financial elite.

I hoped that we weren't going to a dinner party. Surely Theo wouldn't be so reckless. But then, why else would he have asked me to meet him here?

I took my phone out of my bag as I walked back to

the car and started to text Theo to cancel. After this long week, I just wasn't up for any more trouble. My thumb hovered over the send button, but my heart was leaden.

I'd been excited to see him despite my efforts to rein in those thoughts. I turned around and looked up at the building. I mean, it's not every day one receives an invitation to The Winona.

The driver walked me through the arched doorway. Inside the lobby the white-gloved concierge directed me to the elevator that was tucked to the right inside the courtyard. I gave my name, and he pressed the button for the fourth floor.

"You'll be going to apartment number forty-eight," he instructed.

When the doors shut, I looked around the elevator carriage nervously. What was going on, and where was Theo? I steeled myself to be ready for anything as soon as the elevator doors opened.

Stepping out of the elevator, I walked into a long, wide corridor. The walls were painted cream; and the dark hardwood floors were covered in a long, luxurious, blue oriental carpet. Simple crystal chandeliers hung every few yards from the center of the hallway ceiling. Forty-eight was a quarter of the way down the long corridor.

I pressed the small, round, brass doorbell button and could hear the ring reverberating throughout the room on the other side. I'd expected the hush of voices or distant music — a cocktail party perhaps. But all was silent.

I stood there awkwardly in the hallway for what seemed like minutes but was probably closer to a few seconds. The door clicked and opened. Theo was standing on the other side.

"Welcome," he said opening the door further to let me

in. I peeked around his shoulder nervously. Inside, the apartment was nearly empty with the exception of a couple ladders, drop cloths, and paint.

"What is this place?" I asked, walking into the room and toward the large windows on the other side. A single, arched-brass floor lamp stood in the far corner emitting the only light in the space. The walls were white, but the windows were lined in dark timber.

"I wanted to show you my new apartment. Do you like it?"

I swung around, leaving the rest of the way to the window at my back. "What? You bought this place?"

"Yeah, but there was quite a bit of renovation work to do. It's nearly finished now."

Too many different ideas clamored for attention. "You want to move to the U.S.?"

"No, well maybe, but no, it's New York. Who wouldn't want to own a small piece of this magnificent city?"

I couldn't argue with him there. I looked around at the rooms I could see from where I stood, suddenly aware of Theo's wealth in a way I hadn't been before. There was no doubt about it; he wasn't your everyday millionaire. He had joined an echelon that was so far beyond the stratosphere of my own life, I couldn't entirely grasp it. We were in totally different leagues.

The idea should have been attractive, even exciting. Instead, I found it terrifying.

The place was completely empty except for a refrigerator in the kitchen and the occasional random armchair. "Have you been staying here?" I said with a weak smile. "I didn't think you liked camping."

"Oh no. I've been downtown in a hotel, but I come

over to drop off stuff from time to time and check on the progress of the renovation."

How was it possible that this was the same flirtatious consultant I'd met at David's wedding? The light-hearted guy who'd driven me to his grandmother's old cottage and rolled in the grass as if he didn't have a care in the world? Both men looked and spoke alike; but the truth was they were from different universes.

The person quietly watching me now was considered by many a genius whose technology would change the world and a cutthroat entrepreneur fast on his way to becoming a billionaire. But my brain refused to accept the fact.

I let it all spin around in my head for a while and tried to formulate reasonable questions.

Theo walked toward the center of the large entryway that opened into a double living room and beckoned me over to one of the expansive windows. From there we could see the lights of Central Park glowing below.

"Wow." This apartment had to cost at least twenty million dollars — twenty million secrets he's kept from me. I realized with a pang that I was tired of filling in the blanks when it came to Theo. Tonight, I would know who he truly was or I would walk away.

"Are you hungry," he asked, walking toward the kitchen and flicking on the recessed lighting.

"I'm starving, but I guess we need to eat out?" I flinched at the idea of going out in public with him.

"I already ordered in." Opening the refrigerator, he revealed three paper sushi delivery bags. "I didn't want to risk running into another one of your exes."

I couldn't help smiling. Only Theo could be that

obnoxious and get away with it. "Sometimes, I really am crazy about you."

"And the other times?" he asked, leaning over and placing his hands on the marble island that separated us.

I folded my arms and leaned on the island to meet his stare. "It's complicated."

Theo smiled and held my gaze for a moment before turning around and unpacking the plastic takeaway cartons. I went back to the living room and spread out a large drop cloth in the center of the empty space.

"Speaking of complicated," he said, handing me a plastic plate of maki, "What is the story with David?" We sat cross-legged opposite each other with the spread of sushi between us. Theo, chopsticks in hand, was waiting for my story.

I filled him in on how I'd met David and our engagement. "Our plan was a September wedding in Nashville."

Theo quietly dipped a roll into his soy sauce and made sure not to drop my gaze. I took a deep breath and steeled myself for the rest.

"One night toward the end of that summer, I was out to dinner with a girlfriend; and he walked in . . . with a date. He was so completely casual and at ease, as if it was just another night out on the town, kissing her, playing with her hair." I swallowed. "That was it. I left him that night. Staying in Manhattan was too painful: since I'd met him so soon after I'd first arrived, almost all of my memories of the city included him."

Theo placed his chopsticks down on the drop cloth, his eyes narrowing on me.

"My I.P.O. hit the market a couple weeks after our split," I continued, "and just before the financial crisis started to unfold. The offering had been bolstered by a lot of hype from trades, but the company's clients were mostly tied to the real estate boom. The price of my offering came out at fifteen dollars a share; yet one week out, shares were trading down at just three dollars. The entire market was suffering, but this company really suffered. David's fund lost a lot of money."

"He, obviously, blames me, but there wasn't really anything I could have or would have done differently. No one knew what was coming, but David thinks that I should have shared more information about the offering. So with our breakup and the markets a mess, I decided to go do my MBA, and I chose the best school that was the farthest away from New York. Most people saw it as a kind of hit-and-run."

I looked up at Theo who still hadn't touched his food. "So, does it live up to the story you've heard," I asked, already knowing the answer.

"Not exactly," he admitted. "I should have known the reality would be less exciting than the legend." He gave me a small, apologetic smile. "So how do you feel about being in New York now that you're back?"

"It's not my home anymore."

"Do you think it could be again one day?"

"It would take something very special to bring me back here." I focused on my food, tired of sharing and talking about my ex. The thing I disliked about this story was that I came across as the victim of a cheater which I didn't want to be. In that way, the other version where I vindictively screwed David made me feel more powerful. Unfortunately, there wasn't much truth to it.

I picked up a piece of yellowtail sushi and thought about how to shift the conversation. "You know you have a lot to be proud of — yesterday made history. There isn't an organization working in automotive that isn't talking about you today."

"It feels vindicating," he said with a wide smile. "You know — my entire life — people have been discouraging me, telling me things can't be done, or insisting that I'm not the person to accomplish them." He paused to weigh his words. "I grew up with very few people believing in my dreams."

"Really?" Theo always seemed so relaxed and confident. Even now, as he shared this, he casually carried on picking sashimi out of the containers without dropping anything. I, on the other hand, had splashed soy all around my side of the makeshift picnic.

"I mean, you growing up in the U.S., you must have had many champions along the way. It's part of your culture."

That was indeed true. I had countless teachers and mentors to credit for the doors that opened for me.

"I never had that. My teachers thought being an engineer was too much for me to aim for," he explained.

I looked across at the successful entrepreneur in front of me — my heart breaking as I pictured a younger Theo making his way through to university. His route had been much steeper and filled with more obstacles than my own. "And yet you're such an overachiever."

"I guess those experiences motivated me to work harder. I thought that if I could be the best student, then the other students and teachers would leave me alone."

Theo seemed almost embarrassed by his words, fixating on his food. It was rare for him to talk about himself in this way.

"When people expect very little of you, you can try

just about anything. You're already at the bottom, so your situation can only improve, and that's why I started taking risks in my studies and risks in my research. All of that helped me to create my first company."

"And now you risk a major deal just to see me?"

He smiled. "We should get you one, you know?"

"A what?"

"A Volta."

My eyes brightened. "It's already in process."

"What you mean?"

"I ordered one yesterday," I said with a wink.

"You know, I have a connection or two that could have gotten you one. You needn't wait two years."

"Would you believe I did it to help save my deal?"

"Yes," he said with a smile. "But I'll sleep better thinking that you did it for me."

"Maybe you're right. But you'll never know for sure."

He reached his hand across to take mine. "I already know for sure."

We packed up the empty cartons from dinner and folded up the drop cloth. Theo walked me through the apartment showing off all of the work that he'd done to restore the rooms. I enjoyed seeing this side of him. He was more self-conscious tonight than usual — and vulnerable.

Finally, we came to the last bedroom toward the back of the apartment. "This is the master," he said.

This room had more furnishings than the others. There was a simple modern canopy bed at the center of the room with a comforter and pillows that were dressed in no-fuss linen.

A light-grey velvet armchair had been placed in the far corner near a window, and I imagined Theo sitting there watching rain fall outside in autumn. It was a cozy and beautiful apartment; or at least, I imagined it would be once he'd finished furnishing it.

"So you do sleep here," I asserted.

"Well, I may have gone furniture shopping recently," he confessed, unable to meet my eye.

He crossed the room and opened a door to his walk-in closet. It was huge — almost the size of the bedroom in my first New York apartment.

"Wait, there's more," he added, like an eager child showing off an art project.

I laughed at his enthusiasm. He opened another door and pulled me into the darkness beyond. A wave of heat took hold in my chest, spreading throughout my entire body.

"This is the second closet," he murmured.

His eyes pierced mine in the low light of the room, shoulders rising and falling with his breath as he leaned in. Brushing a hair out of my face, he touched his lips to mine. It was the first time we'd kissed since I'd left Istanbul two weeks ago. It was definitely a departure from our agreement, but it was worth it. My heart was his even if I couldn't let him know that yet.

We lingered there — our lips barely touching — the warmth of his breath brushing over my face. It was such a perfect moment that tears began swelling under my eyes. I blinked them back to conceal the emotion. I had to be careful not to get carried away. Our bodies parted a shade, and he looked into my eyes, his back pressed against the closet wall.

"This one is for you if you'll take it," he said, leaning past me to switch on the lights.

THEO

SHE STOOD THERE IN SILENCE — unmoving; and I began to wonder if she'd not heard my words. Her eyes were glistening as she looked away, blinking. "Too much?" I asked.

"No, it's not that, Theo," she said, her voice cracking in the back of her throat. "But what are you asking exactly?"

The truth was I wasn't sure. Having her here with me now — I didn't want her to leave. I didn't want to lose her again. I was afraid she'd walk out the door and never come back — escaping me for the refuge of her career. "Just stay here with me. Stay here whenever you want to."

Her eyes widened; I'd sprung it on her quickly, and I

realized that I needed to stop the analysis she was computing in her head.

"Theo, have you lost your mind?" She took a step back. "We can't even have a relationship right now, let alone live together!"

I pulled her out of the closet and back out into the sparse bedroom. The only light was streaming in from the illumination of the night city. "Never mind, don't think about it tonight," I said, sweeping her up in my arms. "There's no rush to decide anything."

When she started to argue, I picked her up and put her down near the window. I reached my hands up to her neck to kiss her — the soft fullness of her lips pressing into mine.

To my surprise, her soft tongue flicked mine; and she let out a whimper as her lips parted even further. A great amount of restraint was exercised to not take her right there against the window. Then she looked up at me and pushed me away.

"Sorry, I can't do this," she said, walking out of the room.

I stalked after her. "You can't do this now? Or ever?" I could let her go, for now; but I needed to know when she'd be mine again.

"The deal will close faster if you agree to a full technology exchange," she said walking down the hallway back toward the entrance.

"The board is still stuck on this point," she huffed; but I sensed that her exasperation wasn't meant for me.

I stopped in my tracks unable to accept that she was pinning our relationship on me selling out my company. "Are you playing me, right now?" I couldn't tell if she was serious or not.

She turned around and smiled while picking her bag off the floor and placed it over her shoulder.

"It's one big game, Theo; and you're officially in the big leagues. All this . . . " she waved her hand at the half-painted walls and stripped windows, "is just the beginning. It's a dream, but it's fragile. You need partners. The sooner you realize that, the better."

AUDREY

I LOOKED AT THEO ACROSS THE TABLE. This morning he was all business, opting to only make eye contact with Michael Gruner from National Motors and Nick who sat to my left. He didn't look at me once.

I knew that I'd angered him when I delivered my ultimatum about the deal. The way he'd gaped at me displayed a mixture of hurt and betrayal that had haunted me since. But surely he knew that I wanted what was best for him — for this to be resolved so we could be together.

I wasn't the ruthless, career-obsessed woman David made me out to be; but a part of me suspected I had crossed a line that Theo would find difficult to forgive.

There was only one other woman in the room, and Theo was showering her with attention. She'd walked in at his side and sat just behind him in the observer row against the wall. Anna had been introduced to me in London; and I knew she was his head of publicity; however, their warm familiarity was making me ill. I prayed that all of this was lost on my boss and my client.

The table had moved on to the point of technology sharing; and Richard Traub, Volta's lead lawyer, made a declaration that left us all in shock. His client was willing to accommodate National Motors' request; everything they'd asked for, the technology Theo had spent years creating, was on the table.

Theo didn't bat an eye while his gaze fixed ahead across the table. I was sure he'd look over at me to share a knowing look; after all, I was the one who'd pitched it to him days before; but his eyes never wavered in their direct stare.

I'd been stupid to push him; but it had worked. I only hoped it hadn't cost me too much. Any time one mixes business with pleasure, it usually comes out expensive.

While Richard took the room through the specific terms of the technology exchange point, Anna stood from her seat and leaned behind Theo to whisper into his ear. He smiled and whispered back while looking at something she'd shown him on her phone.

Communications staff irked me. They were all party and no content. The woman David had cheated on me with had been an aspiring publicist.

By the end of the afternoon, we had a final outline for the deal. The National Motors' team was relieved to have something worth submitting to their board for the meeting later that week.

Nick was beyond happy. This was a huge win for both of our careers, but I was just grateful to be able to leave the room at the end of the meeting. No one, especially not Theo, bothered to walk me out.

BY THE TIME I'd returned to my hotel late Tuesday night, it was clear that my relationship with Theo was over. He hadn't called or texted, and the inherent message was clear: I had won the deal but lost something potentially more important in the process.

Loss and disappointment were humbling and had a way of leading to making amends. I picked up the phone and rang David. I'd hoped that attending his wedding had put our past to rest; but clearly, it hadn't. With him working on Volta's I.P.O., I couldn't have any continued tension between us.

David met me halfway between his office and my hotel at a small dive bar we'd frequented during our time together. We sat at the old zinc counter just as we'd always done, and I ordered a light beer. David ordered a soda.

"Really?" I asked.

"I think it's best I don't drink around you," he confessed. I smiled, but I definitely needed a drink to have this conversation.

I started by expressing regret for my part in what had happened at his firm. I knew that ethically I couldn't have done things any differently, but it was the olive branch that I suspected he needed.

David apologized for the thinly veiled threats during our last interaction. "You know, even after everything that happened, I wouldn't hurt you," he said. "A part of me will always love you."

I couldn't make sense of how if he'd loved me, he had treated me so badly; but I was learning that love isn't rational, so I played another olive branch.

"Me too," I said. "When you pull back all of the pain, a part of me will always care for you as well." That's the thing about love. True love at its core is forgiving even if it takes awhile for the absolution to come to the surface.

"So are you dating Theo now?"

"No. In fact I think there might be something between him and his PR girl." I gave David a wry smile. "Damn PR girls."

He ignored the jab, shaking his head. "Audrey, wake up. There isn't anything between him and Anna. I mean, the way he was looking at you the other night . . . He's got it bad." He seemed so earnest, I could only nod.

We sat together for a few minutes pulling apart Buffalo wings and catching up, until he pulled his shirtsleeve back and checked his wristwatch.

"Look, I better get back home. Delia is waiting for me. Do you want to share a cab?"

"No, you go ahead," I said. "I think I might walk."

When David left, I continued to sit at the bar finishing my beer. What was I supposed to do about Theo now? Could David have been right? Theo hadn't called me, but I hadn't called him either. Deep down, I was so afraid of getting hurt; it was easier to imagine he didn't really care about me.

I set my beer on the counter and asked for the check. With the deal nearly closed, the only thing I needed to worry about now was making things right.

THEO

LOOKING OUT OVER THE PARK drenched in the peach light of daybreak, I found myself resigned to what had been done. I'd barely slept since Audrey had walked out a few nights before as I endlessly turned each deal point over in my head. With the fresh light of the new day came the certainty of my decision.

The road to where I stood now had been long and full of obstacles. In developing the technology that underpinned my company, I'd battled countless regulatory agencies, patent offices, and legal disputes. Handing the fruits of my labor over to a competitor wasn't easy, but I needed their old factories now more than ever if we were to deliver on the overwhelming surge of pre-orders that we'd received.

I didn't have the luxury of shopping the deal around to the other potential partners who'd reached out. Time was no longer on my side.

If I was really honest with myself, I wanted Audrey to be mine. Even though the reasons to accept deal were solid, perhaps closing it might show her how much she meant to me. That even if I was a work-obsessed entrepreneur like the ones she loved criticizing, I was also ready to change my priorities — for the right woman. In just one month, a possible future with her had become as important to me as the deal that represented my entire life's work.

At 7:30 a.m., Richard was the first person to call. National Motors' board had overwhelmingly approved the partnership. Per the agreement, a hundred and twenty million dollar cash payment would be due to us soon. That, in addition to the five hundred million we'd raised the week before during the pre-order event, meant that I'd raised so far a total of six hundred and twenty million.

It was short of the one billion I now needed, but I was confident that the I.P.O. would clear the remaining cash gap given the new company valuation that had been priced at four billion.

I'd taken Richard's call while I was still in bed; and after hanging up, I thought of all that we'd accomplished these last two weeks. I couldn't deny that I owed Audrey a lot of credit. She'd been the one who'd approached us with National Motors after all.

I wondered where we stood. We made a great team — if only we weren't on opposing sides. I hadn't heard from her since I'd last seen her in our final meeting.

Apparently, my gallant act of goodwill hadn't done as much to sway her as I'd hoped.

My phone rang again. It was Anna. I was due back downtown. There were statements to clear and interviews to give. If I could use the momentum of this deal to generate enough good publicity, it could bolster our success in the public offering.

A heat wave had swept over the East Coast rendering the early summer days nearly unbearable. People leapt from air-conditioned offices to air-conditioned apartments as if they might burn up if they spent too much time outside. I'd wear my linen suit today that I'd purchased in Athens. It was the lightest one I'd brought with me.

I crawled out of bed and glanced at the trees outside in the large expansive park. I was already running late to the appointments Anna had added to my schedule.

On my way to the bathroom, I paused in front of the second closet — Audrey's closet. Would she come back? I'd done everything she'd asked of me, but maybe I'd scared her by asking too much — or maybe she'd never been that invested to begin with. She had her deal now, and perhaps that's all she'd ever really wanted. In any case, the ball was in her court. I would not pursue her further.

I'D TAKEN AN EARLY HAPPY HOUR drink with Anna and Philipp to celebrate the successes of the past week. On my way back uptown, my phone beeped. It was a text from Audrey. My stomach did a flip.

Do you have dinner plans?

An unexpected swell of relief spread through my body, and I caught myself smiling. I'd been missing her; it was impossible to deny. I replied immediately telling her to meet me at my place at 7:00 p.m.

It's a deal, she replied. *Just wrapping up at the office now.* It was 6:00 p.m.

When I got back to my flat, I showered and changed. Flipping open my computer, I racked my brain to think of a nice, quiet place to take Audrey for dinner. Inevitably, we'd have a lot to sort through. Long distance relationships were perilous, and I needed to know just how much she cared for me.

Audrey was special, and I imagined how our lives could find a way to merge together. Would she move to New York — or Istanbul? Maybe I could relocate to London. I was no longer interested in just a casual affair or dancing around the requirements of our respective careers. I was all in, and I needed to find out if she was as well.

I remembered a quiet Peruvian-Japanese fusion spot I'd visited a year ago with Richard, my lawyer. With a little luck, they'd have a robust air conditioning system. It was only a few blocks from the apartment, so we could walk there. Following all of the travel and chaos to see each other, it would be nice to share a discreet night in what I was hoping would one day be our neighborhood.

I went to the closet where I'd taken off my suit and pulled my phone out of my pants pocket. Dialing the number to the restaurant, I had to hang up to take an incoming call from Malik. He was quick to get to the point.

"Theo," he said quickly, "we've just caught one of the

night shift employees leaving the plant with a hard drive. We think it contains something proprietary."

"What?" I asked, stumbling out from the closet into the bedroom.

"It could be some sort of espionage, but what am I supposed to do now? Security is holding him in the employee break room. Should I call the police?"

"You cannot hold him against his will; you have no choice but to call the police, Malik." Nausea struck at my stomach. This might have been a corporate betrayal, but I couldn't help taking it personally. While I was a demanding boss, I was a fair one. The compensation schemes in place were among the most generous in Turkey.

After hanging up with Malik, I called Azra to book me a flight home. Most concerning of all was whether this was an isolated event or not. How many people could've been involved — how big was this?

There was a flight leaving in two hours and another red-eye departing at midnight. Taking the later one would give me time to see Audrey and get to the airport. But I couldn't tell Audrey about this and risk National Motors finding out about the vulnerability. I'd have to find another way to explain my quick departure.

AUDREY

PACKING UP MY THINGS, I looked over my shoulder to calculate whether anyone would notice my ducking out of the office early. Nick had been running from meeting to meeting all day, and we hadn't even had time to catch up following the news that our deal had closed.

The trades were touting it as one of the most exciting transactions of the year. Overnight, Nick had become the world's most popular banker. Everyone wanted to meet with him. I'd heard he'd spent lunch with Alex Thorne, the president of our bank — one of the hardest meetings to get in this city.

I, on the other hand, had been left on the sidelines to comb through the final details of the arrangement with

National Motors' mid-ranking legal counsel. Having caught the wave of self-importance last week and jumping from one high-stakes meeting to another, today the less glamorous aspects of my responsibilities had plunged me back to reality.

My phone buzzed, and my heart leapt seeing that it was a text from Theo.

Hurry home to me, Audrey. I want every minute I can have with you. I've been looking forward to this for a long time.

I was just about to reply when Nick appeared at the door of my temporary office.

"Audrey, can you come with me?" Propping himself up against the doorframe with his arm, I could see his face was muddled with exhaustion. I was confident that we were both anxious to get home to London to reboot.

"I was on my way out. I have another meeting." I skipped the explanation of whom I was eager to go see. I'd see how tonight went with Theo before confessing my sins to my employer. I dropped my phone into my bag. I didn't want Nick to see who I was messaging.

"It shouldn't take long," he said. "I really do need to see you."

I sighed and placed my bag back on the table. "Okay, but let's keep it quick." Rolling my shoulders back, I followed him out of the office and down the hall.

He led me to the elevator bank and pressed the button to ascend. I stood there silently, void of the creativity to float a conversation, but wondered, *where were we going?* Was this good news? *A promotion, maybe?*

I hoped that I wouldn't be delayed. I really wanted to

see Theo and turn our page. I was finally ready to take a step forward, even if I didn't know where I'd be heading.

"HELLO AUDREY," he said with a firm squeeze around my hand. A tall, silver fox stood at the center of an obscenely large office by New York standards.

Nick had forsaken me at the assistant's desk outside the double doors, so I'd entered alone, hiding my disbelief as best I could. I was standing in Alex Thorne's office. Mr. Thorne was the president and Chief Operating Officer of the bank. One of the most powerful bankers in the world, he made over twenty million dollars a year, meaning that the minute he'd given me so far was worth around forty dollars — give or take.

"Please, take a seat."

I took my place on the edge of a grey leather armchair and folded my hands in my lap.

"You know, Audrey, here at Roland Capital our standards of excellence are high; and we don't compromise on them."

My hands grew cold as I studied the serious look on his face.

"And as president," he continued, "my team and I strive to reward those loyal to the company and cut the team members who are playing their own game."

He knows about Theo. This wasn't a promotion — it was a firing.

"The National Motors deal with Volta is unprecedented. It's a feather in our portfolio this year, and my phone hasn't stopped ringing all day from clients eager to discuss their ideas for new transactions." He paused to give me time to blush. "We're promoting you to Managing Director."

I swear my heart nearly stopped.

These were the words I'd been longing to hear for so long — a validation that all the crazy hours and sacrifice had been worth it. I didn't know anyone else my age that held this level of responsibility at a bank — male or female. It would inevitably mean a near doubling of my income.

"That's great news, but Nick is a Managing Director. Would I still report to him?"

"Yes and no. We've offered him a partnership in London."

We'd both been promoted?

"And look, if you want to return to London, you can; but should you consider moving back to New York, I'd be happy to have you leading in this office. It's not a stretch to imagine you joining as a partner in a year or so if this transaction is indicative of your future success."

Move back to New York? No, I wasn't putting that on the table. These last two weeks had been difficult enough. My home was in London now.

I had thought that with a higher position I'd have more freedom in my career; but now, I'd be even more visible at the bank and under the sharp eyes of the executives — as Alex was hinting.

Was that really what I wanted? Maybe I'd be able to squeeze out a partnership from the London office in just as little time as New York. I considered it a bet worth making.

"That's very generous of you; and I really do appreciate it, but I'd prefer to run my deals out of London."

"It's your decision; but of course, I could promote your path to partnership more efficiently if you were here."

"I understand," I said. "But I'll take my chances."

"You really have an appetite for risk, don't you?" he said standing and extending his hand toward mine.

"That's what you pay me for, isn't it?" I said as I took his hand.

Alex smiled a large, white toothy grin as we finished shaking hands, and I swear that I saw a cartoonish sparkle from the corner of his smirk. This guy could charm the dead. "What if I sweetened the deal?"

"What deal?"

"I'll add twenty percent onto your base salary if you come work out of New York."

"Alex, it's not where I want to be right now, but I'll think about it."

"Great, that's all I ask." Walking toward the door, he added, "Look, I'm going out now with Nick to celebrate his partnership. You should come with us."

No, I couldn't. I had to see Theo uptown; but how many times could I tell one of the most powerful men in global capital markets the word "No"? I should at least join them for a drink. After all, Theo wasn't going anywhere.

"Okay, we're just going for a drink?"

"Yes, of course. I have tickets for the Met just after."

The lights in the office flickered and then went black for a second before coming back on. It was well known within the bank and "Page Six," the New York Times' gossip page, that Alex Thorne was one of the city's most sought after bachelors. For an instant I wondered what socialite of the moment he was meeting uptown tonight.

"And we'd better hurry, before the entire city loses electricity in this heat wave," Alex added.

If he thought that he could get up to Lincoln Center for an eight o'clock opera performance, then I'd be able to get to Theo's around the same time. Lincoln Center was just a few blocks away from Theo's apartment. I'd just have to text him quickly to let him know I'd be running an hour late.

Alex picked up his briefcase as we exited his office. "Okay, let's go," he said to Nick.

Shoot, we were going right now. My phone and bag were back in my lower floor office.

Nick and I followed Alex to the elevators where another executive joined us. I recognized him as Nick's boss' counterpart in the US; but now, I was unsure where the contents of the elevator stood in terms of hierarchy — well, aside from Alex Thorne being at the very top and myself representing an emerging bottom.

The executive and I exchanged introductions as the elevator doors shut. I reached my hand out to push the button for my floor. "I'll catch you guys at the bar, I just need to grab my—"

"Nonsense," Alex said brushing my hand out of the way. "Drinks are on me tonight."

I watched the floor that housed my temporary office come and go. I didn't dare press the issue further. I prayed that I'd be back quickly so that Theo wouldn't be left waiting. We were just going around the corner. It wouldn't take long.

THEO

I'D BEEN WAITING for Audrey for an hour before I finally realized she wasn't coming. I was worried sick. It didn't make sense. She'd seemed so eager to see me.

I'd tried repeatedly to reach her mobile, but she wasn't answering nor replying to my texts. Something must've happened. Maybe she was hurt. With the heat wave and blackouts, the city had a weird, post-apocalyptic feel to it.

Jumping into my car, I asked the driver to go to her hotel in the Bowery. Even in the most hellish Manhattan traffic, she would have made it to my place by now, so I guessed that she must still be there.

We were only a few blocks from her hotel when I remembered that she had been at her offices all afternoon. "Actually, we should head downtown — to the financial district," I said, redirecting the driver while I searched my phone to get the exact address.

My mind was racing. What could have happened? Had she been held up at work? She hadn't bothered to call or send a message. Something was wrong.

This wasn't how I'd expected the night to go. I was ready to open up my life to her — finally and completely. I had wanted it to be perfect. With my flight to Istanbul looming, I worried about having enough time with her. I needed to know that she was in with me one hundred percent.

While I didn't want to create a scene by showing up looking for her, maybe I could drop by with the excuse of personally dropping off a couple of the countersigned documents. I rifled through my briefcase to see what I had on me to do the job.

The towering office buildings looked tired under the darkening sky, and pedestrians seemed to stroll the streets with less purpose than they did by day. The driver pulled the car over at the corner.

Ahead off to the right-hand side, I could see the lobby of her building plainly illuminated in its bright, white light. It was mostly empty except from the security desk and an employee who swiped his badge and walked out.

I turned my attention to the window and looked to be sure not to open the door on someone walking by; it was then that I saw their darkened faces through the window of the bar just in front of me.

He was tall and good-looking for his age, and he laughed as she spoke. Audrey peered at him over the rim of her cocktail as he replied by leaning in and whispering behind her ear.

What was she doing?

I continued watching, willing my suspicions to be wrong. Audrey lifted her phone to look at something before laughing and putting it back on the table. So, she'd received my messages. She was just ignoring them.

How could she?

Then it hit me like a fist. Of course she could ignore me now: she'd gotten what she wanted — deal in the bag — her precious career propelled up another rung of the ladder. And from the looks of it, she'd already found a new target to pursue. He was clearly a banker or client, quickly falling under her spell.

"I've changed my mind," I called to the driver without shifting my gaze. "Let's keep driving."

AUDREY

IT WAS EIGHT THIRTY when I came running out of the elevator. The drink with the guys had taken much longer than I'd expected. The bar had been extremely crowded, and our server had struggled to keep up with the orders.

Alex had proven to be remarkably human — sharing photos of his newborn niece with obvious pride and laughing as I cooed at her scrunched-up, little face. For a high-powered executive, I appreciated how personal he could be.

But, I was ninety minutes late already. Opening the door to the office, I saw that my bag was still there. One of the analysts who'd helped with the model for the deal appeared just inside my doorway. I dug through my bag looking for my phone but realized that I desperately needed to go to the ladies room.

"Congratulations, Audrey. I heard there is a celebration in order tonight."

"Thanks," I replied. "But not tonight — I have somewhere I need to be."

To give him the hint that I didn't have time to chat, I led him outside and shut the door to my office behind us. Passing him, I quickly made my way through the maze of cubicles to the bathroom.

"Maybe another time," I said over my shoulder.

There were a few analysts still chained to their desks: eyes thin and strained from the blue glow that radiated from their computer screens onto their faces.

I was now a Managing Director at one of the most storied banks in the world. The rush of impending power and mixed gin streamed through my veins as I walked through the drab floor. I'd made a place for myself in this cutthroat world of finance that'd been built almost entirely by men for men.

Theo would be worried by how late I was, but he'd understand once I explained what— and who — had held me up. This was the start of a whole new chapter in my life — in our lives.

Returning from the bathroom, I seemed to glide over the grey-carpeted floor in my black heels. I'd earned a huge promotion; and now, I was on my way to see a man that I suspected I loved. The complex details of our relationship would be decided later. Tonight, I just wanted to disappear with him somewhere above the canopy of trees that lined Central Park.

Once inside my office, I reached again inside the bag for my phone; but it wasn't there. Panic flushed at my cheeks. Maybe the device had fallen earlier. The lights in the building extinguished again, and the office immediately went pitch black. The guys in the cubicles groaned.

Damn power grid, I thought. *I hope they saved their work.*

I kneeled down to the floor. I couldn't see anything — even when the lights flickered. Crawling under the desk, my hands searched the dusty carpet; it wasn't there.

When the lights roared back on, I tore apart the contents of my bag but also came up empty. My pulse thundered through my ears while the blood at my temples pounded out an intense rhythm. I rushed over to the nearest analyst to my office.

"Hey, hi." He hesitantly peeled his gaze from his screen. "Did you see anyone go into my office? The one over here," I said taking a couple steps in its direction.

"No, I didn't see anyone come by," he replied before returning his attention to his screen.

"Are you sure? There are some important things that have gone missing."

"I'm sure," he said without looking up. "Maybe you should check with security? I think we have cameras all around here."

I didn't have time to call security. I needed to be in a car headed up town. By the time I'd get there, I'd be two hours late. I prayed Theo wouldn't be too upset. Given how much he was always working, maybe he hadn't even noticed my delay.

I took a couple steps back toward the office and shouted to the floor, "Did any of you see someone enter this office?" Three or four heads popped up above their cubicles and shook from side to side. I let out a huge sigh and stepped back into the glass cubicle. *What the hell?*

I picked up the landline phone to dial Theo's number, but I didn't actually know what it was.

Damn technology, I thought. The only place I had my contacts was in my mobile. I didn't even have his email since I'd only corresponded with his staff on the deal points.

My finger hovered over the pre-programmed line to security, but I knew I didn't have time for this. I'd have to deal with it later. Right now, I just needed to get uptown.

Sweeping my bag up around my arm, I hurried to the elevators. On my way out, I'd mention my missing phone to the security officers at the front desk and tell them I'd return later to report the incident.

THE KNOTS in my back emerged and disappeared as I shifted nervously in the car. I'd completely underestimated Manhattan's Friday night traffic, and tonight it was especially hellish.

I was beyond late when my car finally pulled up to The Winona, Theo's building. I leapt from the car while yelling a quick "thank you" to the driver and bolted toward the arched entryway.

The same older, white-gloved doorman was standing behind his counter. "Hello," I said. "I'm here to see Theo — I mean, Aydin Demir."

The gentleman frowned. "Mr. Demir left already."

Maybe he'd gone around the corner? "Is he coming back soon?"

"No, I'm sorry, he's left the country, I believe. I'm not expecting his return."

What! I took a few steps back from the reception

counter. How could he have left? We were supposed to have the evening together.

"I'm sorry, Miss Audrey," the doorman said hesitantly while reaching over his desk, "but he did leave a note for you."

I thanked him and retreated back onto the sidewalk to open the envelope.

Our deal is signed. We both won, but it's time for me to go home —preferably with my heart intact. As you said, it was all just a dream anyway.

Goodbye, Audrey.

I crumbled the note inside my fist and bent over the sidewalk to collect my courage. I was lost for words. His message implied I might break his heart as if that somehow excused him for breaking mine.

Surely he wouldn't have left me just because I'd been late for dinner? If he could drop me so quickly then, obviously, I hadn't meant that much to him after all. Maybe his hints of wanting to share a life together had just been a game to get me back into his bed when I'd insisted we focus on work first.

I should have known better than to trust someone like Aydin Demir, a man who'd built his empire by keeping business partners close and personal relationships at bay. He had never trusted me. Perhaps he was incapable of trusting anyone.

I looked to my right down the sidewalk toward the Westside and then to the left toward the park. Rather than catching a cab from the street, I decided to walk back along the park in the direction of downtown. The streetlights as well as those that emanated from the windows of towering apartment buildings continued to unconsciously flicker.

By the time I'd gone one block, my silk shirt was slickened to my back from relentless perspiration. A cool bath was exactly what I needed to wash away the emotional horror show of the past weeks. How had all of this transpired? And why? Was the gut-wrenching emptiness that plagued me now worth the moments of pleasure we'd shared?

I'd walked ten blocks when the evening heat became too oppressive to continue, so I hailed a cab back to my hotel.

Stepping into the lobby, I caught a glimpse of myself in one of the floor-to-ceiling mirrors. I looked like the nightmare I'd just lived. My hair was plastered to my forehead; my skin was flushed but broken by the dark circles under my eyes. My cheeks were sunken. I must have lost weight closing this deal. I looked at the rumpled shirt that adhered to my body. I was a mess — tossed around again by another man.

David had taken much from me; but Theo, it seemed, had taken whatever had been left.

I needed to start taking care of myself. I'd been following Nick for the last couple years like some tethered ball; and by giving into Alex, I'd missed my date with Theo. *Enough!*

I'd take the promotion but only if I was allowed to stay in London, and I would insist on the twenty percent increase to my base plus a more aggressive bonus structure.

Roland Capital would bend over to keep me. If not, after this deal, I could count on other firms lining up to sign me. Knowing that I'd soon be back in London was especially comforting.

Back in my hotel room after peeling off my wet clothes, I opened my bag to make one last thorough search. Spilling everything onto the bed confirmed that, despite my panicked hope, there was still no phone.

I paged through the files I'd spilled onto the white comforter. The phone wasn't the only thing missing. The detailed notes I'd taken in my meetings with National Motors about our negotiation strategy with Volta were also missing. The trail of compartmentalized information began clicking into place. My phone hadn't gone missing by accident, and Theo's sudden disappearance was probably no accident either. I dropped the papers back onto the bed.

Walking toward the bathtub, I was going to allow myself five minutes. Then I'd call Nick to let him know about the thefts — and about Theo. If someone at work had taken my phone and discovered my affair with Theo, it could unravel my new position at the bank. Seeing as things were clearly over with him anyway, I needed to protect my reputation above all else.

THEO

As I sat in the plane, I tried to turn my rage into rationalization. I'd put nearly everything on the line for Audrey. Maybe that had been her aim all along. I started to question if I'd given up too much — that she had played me. If she had, all of the points I'd agreed to with National Motors including the most painful one, the transfer of our technology, couldn't be rescinded now that the deal had closed.

Even if she hadn't deliberately misled David, it was clear that she'd made a lifelong practice of getting what she wanted — regardless of the price. Her ambition would always outweigh her personal relationships.

Why had I been so careless in opening my heart to

her? I'd offered to share my apartment, and she threw it in my face. It was too early to be rational. While I couldn't make sense of it, the outcome was undeniable.

I exhaled sharply and turned my head to look out the oval window. Baggage handlers hurried to stuff over-packed suitcases into the cargo hold.

The flight attendant shut the forward door and asked her passengers to turn off their mobile devices. I'd already done so having been eager to shut out the complexities of my world. Now, I was right where I wanted to be — feeling sure of where I was going. My company was being threatened, and I felt most assured when I was entering a battle — especially a fight to defend my life's work. Personal commitments were just not in the cards for me: a sacrifice for an even more illustrious return.

"Are you coming or going," the lady next to me asked. I recoiled. I wasn't in the mood for small talk and especially not with a woman.

I hesitated and then looked over at her. "I'm not sure," I responded curtly, glancing back toward the window.

Flying over Manhattan, I searched the city lights as we corrected our course in the air. I tried to find my new apartment next to the dark quadrilateral of Central Park; and as we swung further south, I couldn't help but look for Audrey's hotel.

Searching for her among the glow of the city, I watched the lights of the metro area flicker again in the lower part of the borough. This summer heat wave was testing the city as it had just weathered me. I needed to get over her. She'd taken enough time and energy from me.

I shifted in my seat and turned my attention to the

curious woman. She was my age: mid-thirties. Wearing a white, fitted dress, she looked like she'd just come from the office. Her legs were long, and she sat elegantly in her seat. I studied the seam where her dress ended on her thighs. She was sexy, but I was tired. When I caught myself looking too long, I twisted to look again out the window.

Uptown, the lights also flickered now; and then, in four quick bursts, the lights went dark throughout the entire metro area.

My heart still burned with the smoldering embers of mislaid affection and disillusionment, but one can only sustain so much heat until it oversaturates and the fire burns out. In that regard, my soul was tied with the extinguished city below.

The woman leaned over to look at the scene as other passengers mumbled to each other about the blackout.

"Actually, I think I'm just arriving," I said forcing a smile. "And you?"

KEEPING IN TOUCH

Thank you for buying this book, published by Athenian Press.

To receive special offers, book release news, and
Ava Starke's sensual tips and tricks, sign up for her newsletter at the link below:

It's free – always.

avastarke.com

HEARING FROM YOU MATTERS

Looking forward to read the next steamy book in

THE CONFLICTED SERIES…

Leave Ava Starke some stars and let her know what you liked about *Conflicted Interest* in a review!

UPON REFLECTION

- Discussion Questions -

1. *Conflicted Interest* is a play on "conflict of interest." Have you ever found yourself with a conflict of interest in your professional life? What about your personal life? How do personal and professional conflicts of interest differ or compare?

2. Why do you think Audrey is so determined to bury the hatchet with her ex, David? If you were in her position would you have extended an olive branch by attending his wedding? What does it cost Audrey to seek closure? Is the goal of being a postmodern ex-couple feasible?

3. Theo claims that he wants a family; however, his pursuits and priorities make that difficult. Does he make a mistake in ranking his company over his personal life and friendships? Do you think it is possible for these characters to "have it all?"

4. Audrey states, "Hate as an emotion is much easier to live with than lost love." How relevant is that statement to relationships?

5. How different do you think this book would be if Theo wasn't who he turns out to be? In what ways would Audrey and Theo have an easier path to be together?

6. Theo and Audrey have an intense attraction to each other. Where does the chemistry come from? What do you think draws them to each other?

7. Audrey and Theo grew up very differently with complicated family situations. How do you think the dynamics of their families shaped each of them? How does this affect their relationship?

8. Audrey notes, " . . . I had countless teachers and mentors to credit for the doors that opened for me." How applicable is Audrey's statement to your life?

9. It's important for Audrey to keep a wall between business and pleasure, especially given her past. Does she go too far? Would you have done the same, or would you have chosen to do things differently — why?

10. Audrey is overly sensitive to being able to make her own way financially. What does it cost her? Do you admire her for this principle? How does this play with the power balance between her and Theo?

11. Theo is hell-bent on discovering and honoring his family's history and roots. Have you ever undertaken a similar journey? To what extent is keeping in touch with the past important to you?

12. Discuss the concept of fear as it relates to the main characters. What is the character's biggest fear, and how does that fear impact his or her life?

13. Theo's note to Audrey states, "If I replace what I broke, can I see you again?" How does that statement relate to the novel's conclusion? What will be necessary to mend their fractured relationship?

14. Select a character and detail his or her internal and eternal conflicts. Do the character's choices and actions resolve or exacerbate conflicts?

15. Do Theo's and Audrey's stories, including the choices they make, have applicable life lessons?

16. If you could ask the **author** a question, what would you ask?

17. As he leaves New York, Theo comments that, " . . . one can only sustain so much heat until it oversaturates and the fire burns out." In what ways could this be a prophetic statement?

ALSO BY AVA STARKE

- THE CONFLICTED SERIES -

1

Conflicted Interest

And coming soon…

2

Conflicted Desire

Summer 2017!

3

Conflicted Proposal

Autumn 2017!

ABOUT THE AUTHOR

AVA STARKE is an author, entrepreneur, philanthropist and undeniable feminist dedicated to creating romance novels and serials that help readers find their escape and inspire their sexiest selves. A native of Los Angeles, she now lives in South Florida.

avastarke.com

Made in the USA
Middletown, DE
14 February 2017